BELIEVE

Highland Falls Supernatural Series

— Book 1 —

CATHY SANDERS

Believe: Highland Falls Supernatural Series, Book One
Copyright © 2022 by Cathy Sanders

CS Media
250 Palm Coast Parkway NE
Unit 607-320
Palm Coast, FL 32137
www.csbookdesign.com

This is a work of fiction. Aside from reference to known public figures, places, or resources, all names, characters, places, and incidents have been constructed by the author, and any resemblance to actual persons, places, or events is coincidental.

Unless otherwise indicated, all Scripture quotations are taken from the Holy Bible, New Living Translation, copyright 1996, 2004. Used by permission of Tyndale House Publishers, Inc., Wheaton, Illinois 60189. All rights reserved.

Library of Congress Control Number: 2021918314

ISBNs: 978-1-955632-00-3 (Print)
        978-1-955632-01-0 (Ebook)

Printed in the USA.

For my mom:
The one who taught me
What it means to live by faith.
Faith is the victory; death has lost its sting,
For now you live in complete healing
In the arms of Jesus.

Prologue

Three years ago

"Jesus, please help me!" Sarah screamed, tears streaming down her face. She looked down at the source of the excruciating pain and saw her kneecap bulging grotesquely from the side of her leg. Pain radiated up and down the appendage and eventually through her whole body, as though her entire being was crying out in sympathy to her injured knee.

Slowly she sat up, trying not to move her leg, but even that small movement was extremely painful. Sarah looked around frantically. She was a few miles away from her house and there was nobody around to hear her if she called out for help. Only her horse, Shadow, was in earshot.

Overwhelmed, Sarah collapsed back on the ground as Shadow reached down and nuzzled her with his velvety nose, sensing something wasn't right with his beloved owner. After a frightening experience of losing control over the horse, she had no idea injury would come from getting a foot stuck in the stirrup during her shaky dismount.

Sarah inwardly cried out for God to help her. There wasn't anyone else she could depend on in that moment. Pastor Jake was always talking about how God is ready to help people. She recalled the message he gave in church just the Sunday before, "Faith believes in something, even when it hasn't happened yet. It is trusting that God is in control when everything seems out of control. Maybe you are facing something that you don't think you can do anything about.

The good news is that you can do something; you can believe that God *can* do something. Jesus said that if you just believe, you can see miracles happen!"

Sarah tried to push herself up to a seated position again, wincing as a fresh wave of nauseating pain rolled over her body. The last thought that came to her before she blacked out was how badly she needed a miracle.

Chapter One

Sarah Wright had always loved horses. This was probably because her mother loved them too, but Sarah seemed to grow up reading and watching anything she could get her hands on about horses, and even owned her own horse by the age of seven. Her family lived right on the border of suburban and rural Highland Falls, allowing them to have a few acres and make Sarah's childhood fantasy a reality. While other girls her age were playing with dolls and watching cartoons, Sarah was leading her white horse, Shadow, around the paddock, feeding him sugar cubes, or brushing what she could reach of his silky coat.

This morning Sarah bounded down the stairs excitedly. The summer sun was bright and shiny even at ten o'clock, bathing the house with warmth. She had been asking her parents for months to let her ride Shadow outside of the confines of their small, two-acre property. It got boring going around and around the corral, and as Sarah became a more experienced rider she was ready for some adventure, especially on the miles of trails behind their property on the expansive farmland owned by the Hendersons. She had even walked over to the Hendersons' sprawling farmhouse several weeks back and received permission to ride on their property, hoping that it would further convince her parents that it would be okay to let her explore on horseback. Her persistence had paid off as they finally agreed that when she turned fourteen she could ride the trails by herself. This, of course, was for short periods of time and with a few typical parent-imposed rules attached to the privilege.

She paused at the bottom of the stairs to look out the window by the front door and saw her dad attaching balloons to the mailbox. On any other day she might have felt embarrassed about how childish that was, but now it fueled her excitement.

"I'm taking Shadow out on the trails, Mom. I'm fourteen today, remember?" Sarah said as she rounded the corner to the living room where her mom sat reading.

"Of course I remember, sweetie," Stephanie Wright closed her book and stood, "but you need to be back in one hour, and be careful. You don't know those trails well yet."

"I will, Mom," Sarah rolled her eyes with sass. "I've walked them a million times."

"That may be true, but walking them is a lot different than riding a horse on them; just take it slow." She looked at the time on the clock. "Now by the time you get him saddled and ready it will probably be ten-fifteen, so you need to be back by eleven-fifteen. And wear your helmet." Stephanie was the type of mom who wanted her kids to know all the rules ahead of time and expected them to be followed.

"Okay, Mom. Can I go now?"

Stephanie stepped closer to Sarah, ran her hand down Sarah's long brown hair, and pulled it over her daughter's shoulder to rub her back with one hand. "Yes, and happy birthday, Sarah!"

Sarah gave her mom a quick hug before bouncing out the door. "Thanks, Mom!"

Sarah made speedy work of saddling Shadow and was off to the trails in no time. Just like her mom said, riding was a lot different than walking. What appeared like a slow incline when walking was actually steeper on horseback. Both she and Shadow were used to the flatness of the corral.

They picked their way carefully up a small hill and around a bend shaded by tall maple trees before coming to a flat path that stretched out ahead. Fortunately, the summer had been pretty dry, so the dirt trails were hard packed and the large horse seemed to navigate them easily. Sarah closed her eyes and listened to the constant buzz of the cicadas in the trees above her.

Opening her eyes, she brought Shadow to a stop and checked her phone for the time. Ten forty-five already. Sarah put the phone away and gently squeezed with her legs, urging Shadow to pick up the pace. If she was going to cover all the trails before she had to be home they would have to go quicker.

Ten more minutes passed as horse and rider explored the trails. Suddenly, a raccoon shot out in front of them, spooking Shadow. Rearing up a bit, Shadow snorted, his nostrils flaring. In spite of the surge of adrenaline she felt with the sudden movement, Sarah managed to stay on his back; he had done this a few times in the corral, so she knew how to adjust her weight to keep her balance.

What she wasn't prepared for was when Shadow shot forward, causing her to almost flip backwards off the saddle.

Yanking on the reins, Sarah yelled, "Whoa, Shadow!" but the frightened horse was not to be stopped. Shadow wasn't familiar with the trails yet and left the hardened pathway for the soft field, eventually leading to the tree line.

Now it was time to panic.

Sarah tried to hold the reins tight while getting her feet back into the stirrups. She had lost her foothold when Shadow had darted forward, and now they were moving at a fast pace and all the bouncing was making it hard.

She finally secured her left foot and was working on the right one when she glanced up. She could see from halfway across the field, heading toward the trees, that there were a lot of low hanging branches. she had to stop Shadow or turn him around quickly.

Sarah pulled back hard on the reins but Shadow shook his head violently, causing her to drop one of the reins. With one rein left, she remembered something she had seen in a western movie once and pulled the rein hard. She wrapped the worn leather strap a few times around the saddle horn and forced Shadow's head to the side so he had to slow down.

Shadow pranced in a circle as he slowed and eventually came to a stop, his sweat-covered sides heaving.

Sarah drew in a shaky breath and she closed her eyes to breathe a prayer of thanks to God. When she felt assured that Shadow wouldn't bolt again she slowly unwound the rein from the saddle horn. With her insides feeling like mush, Sarah figured she better get both feet on the ground for a few minutes before they headed back. She swung her right leg over Shadow's back, but as she tried to dismount, her left foot caught in the stirrup, and the balance of her weight caused her leg to bend in an unnatural position.

That's when she dismounted, but failed.

***

Sarah regained consciousness just a few moments after she blacked out. As the memory of what Pastor Jake had said raced through her mind, so did the fact that Jesus rose the dead back to life. If He could do that, and if she could do greater things than what He did by just believing, maybe it was worth a shot. Sarah always believed in God and that the Bible is true, so it wasn't a stretch for her to believe that God could heal her dislocated kneecap.

Sarah closed her eyes and a jolt went through her body, only this time it wasn't pain. It felt like electricity.

Warmth spread through her from head to toe and an unmistakable power vibrated her to the very core. It was like she knew, beyond a doubt, that God was healing her. This surge of faith was so strong that it forced her eyes open and her mouth dropped in amazement as she witnessed her kneecap moving back into place. Somehow, her hands ended up hovering about six inches over her knee as she was praying, and she could feel the power of God flowing through thems to her knee as it was healed right before her eyes.

In amazement, Sarah gingerly touched her kneecap and then ran her fingers all around her knee, noting that there was not even a bit of pain. "Thank You, Jesus. Wow!" was all she could say as the wonder of what had just happened overwhelmed her. She had heard of people being healed before, but never had seen it happen to anyone she knew, let alone herself.

She stood slowly, carefully putting weight on her left leg to find that there was no pain. Nothing felt out of the ordinary! "Thank You, Jesus! This is the best birthday present ever!" she shouted.

Sarah excitedly mounted Shadow and took a safe pace directly back to the stable. As she expected, her mom was standing outside looking for her, arms crossed. Upon her approach, Sarah tried to explain her late arrival before her mom exploded.

"I know I'm late, Mom, but you wouldn't believe what just happened to me," she rushed on as she brought Shadow up to the gate of the corral, "I was way on the other side of the trails and something ran out in front of us and scared Shadow and he started running and I almost fell off."

She saw her mom open her mouth to say something. If only she could get the whole story in first! She quickly continued, "But I got him stopped, then my foot got caught when I tried to get down and my knee..."

"You're almost a half an hour late, Sarah!" her mom interrupted angrily as Sarah dismounted, more carefully this time, and made quick work of removing his saddle and bridle before letting Shadow into the corral to graze. "How do you expect us to give you privileges when you break the rules we set the *first* time we let you do something like this?"

"I would have been back on time if Shadow hadn't gotten scared and if my knee didn't get dislocated!" Sarah insisted as she walked to the stable to put away the tack. Knowing she didn't have time right now to put everything away properly, she set it down on a bale of hay by the door.

"What?" Stephanie's eyes looked suspiciously at Sarah's knees as she walked. "Your knees look fine to me. What are you talking about?"

"I was trying to tell you." Sarah replied as she returned to face her mother, "My foot got caught in the stirrup and I fell off Shadow when I was trying to get down. I guess I was so shook up from him almost running into the trees." She took a breath and continued, "Anyway, my kneecap went off to the side of my leg, it hurt so bad, and there was nobody around."

Stephanie's face clouded with a mixture of concern and disbelief.

Sarah went on, "But I remembered what Pastor Jake said in church last Sunday about just believing and seeing miracles, so I prayed and I watched my kneecap go back into place!" She finished excitedly, "I wish you could have seen it!" Even as she spoke, she could tell that her mom didn't believe her.

Stephanie shook her head, "Sarah, you can't just tell some story and put God's name on it to get out of trouble."

"I'm not, Mom. It really happened—"

"As soon as you get Shadow taken care of you can go to your room for the rest of the day," her mom fumed.

"But Mom, it's my birthday, what about my party? I'm telling you the truth."

Stephanie put her hands up, a good indicator that the discussion was over. "Just go. I'll have to talk to your father about all this." She turned to walk back to the house.

Tears were now once again streaming down Sarah's face for the second time today. "Why don't you believe me? It really happened! Shouldn't you be happy that God healed me?"

Stephanie turned back around as Sarah pointed toward the Hendersons' property.

"I would still be in the field right now if He didn't. You wouldn't even know where I was. I thought you believed in miracles, but I guess not." Sarah stormed into the stable to put the tack away and brush down Shadow from their ride before her mom could say anything more.

***

A few hours later, Sarah lay on her bed staring up at the ceiling and trying to process everything that had happened that morning. She didn't want to get that mad at her mom, but she couldn't believe that her mom thought she was lying.

Remembering how amazing it had felt when God touched her body and healed her, she rolled up her jeans to look at her knee again. She poked and prodded and smiled when there was no pain. It had been so surreal, like she had been watching a sci-fi movie or something when her kneecap had moved back into place on its own.

There was a soft knock on the door. "Sarah, can I come in?" Stephanie cracked the door open and asked in a gentle tone.

"I guess so."

Stephanie opened the door slowly and came in, closing it behind her. She sat on the bed and looked at Sarah's leg, still exposed. "Is that the knee God healed?" she asked quietly.

Sarah looked up at her mom and their eyes met. "You believe me now?"

Stephanie nodded. "I talked to your dad and I called Pastor Jake. I was just so upset that you came back late. And then when I knew you had gotten hurt and I wasn't there, it made me more upset." Her brow furrowed and she reached up to stroke Sarah's hair. "You're growing up, and I can't protect you from everything anymore." She blinked back the tears that threatened to blur her vision. "Pastor Jake talked to me some more about faith and healing and so, yes, I do believe you now. I'm sorry I accused you of lying to me." Stephanie placed her hand on Sarah's leg, "You might do other things that get under my skin, but I know you don't normally lie. And I'm sorry for punishing you on your birthday. The party is still on."

"Thanks, Mom." Sarah smirked as she reached over and embraced her mother.

"Can you tell me again what happened?"

Sarah repeated the story; this time it built faith in both mother and daughter and they marveled together at what God had done.

"Mom, when God healed my knee, it felt like something changed inside me."

"What do you mean?" Stephanie tilted her head to the side.

"I don't know," Sarah shook her head slowly, "I just feel different."

***

Later that day, several of Sarah's friends would be gathering at the Wright home to celebrate her birthday. Sarah tied more balloons to the chairs on the patio while her mom put a plastic table cover over a wooden picnic table, the breeze threatening to blow the tablecloth across the yard.

Her dad was just starting to prepare the grill when the first guest arrived. It was her best friend, Nathan Stone. As Nathan crossed the yard he hit a red balloon as if it were a punching bag.

She watched him, trying not to laugh as he went after the balloon.

Looking over, he realized she was watching him and stopped mid-punch, the red balloon coming back to tap his head as his face turned the same color.

"You saw that, huh?"

"Yup," Sarah giggled. "What did that balloon do to you?"

Nathan cracked a smile as he walked over to her, "Um, it looked at me wrong."

She was glad that he had come first; it would give her a chance to tell him what had happened that morning. "Do you want to come see Shadow?"

"As long as I don't have to ride him." Nathan wasn't much of a horse lover, but he tolerated Shadow for Sarah's sake.

"No, don't worry."

They walked over to the corral to watch Shadow graze, his tail swishing flies off his back as he ate.

"I fell off of him this morning," Sarah glanced sideways at Nathan.

"You did? What happened?"

Sarah told him about how her knee had dislocated and then about the miracle.

Nathan's eyes widened. "So you saw it go back into place?" he asked in wonder. "That must have been crazy! Has anything like that ever happened before?"

"No, never."

They stood silently watching Shadow for a few minutes.

"Do you think it could happen again, like a miracle?" he asked quietly.

"I don't know, why?" Sarah looked over at Nathan, not sure what he was thinking.

"It's just...I woke up with this pain inside my ears that won't go away...maybe you could pray for it?" He looked over at her hopefully.

Now that he mentioned it, his ears looked red and she recalled him pulling at one of them while they walked over to the corral. Sarah looked around; nobody else had arrived yet and her parents were inside. She wasn't allowed to be alone with Nathan or any other guy inside the stable or house, so she would have to pray for him right out here in the open.

"Okay, I guess."

Sarah and Nathan turned to face each other, and she wondered if she should touch his forehead or his ears or if she should just pray without touching Nathan. She remembered Pastor Jake always putting his hands where the pain was when he prayed for people in church. Before she could talk herself out of it, she put her hands gently over Nathan's ears.

As she closed her eyes, she could feel something stirring up inside of her—a deep faith just like she had felt earlier that day in the field. "God, please heal Nathan's ears and stop the pain, in Jesus' name. Amen."

As they opened their eyes, they heard giggling. Three of Sarah's other friends from school had just arrived and were standing there watching them.

"What are you guys doing?" one of them asked. The others still chuckled.

Sarah felt her face turning a hundred shades of red as Nathan responded, "I asked Sarah to pray for my ears."

"Right here in the yard? That's weird," another girl remarked.

"I thought you're supposed to do that at church," said the first girl. Then she turned to the girl next to her and grabbed her head. "Be healed in the *name* of Jesus!" she said with gusto, making fun of Sarah and Nathan. The three girls erupted in laughter.

"You're not turning into a Jesus Freak on us, are you, Sarah?" asked one of them.

Nathan tried to help the situation. "Just because someone prays doesn't make them a freak."

"Maybe not to *you*," one of the girls said under her breath, but loud enough for everyone to hear.

Sarah pulled herself together, wanting to turn the conversation away from what the girls just saw and didn't understand. "Hey my mom made a bunch of cookies, you want to go in and have some?"

"Okay," the girls shrugged and turned to go into the house.

Sarah and Nathan looked at each other as they walked in.

"Sorry, Sarah. I wasn't trying to embarrass you."

"I know," Sarah said, glad the awkward moment had passed.

"My ears feel better, by the way," Nathan added.

Sarah turned to look at him. "Really? Wow," she smiled. As they entered the house, Sarah hoped that the girls would just forget about the whole thing.

***

A few weeks passed and what Sarah had hoped only amounted to wishful thinking.

Those three "friends" spread around the story they thought was so humorous, and soon people at school she didn't even know were calling her "Jesus Freak," both behind her back and to her face. When they passed her in the hallway, they would either pull their sweaters over their heads and pretend to be nuns or they would run up to her and say, "Pray for me, Sis-tuh!"

Sarah could have talked to a school counselor and turned them in for bullying, but she didn't want to ruin the chance to witness to them by doing that, so for now she tried as hard as she could to avoid them and hoped they would forget.

There were times when she took a chance and prayed for someone she knew was hurting, but soon word would spread that the Jesus Freak struck again. Before long, she just wanted things to be back to normal, just another face walking down the hall and not be called names or teased constantly. Others she thought were friends even joined in the mocking until there were only a handful of people she really trusted to not abandon her, like Nathan and a few friends from church. Nathan never teased her and, aside from her family and Pastor Jake, was the only person who believed in the gift she carried.

By the time she was halfway through ninth grade Sarah resolved not to pray for anyone publicly again. The desire to be normal was so strong. It took about a year, but eventually the names stopped and only a passing comment here and there was made about her.

Then something happened that sealed Sarah's position as a normal teenager.

Nicholas Caine moved to Highland Falls at the beginning of eleventh grade. As an excellent football player and one of the best-looking guys in the school, he achieved instant popularity. He didn't know Sarah's past, and by then she was enjoying the fruit of her labor to be a normal student. Nick was admired by most of the female population at Highland Falls, and he could have dated anyone he wanted to—and probably did for a while.

Then one day at the start of their senior year Nick accidentally bumped into Sarah in the hallway and it was like he had noticed her for the very first time. Before long, Nick and Sarah were a couple.

She said hello to her popularity ticket and goodbye to the cruel jesting of the past.

Chapter Two

Present Day

At first glance, Sarah Wright looked like a typical high school girl, and she liked it that way.

By seventeen years old, she had many achievements both socially and academically. Inheriting the smarts from her parents had enabled her to take honors classes and she was in the top ten percent of the senior class. And the fact that she was dating Nick had put her in a good social situation as well. She had been accepted by the general population of the school, though she still held some people at arm's length. If they really got to know her they would see that faith was still a high priority for her, and she couldn't take that chance again.

Working her way down the crowded hallway to her locker, Sarah pulled the shoulder-length dark brown hair out from under the straps of her backpack and took a deep breath. Math had been especially challenging that day, leaving her brain tied in knots on the way to gym class.

Reaching her locker, she absentmindedly worked the combination, threw some books in the top compartment, and stuffed gym clothes in her backpack in record time.

"Hey, Sarah, wait up!"

Sarah turned, even though she knew who it was. Nathanial Stone had been one of her closest friends since third grade and she could pick out his voice anywhere. "Hey, Nathan, I have to get to gym on time. Coach reamed me out because I walked in five seconds after the bell rang last week," she explained as Nathan came up beside her, the familiar scent of his cologne greeting her nose. He had worn the same musky scent since he was fourteen.

"Yeah, you don't want to get on his bad side. Of course, the fact that one of the top players on the football team is your boyfriend should give you some leverage." He elbowed her side as they hurried down the hall, his hazel eyes twinkling to match his mischievous grin.

Everyone knew that Coach Jamison had a soft spot for any of the football players, especially Nicholas Caine. With Nick as running back, Highland Falls had one of the best teams in the area, and it looked like they had a good chance of going to the state championship games this year.

"I wish it did," Sarah responded wistfully.

Aside from horseback riding, Sarah was not what you would call athletic. At five-foot-seven, Sarah could have easily tried out for the girls' basketball team or a number of other sports if she wanted to, but sports did not hold her interest. As much as she tried to excel in gym class—at soccer, basketball, or field hockey—she always ended up on the floor or with bruises on her shins from someone's leg or hockey stick. She didn't even want to think about her time for running the mile. Aside from her lack of athletic ability, taking honors classes and being involved in church a few times a week limited Sarah's available time for practices and games. When she wasn't studying or hanging out with Nick, Nathan, or other friends, she was riding Shadow.

Glancing at Nathan, she silently noted that he had grown taller recently, and the stubble lining his angled jaw was becoming more visible, giving evidence that he had been shaving more consistently and that he had purposely let it grow a bit. His light brown hair had grown longer than she remembered and was almost hanging down into his eyes. The way he sometimes twitched his head to the side to flip his longish bangs out of his vision reminded her of some famous boy-band star, and she couldn't help but chuckle with the realization.

"What?" Nathan eyed her with a lopsided grin.

"When did your hair get so long? It seems like it was like three inches shorter last week!" Sarah reached over to tousle his hair for effect.

Nathan ducked away from her hand playfully. "You see me practically every day and you never noticed that my hair grows? Wow." By now they had arrived at the gymnasium. Most of the other kids were already dressed in their gym clothes and were milling around the far end of the gym, waiting for class to begin.

Rolling her green eyes at him, she headed off in the direction of the girls' locker room. "Better get moving; the bell is about to ring!" Just as she finished talking, the bell sounded, as if to punctuate her statement.

"See ya," Nathan jogged off to the boys' locker room. They had just barely made it in time.

Sarah changed as quickly as she could into a light blue T-shirt and dark blue shorts. There was only one other girl left in the locker room and she was changing just as fast.

She jogged across the highly polished hardwood gym floor to join the rest of the class as Coach Jamison announced that today's agenda was volleyball, which she should have known because the net had been stretched across the room.

Sarah breathed a sigh of relief; volleyball wasn't too bad. She had a fairly good serve and could hit the ball well; it was setting and spiking that she really wasn't good at.

Coach counted them off on different teams and luckily she and Nathan ended up on the same team, but at the same time, so was Maria Romano.

Maria and Sarah had been best friends until the fourth grade and then suddenly Maria had pulled away from everyone she normally hung out with and totally changed, abruptly cutting off all communication with Sarah. It happened after Maria's parents had divorced, and Sarah was sure it had something to do with that, but she really didn't know how to approach Maria again.

In middle school, Maria had joined the junior cheerleading squad and became stuck up, hanging out with the popular people and wanting nothing to do with Sarah. With her long jet-black hair, deep chocolate brown eyes, and perfectly shaped body, Maria was the envy of a lot of girls in school, getting a lot of attention from the male population, which she seemed to enjoy. Being a cheerleader seemed to accentuate her change in attitude.

Sarah had even tried to talk to Maria on a few occasions, but was immediately shot down, hung up on, and left with no more answers than when she started. Even though Sarah had a lot of other girls who were good friends, none of them were as close to her as Maria had been.

Now Maria looked at Sarah over her shoulder from the row in front of her with narrowed eyes and a disgusted snort as they took positions to start the first game.

Looking away, Sarah breathed a prayer, asking God to help her— once again—try to bridge a relationship again with Maria.

As the class progressed, the mere proximity of Sarah seemed to drive on the bitterness she could feel emanating from Maria. It was as if just being in the same room aggravated her more and more. Trying to push aside the hurt that wanted to surface, Sarah made a mental note to get to her next class as soon as possible, even if it meant not waiting for Nathan, to avoid a potential confrontation.

When it was Sarah's turn to serve, Maria's evil glare was strong enough to drive bullets right through her, causing her to squirm despite her attempts to not let it bother her. It was unnerving. Trying to block out Maria, Sarah prepared for her typical serve. She twirled the ball in her hands three times, took a step forward, and threw the ball straight up with her left hand to hit it hard with her right.

At the last moment, Maria straightened suddenly in her line of view, the momentary distraction causing the ball to soar into the net.

Frustration mounted in Sarah's chest, heightened by Maria's satisfied smirk. *Really? I thought we were on the same team here,* Sarah thought, knowing that quite the opposite was true. Maria should at least be able to put aside their differences for the sake of the score in gym class.

The rest of gym went much the same and Sarah was relieved when Coach dismissed class. Fortunately Sarah's gym locker was on the opposite side of the locker room from Maria's.

Changing at Mach speed and jetting out of the gym, Sarah headed to her locker to drop off her sweaty gym clothes before going to the cafeteria to find Nick for lunch. Behind her she could hear Nathan calling her name.

"Sarah! Hey, slow down. They won't run out of pizza before you get to lunch." Nathan grinned as he sprinted, dodging around other students in the hall to catch up to her. He always knew how to defuse her anxiety and calm her down.

She let him catch up to her. As they neared the cafeteria, the smell of chicken nuggets and pizza hung in the air.

Turning as she walked, Sarah slowed a bit. "I had to get out of there. Did you see how Maria was treating me all through gym? I wish I knew why she hates me so much!"

"I figured that was what had gotten you so worked up. Hey, don't worry about her. She just wants you to get mad back at her and give her more of a reason," Nathan responded, this time more loudly as noise from the cafeteria made it next to impossible to carry on a conversation. "Well, it looks like Nick is waiting for you. I gotta run to English class, quiz today, wish me luck!"

"I'll do better than that, I'll say a prayer for you," Sarah smiled. "You'll do great."

"Thanks!" he returned her smile as he retreated backward a few steps, then turned to head to class.

Sarah watched as Nathan was enveloped by the mass of students moving through the hallway, then turned to see Nick in the entryway of the cafeteria. She started in his direction.

"Hey, baby, what's going on?" Nick glanced in the direction Nathan had gone. "Is he in *all* your classes? He seems like he's always around you." He looked at her suspiciously for a second.

"No, just math and gym, oh, and study hall later," Sarah added, linking her arm in Nick's. "He's just a good friend, you know that. We've been friends since third grade." Because she had only been dating Nick for a few weeks he hadn't learned her whole schedule yet, but it bothered her how Nick questioned her friendship with Nathan.

"Whatever. Hey, we have a table over here." Nick motioned to a table where it looked like half of the football team was already wolfing down cafeteria pizza.

She set her backpack down and got in line, deciding whether to get pizza or the chicken sandwich.

***

Nathan had walked down the hall just far enough not to be seen before he slipped to the side of the hallway next to a row of dark blue lockers and turned around to get another glimpse of Sarah.

Pushing his hair to the side out of his eyes, he stretched his neck up so his vision reached over the heads crowding the hallway. Uneasiness came over him as he saw her and Nick walking arm in arm into the cafeteria. He wasn't sure if it was because of Nick's reputation in the locker room or because of his own growing feelings for Sarah.

Frustrated, Nathan exhaled sharply as the couple disappeared from his line of vision. The last thing he wanted was for Sarah to get hurt. It seemed so odd that she would gravitate to someone like Nick, whose beliefs and morals were the complete opposite of her own. Nick put on a good front, but the rumors about him coupled with overheard comments Nick had made gave him cause for concern.

Turning, Nathan headed for English class, which was just around the corner, trying to shake his thoughts off of Sarah and Nick and on to his upcoming quiz.

***

While Sarah filed into the lunch line, Nick sat back down, his dirty-blond hair curling slightly at the ends with the humidity in the building. His blue eyes found hers from across the room as she shuffled forward in line. He winked at her, and her stomach flopped.

Sometimes she wondered why someone like Nick was with her. Her hand went to the delicate chain hanging from her neck, fingering Nick's school ring that hung on it like a pendant. He could be with any girl in the school, but he had pursued her. Maybe it was because at first she had ignored him, or because she had made it a challenge to get to know her.

She had always had a bad feeling about dating someone who didn't really seem like a Christian, but dating Nick was definitely a way to make sure other kids wouldn't start calling her Jesus Freak again. Enough time had passed that only a few people in school knew about the gift of faith and healing she had, Nathan included. She didn't dare tell Nick about it or he would really think she had gone crazy. It was hard to talk to him about God, but the few times that the subject had come up he reassured her that he believed in God and that he was a Christian. Even then, it didn't come across as though he was sincere, but maybe just telling her what she wanted to hear.

For now, she stuffed down her doubts and was grateful that she was able to appear normal to others around her.

Choosing the chicken sandwich and a salad, she scanned her ID card to pay for it. Sarah glanced again at Nick as she made her way back to the table. He looked up and winked again, causing heat to rise up her neck and flush her cheeks.

When she sat down by him, Nick ran a finger along her jawline and lightly kissed her cheek, whispering in her ear, "Do you know how beautiful you look today?" His warm breath on her skin gave her goose bumps and now she knew for sure that her face came close to matching her red shirt.

He sure knew how to make her feel special, but his outward display of affection always drew a red flag inside of her. She knew it was a dangerous line to walk. Her mother had always made comments when seeing young people kissing or caressing each other publicly, like, "If they are doing that in front of everyone, who knows what they are doing when nobody is around." Sarah had made a pact with herself and the Lord that she would never let things get so out of hand emotionally that it would go too far.

Shaking herself from her thoughts, Sarah lowered her voice and leaned over to Nick, "Hey, you know I don't like doing stuff like that in public, but thank you for the compliment." Making herself sound more like a parent she added jokingly, "Now behave yourself, young man!"

"Yes, ma'am!" Nick played along with her.

She wasn't sure if he meant it or not, but she was determined not to let his charm carry her emotions away.

In mock seriousness he straightened up, folding his hands on his lap, and looked over at her for approval.

Laughing, Sarah elbowed him lightly before grabbing her sandwich to eat it. "You're so weird. Better finish your lunch before the bell rings."

Chapter Three

After school Sarah changed into a gray long-sleeved T-shirt and faded jeans and headed to the stable. She was determined to put all her worries aside as she swung up on Shadow's back, the white horse shifting from side to side as she settled into place in the saddle. Clicking her tongue to encourage the animal into motion, Shadow eased into a comfortable lope and Sarah breathed in the scent of the pine and maple trees that dotted the hillside in front of them.

Riding had always been a form of therapy for Sarah, refreshing and exhilarating at the same time. Although Shadow was not a show horse or a jumper, she had worked with him on small jumps over fallen logs on the trails and basic maneuvers that she had seen in horse shows.

Today she noticed that the leaves were painted with red, orange, and golden hues. September was coming to a close and the colorful view was spectacular.

The particular trail she rode today on the Hendersons' property was so familiar to both horse and rider that Sarah could have closed her eyes and they would have ended up back at the stable just fine. The gurgling of Hanson's Creek met her ears as she rounded the bend about a fourth of the way into the trail. A contented sigh escaped Sarah's lips as she listened to the sound of water rushing over the mossy river rocks, washing over her like a cleansing stream.

Not able to resist getting lost in the beauty of the moment, Sarah pulled back on the reins and turned Shadow off the trail to a small clearing beside the sparkling water. After tying him to a low-hanging branch, Sarah secured her hair in a ponytail as she found a spot on a fallen log near the creek to sit and take it all in.

Here in the forest the colors were even more vibrant than near the house. A striking red maple draped in deep burgundy across the creek was perfectly complemented by the bright yellow leaves of the birch next to it.

After letting her senses drink deeply of her surroundings for a few moments, Sarah's thoughts turned back to the events of the day and she found herself talking to the only One she knew who could make things right.

"God, I don't know what to do about Maria. She seems to hate me, and I don't know why. Please show me what to do."

See her with My eyes, was the answer that came to her heart.

"I don't know what that means, Lord." She sat silently in thought and then continued, "Help me to get through to Maria. It still hurts my feelings how she treats me. We used to be such good friends. Help me to see her with Your eyes, God."

As she sat, deep in thought, the nagging issue deep inside of her began to come to the surface. "God, I know You gave me a special gift, and I want to make a difference, but I don't want to look weird or have people think I am some kind of religious nutcase. I can't go back to people calling me Jesus Freak and mocking me all the time, but I still feel like I should be helping people sometimes. Is that even possible?"

Use your gift, God whispered gently.

Sarah knew exactly what God was saying, but this was the thing she warred with so much. How could she use her gift of healing without other people ridiculing her? There had been times in the past she had let the gift flow, under very controlled circumstances, like the time Nathan had asked her to pray for his ears at her fourteenth birthday party. She could remember the feeling of God's healing flowing through her; but she also remembered the cruelty of those three girls when they saw her praying for Nathan. She closed her eyes and reminisced about the event.

Shadow's whinny brought Sarah back to the present. Standing, she stretched and brushed off the dirt from the back of her jeans as she returned to where she had tied the patient horse. He pawed the ground as she stroked his velvety muzzle, then used her fingers to brush through his coarse gray mane.

"Sorry boy, I got lost in my thoughts." Wrapping her arms around Shadow's soft neck, she breathed in the scent of horse and the outdoors before patting his hindquarters, which sent a swirl of dust up from the movement. "Ready to head back home?"

She untied the reins from the branch and led him back to the trail. Hiking her left foot up into the stirrup, Sarah swung her right leg over Shadow's broad back and turned the animal toward home, squeezing her heels into the horse's flanks to tell him to pick up speed. In a few minutes, she was approaching the stable and saw Nathan leaning against the fence, waiting for her to return.

"Hey there, cowgirl," Nathan greeted her with a wide smile as she approached. He was still wearing the same green shirt and dark blue jeans he had been wearing at school earlier.

"You been here long?"

"Just a few minutes. Figured you'd be back soon." Nathan followed her as she dismounted and led Shadow across the yard and into the stable to brush him down after their ride. He gently rested his arms on the stall and watched in comfortable silence as Sarah began the routine of brushing down the sweaty horse and picking out debris from his hooves.

After a few minutes Sarah looked up, curry comb in hand. "Do you remember that time when you asked me to pray for your ears when I turned fourteen?" She smiled at the memory as she continued to brush Shadow. "I was just thinking about that today."

"Of course I remember that; how could I forget it?" Nathan returned the smile. He gazed off, as his mind replayed the events of long ago. After a few minutes he looked down, moving around some stray pieces of hay with his shoe.

When he looked up, he asked, "Why don't you ever pray for anyone? There are so many people you could help. I think about it every time my friend, Brad, gets a migraine or whenever I hear about someone who's really sick." Nathan paused for a moment. "I know you don't want people to know about it. But something like that shouldn't be hidden."

Sarah sighed, now positioned next to Shadow's withers with one of his front hooves secured between her knees to pick out the packed dirt from the trail. Some of her hair had escaped from the ponytail and framed her face as she glanced at Nathan. "I guess I feel like everyone at school will think I'm some type of freak again. I got so tired of people calling me names or making jokes about me. I don't think I can handle that again."

She took a deep breath as she straightened Shadow's leg back to the floor, her hands feeling the powerful leg muscles to make sure there were no injuries going unnoticed. She glanced his way again. "Sometimes it bothers me when I know someone is sick, but I see how everyone treats the other kids who talk about God all the time and I...I just can't do it. I would lose everything I've worked so hard for..." She trailed off as she moved to the next hoof.

"You wouldn't lose me," Nathan said softly, then quickly added, "I would still be your friend."

"Well, duh," Sarah turned to look at him, smiling. "I know *you* wouldn't look at me that way, but I think everyone else would though."

After a few moments, he added, "You might be surprised." Nathan watched as she finished up with picking out the last hoof. "I think if other people knew you had something real, they would probably respect it."

"They didn't when we were fourteen...and maybe things have changed, but I'm not ready to find out yet." She led Shadow back into his stall and kissed his soft muzzle before shutting the stall door. "Wanna come in for a bit?" she asked, hoping to steer the conversation elsewhere, "My mom was making chocolate chip cookies when I left."

"Of course!" Nathan followed her the short distance from the stable to the house, "When have you ever known me to pass up your mom's chocolate chip cookies?"

As they entered the back door into the family room, the aroma of freshly baked cookies hit their noses, the chocolaty, sugary fragrance making Sarah's stomach growl.

"Hi there, Nate," Sarah's mom said as she emerged from the kitchen. "You must have a cookie sensor. Just in time." She gave Nathan a friendly rub on the shoulder. Then she turned to Sarah and gave her daughter a warm embrace. "Your dad should be back with Jordan any time now; he's picking him up from basketball practice. Did you have a nice ride?"

"Yup. The creek is beautiful right now. The leaves are really colorful deeper in the woods."

"I love autumn," Stephanie smiled wistfully. "We should have a bonfire soon and make s'mores." She turned to Nathan, "Maybe you and your family can come over, Nathan. I'll have Sarah let you know when we plan to do that."

"That would be fun, Mrs. Wright; my parents would like that," Nathan grinned.

Just then Sarah's brother, Jordan, came in the front door with her dad following close behind. Jordan's light brown hair was damp from practice and the ends curled out. Sweat marks in his white and orange basketball uniform showed signs of a rigorous practice and his weary blue eyes gave evidence that the coach had worked the team hard.

"Hi, Mom. Hey, Sarah. Oh, hey, Nathan, what's up?" He gave Nathan a fist bump as the trio in the kitchen echoed their hellos. Jordan headed through the kitchen, grabbing a handful of cookies and stuffing one in his mouth, "Hard practice today. Need a shower. Catch you all in a bit," he managed between bites as he headed down the hall to the bathroom.

David Wright entered the room next, pecking his wife on the cheek and wrapping his strong arms around her. Stephanie smiled and leaned into his embrace before he released her.

When David saw Nathan he crossed the room to enfold Nathan's hand in a manly handshake. Nathan was now just an inch shy of Sarah's five-foot-ten-inch father. David's deep blue eyes twinkled as he greeted Nathan. "Good to see you again, Nathan. You watching out for Sarah at school for us?" he winked.

"Yes, sir, I try to," Nathan answered playfully. Nathan had always fit into the Wright family with ease. Her house had almost been a second home to him; in fact, his parents joked with him that the Wright house was his second home.

"Good, that's what I like to hear." David caught Sarah in a warm side hug. "See, told you we have spies everywhere." He kissed the top of her head. "Anyone tries to mess with you, and Nathan here will knock them out for me."

"That's right, Mr. W., they're no match for me." Nathan pounded his fist in the palm of his other hand, amused at the insane idea of him beating *anyone* up.

The group laughed together and David made his way back to his wife. "Hey, Steph, if you need help with dinner, let me know. I'm gonna sit down for a few minutes," he said before retreating to the family room to catch up on the football stats.

"I better get home or my mom will wonder if I'm eating with you guys again for dinner."

"Well, you are certainly welcome to stay anytime, Nathan," Stephanie smiled.

"I know." Nathan grinned. "See you at church tonight, Sarah."

"I'll be there!" Sarah responded enthusiastically, watching at the doorway as he headed down the walkway. As usual, he turned to wave as he rounded the corner and disappeared behind the neighbor's wall of thick bushes.

"I'm so glad you have such a good friend like Nathan, Sarah," her mom said as Sarah shut the door.

"Yup, he's the best," Sarah agreed as she bounded upstairs to get her homework done before dinner.

Yes, she had a lot of friends, but Nathan was the most faithful one she ever had. What would she have done without him around?

Chapter Four

Sarah opened the door to the youth hall at Highland Falls Community Church and was met by loud, upbeat music and the sounds of a video game tournament in progress. Even with the low, colored lights she could tell that her youth pastor, Thomas Matthews, and about five to six other kids in the youth group were battling each other in a virtual paintball tournament before the service started.

All around the room there were posters of Christian bands along with signs, T-shirts, and banners with their youth group's name: R.I.O.T., which stood for Restoration In Our Town.

A small basketball court, separated by floor-to-ceiling glass walls, sat on the left side of the youth hall. It looked like a game had just come to an end as several of the guys filed in from the court, laughing and patting each other on the backs or shooting imaginary basketballs in the air as they relived highlights of the game they had just finished.

Sarah walked across the room, greeting friends as she went, to the coffeehouse-style tables situated on the far side of the room where she was welcomed by Nathan and some others who had gathered there. She smiled a greeting to Pastor Jake's son, Colton Martin, who gave her a half-smile in return.

Colton didn't strike her as a typical pastor's kid with his black hair and Goth-style clothing. Sarah felt like something was always bothering Colton, but never felt like it was her place to ask him about it all. For now she just prayed for him, as well as the whole Martin family.

With about twenty minutes to go before the service, she bought a soda from the snack bar and sat down by Nathan, who was wrapped up in a conversation with the rest of the group.

She glanced at two best friends sharing a secret at the next table and giggling together. Looking away, Sarah sighed inwardly. Even though she had a lot of friends at church, she missed the close friendship she used to have with Maria.

Before Maria's parents had divorced, she was at church all the time, and she and Sarah had been inseparable. There were so many memories they had shared here in this building. After the divorce, Maria had alienated herself from everyone—even Sarah, despite all the times Sarah had tried to reach out to her. Once Maria had seemingly recovered from her parents' falling out, she showed a strong bitterness and hatred for Sarah that struck deeply. Sarah suspected that it was coming from a jealousy of the tight family ties that she had with her own parents. It seemed that every time she came to church she was reminded of the closeness she and Maria had once shared.

She glanced at the two giggling friends again with a wistful, forced smile. It did no good to think about what had been and could be; only the future could be changed.

Taking out her smartphone, Sarah opened her Bible app to read a bit before service. It opened to where she had left off earlier in the day in 1 John 5 so she started reading from there.

As she read, verses 14 and 15 really caught her attention, "And we are confident that he hears us whenever we ask for anything that pleases him. And since we know he hears us when we make our requests, we also know that he will give us what we ask for."

Sarah paused to think about this passage. She definitely understood what the apostle John was saying and believed that God answered prayer. It still blew her mind to think that the God who made the universe would listen closely to her. Whenever she thought about this, she could not help but feel very small, but at the same time, extra special.

***

Nathan glanced over at Sarah as she was reading on her phone. She was beautiful. Her dark brown hair was smooth and silky, and her vivid green eyes captured him every time she looked at him.

They had been friends forever, it seemed, but about a year ago he started seeing her differently. It was like one day she was his buddy, and the very next day she started looking like a woman. He could clearly remember the moment it happened, although she probably had no clue. She had been walking down the hall with some friends at school and when she saw him she smiled and waved like she usually did, only this time his stomach started flip-flopping. He had managed to maintain his composure when it happened, but over the last year, his admiration for Sarah had grown, as well as his attraction to her.

Right now he tried to keep his attention on the conversation with his friends, but just having Sarah sit so close to him was both comforting and unnerving at the same time.

Nathan had grown more and more uncomfortable with Sarah's relationship with Nick. He saw how sometimes Nick said or did inappropriate things to Sarah, which really bothered him. She would playfully put Nick in his place, but he wondered what would happen as their relationship progressed. Being a guy, he knew how powerful hormones could be, especially with someone as attractive as Sarah around. He had not said anything to Sarah about his perception of Nick; not wanting to come across as jealous or controlling, but he prayed daily that God would show Sarah if she wasn't supposed to be with Nick.

Inwardly, Nathan wished that she would one day have feelings for him instead of Nick—or any other guy, for that matter. He always had a sense that they were supposed to be together, but did not want to risk losing her friendship if he ever told her how he felt.

With Sarah sitting just inches away, Nathan could smell the fruity fragrance of the strawberry-kiwi body spray she normally used. He slowly drew in a deep breath through his nose and allowed it to fill his senses. *Okay, Nathan. You have to get a handle on this. Church is about to start soon.*

He forced his attention back to what his friends were talking about for a moment before turning to Sarah, who was now putting her phone away.

"Reading something good?" he arched an eyebrow with the question as he tilted his head to look at Sarah.

"Of course, the Bible is always good reading." Sarah smiled, her features brightening. "Hey, I think service is getting ready to start, wanna head over?"

"Sure, let's go."

They got up and headed to the youth sanctuary located across the room from where they had been sitting. The auditorium held seating for about three hundred people, most of which was filled up every week with teenagers. They entered through a set of double doors and saw that the worship team—composed mostly of teens and a few college-age leaders—was already beginning to play some music, signaling that service was about to begin.

Sarah, Nathan, and some of the others from their table filed into the third row from the front, eager to worship. This was Nathan's favorite part of the service; he loved to listen to the music and unload the burdens of the day as he worshiped God. Of course, it was a bit more difficult to focus with Sarah next to him.

Today she occasionally brushed against his side as they swayed out of sync with each other to the music. Once her hand ran across the back of his hand when she had lowered her arms, sending a warmth that spread through his whole body. She must not have noticed because her eyes remained closed as she continued to sing.

***

Sarah forced her eyes not to open as she tried to evaluate what was going on inside of her.

How could one small accidental touch cause such a stir? It was like electricity had shot through her the instant her hand had brushed against Nathan's. How many times in the past had that happened and she didn't think anything of it? What about all the times they hung out after school or on the weekend without any strange feelings surfacing?

It had to be nothing—she was dating Nick anyway, right? He was the one she was supposed to have feelings for. Maybe she was just missing Nick because she had not been able to spend much time with him lately. Maybe she should spend some more time with Nick to make sure her feelings weren't being displaced.

She took a quick glance at Nathan, who seemed to be focused on the music. He probably didn't feel or sense anything. Sarah determined not to make it anything more than what it was—an accidental touch.

At that moment the drummer really got into the beat and his drumstick cracked, sending the splintered end flying over two rows of seats into the audience.

Sarah clapped her hand over her mouth to stop from laughing out loud as she and Nathan looked at each other with wide eyes before the whole room exploded in laughter.

Eric, the drummer, raised up his remaining stick like a trophy and nodded before reaching into his bag to grab a new stick and tapped his sticks back into the song.

Pastor Thomas just shook his head and chuckled, motioning to everyone to settle back down as worship continued.

The rest of the worship service was sweet and non-eventful, and before long, Pastor Thomas came up to the stage to transition the service into teaching. She looked forward to his message every week because it was always something that spoke right to where she was at, something she really needed to hear. She knew today would be no different.

Thomas Matthews had grown up in southern California before going to Bible college in Florida, and his style was proof of his tropical origins. His blond hair and laid-back attire, complete with brown leather sandals, made Sarah think that any minute he was going to grab a surfboard and head for the nearest ocean, several hundred miles away. Okay, maybe not at this time of year, but she imagined that he missed the sun-kissed states he used to live in. For now Pastor Thomas seemed content to dig in his heels in chilly central New York as he poured his life into the teens at Highland Falls.

"Turn in your Bibles to Matthew 21," he began.

Sarah already had her smartphone out and was quickly tapping the screen to get to the place where Pastor Thomas had said to open to.

Pastor Thomas began to read verses 18 through 22.

"In the morning, as Jesus was returning to Jerusalem, he was hungry, and he noticed a fig tree beside the road. He went over to see if there were any figs, but there were only leaves. Then he said to it, 'May you never bear fruit again!' And immediately the fig tree withered up. The disciples were amazed when they saw this and asked, 'How did the fig tree wither so quickly?' Then Jesus told them, 'I tell you the truth, if you have faith and don't doubt, you can do things like this and much more. You can even say to this mountain, "May you be lifted up and thrown into the sea," and it will happen. You can pray for anything, and if you have faith, you will receive it.'"

Pastor Thomas moved to the side of the small black podium his laptop was sitting on and pressed a knuckle to his lips, his other hand still resting on the podium as he assessed the group with his eyes. After a moment, he asked, "How many of us have this kind of faith, the kind where you can ask God for anything and know it will happen?"

Out of the corner of her eye, Sarah noticed Nathan glance over at her. She was very careful not to look back. She had never told Pastor Thomas or anyone else in the youth group about her gift—only Nathan. In fact, the lead pastor of Highland Falls Community Church, Pastor Jake Martin, was the only one who knew about it other than her family. Sarah knew that she possessed this type of faith, but was not sure how to use it without being labled as strange or crazy.

Once again, she focused her attention on Pastor Thomas as he continued.

Pastor Thomas hopped down off the stage to walk in the open area at the front of the room. His face became animated as he spoke, "Imagine what the world would be like if we really believed what Jesus said and demonstrated this type of faith. When the world realizes that the church has the answers that they have been searching for, they will be lining up out the door to experience the power of God that we know," he said excitedly, sweeping his arm in the direction of the door.

Pastor Thomas continued his message, but Sarah couldn't clear her mind from what he had just said. Could she take a chance on letting God use her to touch other people publicly? She didn't think she was ready to find out yet.

As she thought about it more she could feel healing power surging through her hands again.

***

A little while later, Sarah was heading out the door of the church with her mom to go home as she greeted Pastor Jake and Charlotte, who were holding the door open for people as they were leaving. Pastor Jake was wearing dark blue jeans and a maroon designer shirt. His short, dark hair was pushed up to little spikes right at his hairline, which, paired with his black-rimmed modern glasses, made him look younger than forty-five years old. Charlotte was dressed to match and her wide smile exuded warmth.

"Just the Wright ladies tonight? Good to see you, Sarah, Stephanie," Pastor Jake said as he gave them each a quick side hug.

"Yeah," Stephanie replied as she hugged Charlotte next, "Jordan had a big game tonight so David is there cheering him on."

"Great. I hope he does well," Pastor Jake sincerely stated.

Charlotte interjected, "I don't know if either of you were in the main service to hear the news. There's a member of the church you might know, Anna Clark, who is in the hospital. She was in a car accident yesterday and had a lot of internal damage. The doctors don't think she will live much longer."

"Oh my," Stephanie gasped, "I didn't know!"

Pastor Jake added, "We've been praying for her, and a few people have gone to visit her, but there hasn't been much progression in her condition. Charlotte and I were going to go visit her tomorrow and I would love for you ladies to come with us and join your faith with ours to pray for her healing. Would you be able to come with us after school?"

Charlotte spoke up, "I know God sometimes uses your faith to touch people who need healing, Sarah, and we were thinking this could be an opportunity for you to grow in that gift." She turned to Stephanie, "And you know Anna, so we figured you'd like to come along too."

Stephanie frowned. "I really wish I could but there's a PTO meeting tomorrow and I'm on the board so I need to be there."

Sarah could see the internal struggle in her mom's eyes. Stephanie always wanted to help others in need but her dad had told her that her mom tended to try to do too much for other people, getting way too involved in other people's business, at least from his perspective. Right now she could see that longing to help again.

"How about you, Sarah? We can pick you up if you need a ride," Charlotte asked.

Sarah bit her lip and her brow furrowed, "I don't know...um....it depends on how much homework I have." She searched her mind for anything else, not sure if she wanted to expose her gift just yet.

She had seen Anna around the church quite a bit and knew she was a great lady. It wasn't that she didn't want to help her; in fact, her heart was moved just from hearing about Anna's situation. And it wasn't that she didn't know if Anna would be healed—Sarah was confident that God would touch her if she went with Pastor Jake and his wife—

the real issue was that she still was not sure if she was ready to display her gift to the public eye. When God healed Anna, it could be all over the church, maybe the news, and who knows where else?

How in the world could she keep it quiet if an amazing miracle like *that* were to happen?

"I don't see why you couldn't go," Stephanie interjected, "it usually doesn't take you too long to do your homework, and this is a serious situation."

"I will have to let you know tomorrow," Sarah responded.

Charlotte reached to rub Sarah's shoulder lightly, "I hope you can. Have a good night."

"Please let me know if there's anything I can do," Stephanie said as they exited the building.

"I will. For now, just pray," Pastor Jake replied.

"We will. Goodnight," Stephanie said.

A war started inside of Sarah. Deep down she knew she probably should go. But if the woman was healed, how could she prevent people from talking about it? News could travel fast in a smaller community like theirs.

***

Sarah woke with a gasp, her chest heaving from the disturbing dream that played through her mind. Closing her eyes, she took a few deep breaths to calm herself down.

A glance at the clock revealed that it was just after midnight. She had only gone to sleep at eleven.

The dream had started out with her going to visit Anna with Pastor Jake and Charlotte, but she made a wrong turn and when she turned around Pastor Jake and Charlotte were gone. The hospital turned into and endless maze of hallways and passageways until she started running and calling out for Pastor Jake and Charlotte.

At the end of the dream she saw a door at the end of a long hallway and knew it was Anna's room. Sprinting there she entered to find Anna's body covered in a white sheet and Pastor Jake shaking his head saying, "You were a few minutes too late…"

It was long after this when Sarah was able to get back to sleep—and even then she was tossing and turning. By the time she woke, guilt had set in and she was leaning more toward joining her pastors later on. When it came down to it what was more important, her reputation or someone's life?

The answer seemed simple enough, but acting it out would probably be a different story.

Chapter Five

After losing sleep the night before, school was dragging on. By third period Sarah was having a hard time keeping her eyes open and her Spanish teacher was starting to notice.

When the end of class signaled, she gathered her books and papers and joined Nick, who was waiting outside her classroom and texting someone as he waited for her. His class was conveniently just across the hallway and they both had a study hall next. He wore a jersey emblazoned with the bright orange and black school colors that had "Highland Falls High" embroidered in an arch across the back along with his last name and number, which for Nick Caine was 31. All the football players wore their jerseys on game days.

As she approached, he quickly put his phone away and ran a hand through his blond hair, his usual sly smile spreading across his face.

"Hey, beautiful, you look tired," Nick said over the noise of the other students in the hallway.

She interlaced her hand with his and as they started down the hall, she leaned her head against his strong shoulder.

"I had a hard time sleeping last night," she yawned.

"Couldn't stop thinking about me?" He let go of her hand to put his arm around her waist.

The warmth of his hand through her clothes made her pulse race a bit.

"I have an idea," he said. They walked a bit longer in silence, his thumb stroking her waist. "Come with me." He shifted directions, guiding her down a less crowded hallway, her heels clacking on the shiny, white tiled floor. His blue eyes lingered on hers as they walked, making her cheeks flush.

She wasn't sure where Nick was headed with this.

"Where are we going?" Sarah asked, his touch starting to waken her senses.

"Somewhere to help you wake up."

He stopped in front of a wooden door labeled "Sports Department Storage," pulled a set of keys from his pocket without removing his arm from Sarah's waist, and opened the door. From the hallway she could see it was halfway full of used football equipment; a musty smell of sweat and old gym clothes met her nose.

Nick looked both ways and pulled her into the closet before she could protest. He shut the door behind them and pressed her to the wall of the darkened closet, sending her pulse into a frenzy. The only light in the closet came from some wooden slats in the door for ventilation purposes; she could just barely make out Nick's features in the dim light.

He rested one arm on the wall above them and lifted her chin with his other hand as he kissed her, lightly at first, then with an intensity she had never experienced before, and made her a bit frightened.

Pushing aside her fears, she brought her arms up around his neck and down to his muscular chest as she responded to his passion.

Nick brought his arm down and framed her face with his hands as the kiss deepened.

Her strong reserve started to chip away as his hands traveled down her back and to her waist, his thumbs circling at the top of her jeans where the edge of her shirt was.

She knew she had to put a stop to this soon, but her head was feeling light from the strong emotions racking her body.

Nick pressed himself against her body even harder and groaned as the intensity of his kiss heightened.

As Sarah felt his fingers shift from the edge of her shirt to her skin, the red flags that were waving in her head suddenly became a flashing neon warning.

She dragged her mouth away from his and pushed his hand out from under her shirt. "Nick…this isn't right…you know I don't believe in letting things go too far. We should get out of here." Her breathing was ragged and her chest heaved as she tried to compose herself.

"I told you I would wake you up." His voice was thick with emotion and his blue eyes smoldered in the dimly lit closet. He traced her jawline with his thumb, looking like he wanted to dive into another kiss. "I promise I won't let things get too heavy."

He moved in closer again, but Sarah was already squeezing out from between him and the wall. She opened the closet door, poking her head out to make sure nobody was around to see them exiting together. Now she vaguely remembered hearing the bell ring while Nick was kissing her.

With the coast clear, she ducked out quickly into the bright hallway before Nick could pull her back into the closet.

"I have to study for a test I have later. Come on." By his body language she could tell he was disappointed that she had ended things when she did. Sarah took a deep breath and quickly led the way down the now-empty hallway and back into the safety of the small cafeteria which was left open for students to go during study hall.

Because they were late, Nick gave the study hall monitor a pre-made excuse, which Sarah assumed they believed to be valid because of his popularity.

Sitting down at a long white table, she sat her backpack down between her and Nick to put some distance between them. Their study hall was pretty laid back and the teacher on duty didn't mind if they talked a bit or walked around. Most of the students were clustered in groups and talking among themselves. By now Nick had engaged himself with a game on his cell phone.

Sarah opened her textbook, trying to calm her mind enough to study. It took a few minutes for her pulse to stop racing.

That could have been really bad. What if she didn't have the same resolve next time Nick kissed her in private?

As these thoughts churned in her head, she noticed Nathan with a few of his friends across the room. She lifted her textbook a bit and slouched down, trying to avoid eye contact. In a way, Sarah hoped that Nathan would stay over there with his friends. She was feeling guilty for things almost getting out of hand a few minutes ago and felt sure that if Nathan saw her face he would be able to tell something was wrong.

She glanced over the top of the textbook to see if Nathan was looking at her. Sure enough, he was glancing at her every few minutes from across the room. There were twenty minutes left to the period so she tried to avoid Nathan's eyes. She knew he still felt uncomfortable around Nick so maybe he wouldn't come over. Nick stayed nearby, but he was now chatting with some of his friends. She hoped the rest of the period would go by quick.

Fifteen minutes before the bell rang Sarah peeked around her textbook again only to find Nathan's eyes seeking out her own. Not only that, but he was up and walking in her direction. Sarah sat up and put her textbook down, trying to stuff down her feelings of unease as Nathan approached their table.

"Hey, Sarah, Nick, how's it going?" Nathan asked with a smile. He was wearing a black and white checkered shirt and black jeans.

Sarah made a mental note of how good Nathan looked then immediately scolded herself. Glancing up shyly she returned a quiet, "Hey, just studying for a test." Nathan seemed to inspect her face with concern, but didn't say anything.

"Hey, Nathan! You moving in on my woman?" Nick said, half joking. With a sneer he put his phone away, moved her backpack aside, and scooted closer to put his arm protectively around Sarah's shoulders.

Nathan's face reddened and his eyes narrowed, something Sarah hardly ever witnessed. It took quite a lot to get Nathan mad, so why was he so bothered right now?

"Chill out, man. I was just saying hi to my *friend*. Sarah can be friends with whoever she wants; you don't own her. And by the way, Sarah and I have been friends much longer than *you've* known her," Nathan replied, straightening himself to his full height.

Sarah didn't think she had ever seen Nathan this perturbed before. He was normally laid back. *What has gotten into him?*

Feeling the need to defuse the situation, she took Nick's arm off her shoulders. "Come on, you guys. Nathan's not trying to take me away from you, Nick. He's just my friend. All he was doing was saying hi."

Nathan looked down at the ground, and she caught a hint of something else in his face, but she could not put her finger on what it was.

***

Nathan tried not to let his face give away his emotions. When Nick had put his arm around Sarah, it had ignited something deep inside of him. Then when Sarah emphasized that he was only her friend, he suddenly wished that *he* had been the one with his arm around her. He wanted to protect her *from* people like Nick. Guys like that typically just wanted one thing, and it wasn't a chaste little kiss, it was the most precious thing—their innocence—and they would normally keep seducing their girl until they got what they wanted. Nathan wished that girls, especially Sarah, would know to steer clear of those types of guys. They were trouble; and every single relationship that he had witnessed always ended with a tarnished female reputation. That was the last thing he wanted to see happen to Sarah.

When he first walked up to them today, he could tell that something wasn't quite right. Other people probably couldn't decipher Sarah's feelings, but he could read her like a book. Her eyes were hiding something, and he wanted to find out what it was.

Maybe he would text her later and find out what was going on.

Nick put his hands up, eyebrows raised. "Well I won't get in the way of your *friendship* then," he said dramatically.

Apparently trying to keep the mood light, Sarah chimed in, "You don't have to fight, boys. There's enough of me to go around."

Nick leaned over to Sarah and said in a low voice, "Wasn't enough for me earlier," nuzzling her neck.

He probably didn't realize that Nathan had heard it. In addition to having good hearing, Nathan had a cousin who was deaf and had taught Nathan how to read lips, which came in handy in situations like this.

Sarah moved away quickly and told Nick to stop. By the look on Sarah's face, Nathan knew this had something to do with whatever it was she was trying to hide.

The innuendo wasn't lost on Nathan and his anger boiled even more.

Nathan took a deep breath, his hands clenching his backpack straps a bit too tightly. Exhaling, he tilted his neck to the side, popping it. "I have to go study anyway. Mr. Moore is giving us a test later." He looked Sarah straight in the eyes. "I'll see you later, Sarah." Then he turned on his heel and went back over to his friends, sitting down and taking out a textbook to study without looking back at Sarah or Nick the rest of the study hall.

He was definitely going to find out what was going on.

***

Sarah watched Nathan as he went back to the other side of the room. She could tell by the way he walked and how his jaw was set, that he was very upset. Between what had happened with Nick earlier and Nathan's strange behavior just now, she didn't know what to think.

"Well, that was weird, looks like your friend doesn't like me after all," Nick ran his hands through his blond hair and chuckled. Leaning forward he looked Sarah in the eyes. "I still think he likes you; I mean, he is *always* around! He goes to church with you too!

Who knows what goes on there that you don't tell me about?" Nick sat back with his arms crossed, inspecting her. "Why *do* you go to church so much anyway?"

Sarah didn't like how this conversation was turning out. She took a deep breath. "I believe in God, Nick. You know that. Church is where I can learn more about Him. Nothing weird happens there, nothing between Nathan and me. I keep telling you that he is *just* my friend," she said, hoping the end of the period was soon.

She checked her cell phone. *Good, only a few seconds left.* She definitely wouldn't mention that she sat by Nathan in youth group each week, or that he came over to her house to hang out frequently—that would only fuel the fire.

"Well, guys can tell how other guys look at a girl. If you didn't keep telling me that he is just a friend, I would think he likes you...a lot."

The bell rang. *Good timing.*

"I have to run, catch you later." She gave him a quick peck on the lips and hurried off to her next class. She needed to clear her head.

Deep in thought, Sarah traveled down the crowded hallway mechanically as she tried to sort everything out in her head.

On top of the closet encounter with Nick and how Nathan was acting a few minutes ago, she hadn't mentally prepared herself to go to the hospital later to pray for Anna. This morning at breakfast she had asked her mom to pass on to Pastor Jake and Charlotte that she would go with them. She thought back to when she was fourteen and all of the junk that she went through just because she wanted to help a few people and see them healed. Was she setting herself up for something like that to happen again?

A shoulder knocked into her unexpectedly, jarring her out of her thoughts. "Watch where you're walking, dork," a familiar voice sneered.

Maria Romano.

Sarah picked up her backpack, which had slipped off her shoulder from the blow, and lifted her eyes to meet Maria's menacing gaze.

"Wow, the happy-go-lucky girl looks sad," Maria said with mock compassion. She flipped her long black hair over her shoulder and took a defiant stance, hands on the hips of her too-short cheerleading skirt. "What's the matter, Sarah? Lose something…or someone?" Maria laughed as she turned on her heel to catch up with her friends.

Confused, Sarah looked after Maria and muttered, "What is she talking about?"

She repositioned her backpack on her shoulder and kept moving, shaking her head as she went. She didn't want to kindle any more hatred, and she didn't have a clue what Maria meant by that either.

Lose something or someone? Great, something else for me to figure out. Just what I needed, Sarah thought as she continued to her fifth period ELA class.

She couldn't wait to get home later. Maybe her mom could help sort it all out.

Chapter Six

So how was your day, sweetie?" Sarah's mom asked, placing a plate with a hot cinnamon roll slathered in melted frosting in front of her as she situated herself on the stool at the kitchen counter. Stephanie came around the counter to enfold her daughter in a motherly embrace, combing through Sarah's hair with her fingers for a moment before letting go. "You look like you need to talk."

Was she *that* transparent?

"Yeah, Mom, it was a weird day." She told her mom about Maria, and how Nathan got really mad at Nick, purposely leaving out the part about the storage closet. That would have to be a whole different talk altogether. Then she unloaded her concerns about going to pray for Anna.

When she finished, she nibbled at the cinnamon roll while her mom came over to sit by her at the counter.

"Well, let's start with Maria. Obviously that girl is hurt. For her to treat you that way when you used to be such good friends tells me that something wounded her deeply and this is how she is coping with it."

"But I didn't do anything to her, Mom. All of a sudden one day she hates me. We used to be best friends, and honestly, I miss that." Sarah's stomach clenched as she fought the tears that sprung to her eyes.

Her mom placed a hand on Sarah's back, rubbing it gently. "I know you didn't do anything to make her hate you, sweetie. God can heal her heart and your friendship, but in the meantime, just love her.

You may not see a difference at first but if you persist and show her love, it will melt that hatred and bitterness."

"It shocked me so much today when she ran into me that I didn't even say anything to her. I felt like an idiot. Then she asked me if I had lost something or someone; what did she mean by that?"

"Maybe the answer to that will unfold eventually. For now, start asking God to show you what to say and do, and listen to your spirit. Many times you probably already know what to do. You know the Bible pretty well, so the Holy Spirit can take the Word and bring it to light when you need answers. Sometimes those first instincts are really the Lord telling you what to do."

Sarah turned this over in her mind as she finished her cinnamon roll, swiping a dollop of frosting off the plate with her finger and transferring it to her mouth. When Nick was getting his keys out, she'd had a feeling that she should just leave and get to study hall. Maybe that was God telling her to stop something before it turned into a sticky situation.

Thank God she finally listened when He flashed the big warning sign in her brain.

Her mom continued, "Now with Nathan, that could be several things."

She pulled the cinnamon roll pan over and cut herself a piece, lifting it out of the tray, icing drizzling on the plate.

"Maybe he knows something about Nick that you don't know and is trying to protect you. Your dad and I don't know very much about Nick. He seems nice enough when he came over a few times, but he has a different set of beliefs, which may be a distraction for you; you said he's Catholic, and you also shared that he is not very committed to his own faith either." Stephanie cut a piece of the cinnamon roll with her fork. "Or maybe Nathan was just having a bad day and Nick's comment threw him off."

Stephanie paused, taking time to chew and swallow her next bite before continuing. "Or…maybe Nathan has feelings for you, and doesn't know how to act when he sees you and Nick together." She glanced at Sarah from the side, her eyebrows raised and a small grin on her lips.

Sarah turned and scrunched up her face. "Mom, Nathan and I are like best friends. I don't think he likes me like that."

Her mind went back to church the night before, when her hand brushed his, and the flurry of emotions she felt then returned with the memory.

"Well, suddenly you are blushing, my daughter." Stephanie smiled, rising to throw away the paper plates and wash her hands.

Before her mom could go any further with that conversation, Sarah thought it would be a good time to gear up to pray for Anna, being that it was already four o'clock. "Well, Pastor Jake and Charlotte should be coming by after a while to pick me up."

"I'm glad you're going. I wish the PTO meeting was on a different night so I could come with you. Anna is in a serious condition from that car accident. From what I hear, there's not a lot of hope for her. Grace called earlier today with the prayer chain. I've been praying for her on and off all afternoon." Stephanie dried her hands on a kitchen towel and placed it back over the handle on the stove where it normally hung. "I wish there was something more I could do."

Stephanie took a deep breath. "But there's something you *can* do. Sarah, God's given you a great gift to be able to pray for people and see them healed—that's rare! I don't totally understand that level of faith, but you should definitely use it when you have the chance. Don't be afraid to use your gift today." She poured herself a cup of hot coffee from the pot she had made earlier, pulling out some French vanilla creamer from the fridge. "You want a cup of coffee?"

"Sure, I think I have enough time. Thanks."

Sarah paused and looked down while her mom grabbed a second cup and filled it, adding some creamer and setting the steaming cups in front of them as she sat back down next to Sarah.

"Like I said earlier, I don't know how I feel about praying for people and stuff. I want to, but I keep remembering how people used to call me 'Jesus Freak' all the time. I don't want to be labeled with that again." Sarah stirred her coffee with a spoon that her mom offered, as Stephanie answered.

"Doesn't that seem a little selfish? You're worried more about your own reputation than helping that poor woman who is lying in the hospital fighting for her life. The Bible says that to know to do good and not do it is actually sin."

Sarah remembered back to the dream she had the night before as she slowly sipped her coffee. She hadn't told her mom about it because it was still so haunting. She could still clearly recall it in detail and she shuddered.

The memory of the dream combined with what her mom was saying to her now brought a fresh desire to do the right thing. "I know, Mom. You're right. I need to stop making this about me and get focused on what God wants me to do."

Stephanie smiled over her cup and they finished their coffee together in reflective silence.

A few minutes later, Sarah ran a brush through her hair and cleaned her teeth, not wanting to pray for someone with cinnamon roll and coffee breath. The Martins had called to say they were on the way and would be there within ten minutes.

As Sarah looked out the front window, her mom came in the room.

"I'll be praying for you all while I'm at the meeting," Stephanie said as she came closer. Tilting her head, Stephanie seemed to struggle to put her thoughts into words. "Since we started seeing God use you to bring healing and do miraculous things, it made me wonder how those things happen when *you* pray, but not as much for other Christians. Sometimes I wonder about it all, you know?"

Sarah nodded slowly. "Yeah, I don't completely understand it. I think it has to do partly with faith. It's hard to explain, but I just know that God can do it. I can tell when He wants me to pray with that special faith; it's almost like I can't *not* pray. I have such an overwhelming feeling that something is about to happen. I can normally tell the moment that God touches the person. I feel this power move through my body and into theirs; it's wild."

She exhaled slowly and checked out the window for signs of her pastors, and spotted their black sedan making its way up the street to her house.

Her mom had noticed too. "Oh, there's the Martins, you better get going. I'll have supper done before I leave for the meeting, so it will be there when you get home—meatloaf and garlic mashed potatoes with corn."

"You're making me hungry already! Love you, Mom." Sarah grinned as she rose to give her mom a quick hug before bounding down the driveway to the Martin's car.

Pastor Jake had stepped one foot out of the car and waved to Stephanie before greeting Sarah. Charlotte was in the front passenger seat looking as lovely as she always did.

Even though they were in their mid-forties, they groomed themselves in a way that made her feel comfortable around them. The only things that seemed to give away Pastor Jake's age were the lines that appeared at the corners of his eyes when he smiled. Sarah felt at ease around him, like a second dad. Charlotte was slim and kept up on the latest fashions, her short, dark hair always in place and nails nicely manicured.

They had a son, Colton, who was about a year younger than Sarah. Even though the Martins lived in the same school district, Colton went to a private school. She didn't know him as well, except that Colton didn't seem to like the church scene and mostly kept to himself.

Sarah got in the back door that Pastor Jake was holding open for her and made herself comfortable. This car was the one Pastor Jake normally used, which he kept fairly clean except for a few gum wrappers sticking out of the console in between the front seats. He was an avid gum chewer, probably because he talked to people all day long. The midsize car had a light tan leather interior and all the latest gadgets on the dash. He must have stashed an air freshener in a vent or under a seat because the fragrance of vanilla wafted through the car; it smelled good.

"I'm so glad you decided to come." Charlotte turned around in her seat to smile at Sarah. "Do you know Deanne Campbell? She works at the hospital on the same floor that Anna is on. In fact, she's one of the head nurses for the floor."

"Yeah, I know her. Mrs. Campbell used to be my Sunday school teacher when I was little. She's nice. I didn't know she worked there." Sarah was glad that there would be a familiar face at the hospital to meet them.

Most pastors did their visitations alone, but Charlotte loved to accompany Pastor Jake when he made his rounds. Once, Sarah had overheard Charlotte tell some other ladies in the church that going with her husband to pray for the parishioners helped her feel more connected. Sarah admired this about her pastors.

They drove in silence for a few moments, and Sarah felt like she better talk to the Martins about what might happen before they arrived.

"Can I ask you guys a favor?"

"Sure thing, Sarah. What is it?" Pastor Jake glanced at her in the rearview mirror.

"I have a feeling that something will happen when I pray for Anna, but in the past when other people, especially kids at school, found out that I pray for people, they looked at me differently. Some of my friends even called me names and stuff. I just don't want to have that happen again."

She picked nervously at some old pink nail polish on a fingernail, "If something does happen, can you guys *not* tell people that I was there? I know it is a strange request, but I would really appreciate it." She glanced up with a hopeful look.

Pastor Jake looked a bit confused for a moment, but then his eyes softened. He glanced at Charlotte, then returned his gaze to the road ahead.

"No problem, Sarah. I can just mention that we had a prayer time and we will give God all the glory for it. It's not really about us anyway."

"We can do that, Sarah," Charlotte confirmed with a smile.

Sarah breathed a sigh of relief. "Thanks."

Remembering her conversation with her mom before she left, she thought she would take advantage of having a theologian nearby. With all the traffic, they had a few more minutes before they got to the hospital.

"Can I ask you a question, Pastor Jake?"

"Sure, I'll try to have an answer."

"My mom asked me something that I really have wondered for a long time. How come more people get healed—and so much quicker—when I pray for them? I know some people who pray for healing for months or years before they see an answer, if any. It seems like I pray just once, or maybe twice, for someone and they get healed! It just doesn't seem normal."

"Well, actually it's not, right, honey?" he said to Charlotte.

She shook her head no as he continued.

"There are gifts that God gives specific people that are supernatural types of gifts. Some people call them manifestation gifts. We read about them in the Bible in First Corinthians twelve. There are nine of them—you should read about them and study them when you get a chance—but I see three of those in particular that operate through you: special faith, workings of miracles, and the gift of healing. You see, often when God gives one of these special gifts to someone, it spills over to other special gifts as well. I believe there are times when God may use any Christian in one of those areas, but when He gives someone the *gift* for that particular area, they will operate in that gift on a regular basis, like you do. But many people who have gifts like yours either don't realize that they have them, or don't know how to use them properly, like you're learning how to do. In my lifetime, I haven't run across very many people with the gift of special faith like you have. So you see, the gifts you have are very special."

They were nearing the hospital now.

"Yes, Sarah," Charlotte interjected, "I don't think you realize yet how important the gifts that you have are!"

Sarah decided she would look that Scripture up very soon and do a study on the manifestation gifts. "Do you have any books that tell more about the gifts I have? I would love to find out more."

Pastor Jake's face lit up in the rearview mirror, "Sure, I even have books that tell about the lives of famous healing evangelists like Smith Wigglesworth, Kathryn Kuhlman, John G. Lake, Charles Finney, and some others. I would be happy to loan those to you too," he said as he grabbed the parking ticket for the garage and found a close spot labeled for clergy parking.

Feeling a new excitement about the special things God had put in her life, Sarah could feel the apprehension chipping away as she and the Martins made their way to the main doors of the hospital.

Chapter Seven

E ven if she had her eyes closed, Sarah would be able to tell that they were in a hospital from the strong odor of antiseptic and rubbing alcohol in the air.

Pastor Jake greeted the older woman at the receptionist's desk and they headed to the elevators that would take them to the fifth floor where Anna's room was.

Sarah was glad Pastor Jake led the way, obviously familiar with the maze of hallways in the hospital from the many visits he had made to parishioners over the years. The wide hallways and pastel framed pictures on the walls helped lighten the mood of the hospital along with the soft music playing through the speaker system.

The staff seemed nice enough; the nurses they passed along the way greeted them with a smile and a nod or a friendly "good afternoon" as they passed.

Sarah felt excited as they walked, anticipating what was going to happen.

After a few minutes they arrived at the elevators. Pastor Jake pushed the button to go up, and they waited for one to arrive.

Sarah wrapped her arms around herself and looked about as they waited. Highland Falls Memorial Hospital had originally been built in 1957 by a local Catholic church and was first run by a group of priests and nuns, according to a large framed painting of the original building on the wall opposite the elevators. There had been a lot of updates since then.

Sarah moved closer to the picture and studied it.

The hospital as it looked today was much larger and more advanced than the one sketched in the picture. The entryway had been totally redone and the smaller black-and-white pictures to the right side of the painting that showed the original interior looked very plain and white compared to the moss green and light cranberry accent colors on the walls and floors today.

"Looked a bit different back then, huh?" Charlotte stepped up alongside her.

"Yeah, it did. When did they make all the improvements?"

"I'm pretty sure most of them have taken place in the last ten years." They heard a ding announcing that the elevator had arrived.

They turned around and waited while a nurse carefully wheeled out an elderly man in a hospital bed.

"It happened a little bit at a time," Pastor Jake interjected as he reached his arm across the elevator entrance, preventing the doors from closing and letting Charlotte and Sarah go in the elevator first. Once inside, he hit the button for the fifth floor.

"I think the new entrance was the last thing they modernized. Unfortunately, as the building became more modern, the staff became more liberal." He explained how over time the spirituality had faded and that even though the hospital still had a chapel, it was rarely used by the staff, only by desperate families praying for their loved ones to pull through a tragic time. There was a chaplain on staff, but he represented a whole array of different beliefs.

After the elevator doors opened on the fifth floor, Pastor Jake led the way around a few bends in the hallway to a large nurse's station.

Deanne Campbell was there, looking over a patient's chart. As they approached the desk, she looked up and a wide smile broke out over her face.

"Pastor Jake and Charlotte, Sarah! So great to see you guys! Have y'all come to check in on Anna?" Deanne put down the chart and moved around the desk to give the Martins and Sarah a hug.

Sarah always loved to hear Mrs. Campbell talk. Even though she had moved to New York state years ago, her voice still had a strong Louisiana accent. The distinctive drawl reminded her of the movies with the southern belles wearing poufy dresses and drinking English tea on the veranda.

Sarah smiled at the thought. Even though she was in her mid-thirties, it was easy to picture Deanne in one of those dresses with her tiny figure, blue eyes, and long wavy blonde hair that fell to the middle of her back. Here at work she fixed it into a neat bun at the back of her head, and her light blue and pink scrubs were a far cry from a flouncy dress.

Pastor Jake spoke first, "Yup, we came to see Anna Clark and pray with her. How is she doing today?" Concern was laced in his voice

"A little better, but she's not out of the woods yet." Deanne frowned. She shook her head slowly. "It's just so sad. I keep praying that she gets better. Her family has all been here, just in case..."

Her voice trailed off as she thought about the implications of what could happen if Anna's condition didn't change soon.

Sarah could feel something starting to rise within her as Deanne talked.

She didn't know if anyone else could feel it or not, but there was an electricity in the air. God was going to do something; she just knew it. Anticipation started to well up and faith grew in her heart as they walked to Anna's room. She felt a joy bubbling up that she could barely contain, and she could sense the Lord's presence very close.

Fortunately, Anna's condition required her to have a private room.

A few of Anna's relatives greeted them with somber faces as Sarah and the Martins entered the room and came alongside Anna's bed.

A frail looking woman in her upper fifties lay on the bed, her salt-and-pepper gray hair spread over the pillow. Sarah barely recognized Anna compared to what she looked like the last time she saw her at church. A myriad of tubes and sensors were attached to Anna in different places and a monitor beeped constantly in the background. She had on a clear plastic mask to help her breathe.

Without knowing that God was at work, it would look like a tragedy indeed. The family, who were also believers, played soft worship music in the background, bringing a peaceful feeling in midst of the tragedy.

Anna's skin had an ashen look and her face was very pale—not a good sign.

Charlotte stepped closer to the bed and gently took Anna's hand, covering the top with her other hand, being careful not to get too close to the IV that was securely taped near the base of her wrist, attached to a slow dripping bag of fluids and medicines to keep her hydrated and help with the pain.

"Anna, it's Charlotte Martin. Pastor and I came by to see how you are doing," she said loudly enough for Anna to hear over the machines and beeping.

Anna's eyelids fluttered for a second, then she slowly opened her eyes about halfway. A tiny smile came across her face as she recognized Charlotte and Pastor Jake and she nodded slightly and squeezed Charlotte's hand a bit.

Anna's gaze moved to Sarah standing nearby and she nodded again in Sarah's direction.

"I asked Sarah to come with me today and pray for you, if that's okay. Sarah is Stephanie and David Wright's daughter. She is practicing praying in faith." Pastor Jake smiled as he glanced over at Sarah.

Deanne had stayed in the room as well, checking some papers at the foot of Anna's bed. It was obvious that she was praying quietly as she looked at Anna's charts. How wonderful it was to know that a solid Christian was taking care of Anna and the others on this floor.

"Thank you." Anna's weak voice was barely audible through the clear plastic mask.

Sarah spoke up, "Anna, I feel like God wants to do something special for you." Her faith was so stirred that she couldn't wait to see what was about to happen!

Feeling led by God, she moved around Pastor Jake and Charlotte and stood by the head of Anna's bed, already interceding quietly under her breath. Placing her right hand gently on the woman's head, she grasped the rail on the bed with her left hand, because there was already a surging of the power of God moving through her body. It grew stronger by the second as she began to pray, "Father God, I lift up Anna to You, asking You to bring total healing into her body. Heal everything that's broken, Jesus."

The atmosphere in the room had changed.

Sarah opened her eyes for a second as she paused to see what was happening. A tear trailed down the side of Anna's face and dampened the pillow.

Sarah closed her eyes again and continued, "God, You love Anna so much, and said that by Your stripes we are healed, and that if we ask anything in Your name, it will be done. So right now I ask that You heal Anna, in Jesus' name."

At that very moment, Sarah felt a rush of supernatural energy flow out of her hand and into Anna, causing the woman's body to jolt slightly. Warmth and release washed over Sarah; it was done, she knew it.

Whether the results were instant or delayed, God was touching Anna.

The hand that had felt so light and weak a moment before now began to grip Charlotte's hand tightly.

"Oh, thank You, Jesus!" Anna whispered slowly as more tears flowed and her trembling lips curled up in a smile. Color was already coming back into her face and skin.

The monitor that had been beeping slowly in the background, low from Anna's weak vitals, suddenly jumped in frequency. The beeps closer together and stronger.

In a few moments another nurse poked her head in the room. "Everything all right in here?" Seeing Deanne she asked, "Did you check on the other patients on this hall yet, Deanne?" seemingly annoyed for some reason.

Shifting her focus to the monitors next to Anna, the nurse noticed something had changed. With a confused look she narrowed her eyes and said, "Huh, that's weird, things sound different."

She gave Deanne a sharp look as she moved around to the opposite side of the bed from where Sarah and the Martins stood, as though Deanne must have noticed something happen and should have alerted the rest of the staff that there was a change.

"It's okay, Rachel." Deanne smiled and moved from the end of the bed to the side by Rachel. "It's a change for the better, not the worse."

"Well, I should check, just in case," she said pointedly as she looked closely at the monitors next to Anna. After a few seconds her eyebrows raised. "Wow, her blood pressure is almost normal. And her color looks better."

Then seeing the tears on Anna's face, she frowned. "You okay, honey? Do you need some rest? We can have everyone leave if you want." She smoothed Anna's hair down and wiped a tear away.

Anna shook her head slightly, "No, please let them stay," she said slowly, her voice already sounding a bit stronger.

Rachel nodded slightly, "Okay, they can stay for a bit longer, but you need some rest soon." She looked at Deanne matter-of-factly.

"We'll make sure she gets her rest. Don't worry," Deanne replied to the unspoken hint as Rachel made her way out of the room.

Turning her attention to the Martins and Sarah, Deanne said, "Don't worry about her. I think she knows we were praying in here. She gets bothered when God comes into any equation."

They visited with Anna a few more minutes. Her family was ecstatic and amazed at the noticeable change in Anna within just a few minutes after they had prayed. They thanked Sarah and the pastors over and over for coming.

Deanne even said that it looked like Anna's vitals had gotten so much stronger in such a short time that the doctor would probably give the okay to stop using oxygen later that day.

Before leaving, Sarah came alongside Anna to say good-bye.

Anna tried to sit up, obviously feeling better than when they came in, but Deanne placed a hand on her arm,

"Whoa there, take it easy, Anna. Let me help you." Deanne brought the head of the hospital bed up so Anna could sit comfortably.

After getting herself situated, Anna reached for Sarah's hand and said through the mask, "Thank you for coming today." Her eyes welled up with tears again and Sarah leaned over carefully to give Anna a hug. "I can feel God healing me; the pain has gotten much better already!" She pulled Sarah into a stronger embrace. "God bless you!"

Pastor Jake turned from talking with the excited family. "Praise God! Isn't it amazing how God can use us to touch other people? And glory to Him for healing Anna today," he said as Sarah stepped back from the bed. "Sarah told me earlier that she doesn't want a lot of people knowing that God works miracles through her just yet." Then he added playfully, "I guess she doesn't want people thronging her for prayer." He winked at Sarah.

Sarah felt her face redden slightly; she knew it must be a strange request to keep something so great a secret.

"I'm still trying to sort it all out; even amazing things are hard to understand, especially to people who don't know the Lord. They look at you differently." She shrugged. "It's God who did it anyway, not me."

Charlotte chimed in, "In time it will be evident how God works through her. And as Sarah is being used more and more by the Lord, we're guessing that she won't be able to hide it. Until then, we want to respect her wishes. Like Sarah said, it's God who touches people, not us. We're just the channel, the vessel He uses."

Anna focused on Sarah and spoke softly and slowly, but with conviction, "You should never be ashamed of what God is doing in your life. Don't hide your light. Let it shine."

***

The words Anna spoke stayed with Sarah all the way home, and gnawed away at her as she brushed Shadow down after dinner. Here in the stable she could pour out her heart to the Lord, sometimes out loud; sometimes as silent prayers while she cared for Shadow.

Deep down, she knew she needed to make some decisions soon. One thing would lead to another. Admitting that God had given her a special gift and letting it flow without trying to hide it would mean that she wouldn't fit in at school like she'd tried so hard to do.

She didn't know what Nick would think of that, or if she should be with him once she made a stand. Her mom had voiced her concerns about Nick not holding the same faith as she did, and that part of their relationship seemed strained. He never came to church with her when she invited him. He always had some excuse for not being able to go.

"Hey, you," Nathan's voice and the stable door closing interrupted her thoughts and made her jump. "I knew I'd find you here."

She hadn't even heard the door open. He had changed clothes since school and was now wearing blue jeans and a button-down olive green shirt that brought out the green in his eyes. The light in the stable accentuated out highlights in his hair that mingled in with his natural color as he swiped his bangs out of his eyes.

He came up next to the stall and leaned on the top rail a few feet away from her.

"You scared me!" She placed her hand over her chest to still her rapidly beating heart.

"Sorry." Nathan just grinned. Apparently he enjoyed making her jump. He took a step closer to her.

Sarah breathed deep through her nose and captured the familiar scent he brought with him before she even realized that she did it.

Do I do that every time Nathan's around? she wondered. Inwardly chiding herself, she turned and smiled. "What's up?"

"I came by earlier, but your mom said you went to the hospital with Pastor Jake and Charlotte to pray for Anna. How did that go?"

"Really good!" She turned back to finish grooming Shadow. Just a little more brushing through the mane and she would be done. "She already seemed better by the time we left," she added with a big smile.

Nathan grinned back, "I had a feeling you'd be saying that. I bet her family is really glad you were there."

"Yeah, they were. I wish you could have seen God touch her like that. She could barely talk or move when we came in the room and by the time we left she was sitting up and hugging me! It was amazing." Her eyes danced with delight as she spoke.

"So we should be hearing a big praise report Sunday, I guess?"

"Yes, but not about me praying and she was healed. God is getting the glory," Sarah added quickly as she worked the comb through a tangled spot in the gray mane.

After a moment Nathan said softly, "You know, it's not a bad thing if people know that God uses you in a special way."

"I know, I know. Everyone's been saying stuff like that to me lately." Wanting to change the subject, Sarah thought she would ask about how he was acting earlier.

"By the way, why did you get so mad at school today in the lunchroom? I don't think I've ever seen you get that mad. At least not since my brother put a bunch of worms in your pocket six years ago."

She smirked at the memory of the horrified look on Nathan's face when he discovered the worms and pulled out a dirty, mushy mass from his jacket pocket. That shock had quickly turned to anger and he had chased her brother, Jordan, down the street, yelling and throwing bits of worms and dirt at him as he went.

"I don't know." Nathan looked down and toed the dirt and straw on the stable floor. "I know Nick is your boyfriend and all, but I just don't trust him. You don't hear all the stories I do about him from the other guys." Sighing, he looked back up. "What *I* want to know is what happened before I got there. I saw the look on your face, and I know what he said to you, Sarah." He straightened. "Did he hurt you?"

Sarah took her time getting the final tangle out of Shadow's mane, thankful that he couldn't see her face from that angle.

"Nothing happened." She hoped her voice held steady enough as the memory of the equipment closet came rushing back. She could feel Nathan's eyes on her as she worked at the tangle.

"I don't buy it, Sarah. I *know* something happened. You might as well tell me now so I don't have to bug you about it every day until you tell me." He came around the stall to face her.

Sarah glanced up at Nathan's inquiring eyes, then back down at her hands fingering the horse's smooth mane.

It was no use hiding anything from Nathan; he *would* find out eventually. What if Nick told a different story than what really happened; that would be even worse. She had heard rumors of things he did in the past, but Nick had assured her that he wasn't like that anymore.

"Nick...well...he said he was trying to help me wake up because I was so tired this morning...I didn't know where he was taking me and...the next thing I knew we were in an equipment closet." She looked the other way at the far end of the stable.

She glanced back at Nathan's concerned face, then looked down. "He kissed me but he wanted more than a kiss, so I got out of there as fast as I could and headed to study hall. That was right before you came in. Nothing else happened; I just didn't think he would be like that. He knows where I stand on it."

Embarrassed, she kept her eyes down.

Nathan let out a frustrated breath. "It doesn't matter with guys like Nick. They only want one thing, and it's...I just..." Nathan looked her square in the eyes. "Why are you with him anyway? He doesn't treat you right. What if he tries something again? What if he hurts you?"

Nathan took a step closer and said in a soft voice, "You deserve so much better than that."

Sarah's skin prickled at his nearness, and she looked up into Nathan's eyes, their gaze locking for a moment before his eyes flicked down to her mouth and back to her eyes.

For a moment, time stood still.

Nathan swallowed and looked down at his boots. He cleared his throat and said softly, "I really care about you, Sarah. I don't want to see you get hurt. You deserve better." When he looked up at her again, his eyes were full of emotion.

Slowly he reached up and tucked a loose strand of hair behind her ear, his thumb gently stroking her cheek as he did. Dropping his hand, he exhaled slowly. "I have to get home. See you tomorrow."

He held her gaze for a moment longer before turning to leave.

"See ya," Sarah responded as he left.

Sarah watched him walk until he disappeared from sight, trying to figure out what was going on in her heart.

A flood of emotions coursed through her, but this was different than what she had felt this morning in the equipment closet. That had been a sensual, lustful wanting, but this felt pure and hopeful. Sometimes around Nick she felt like a piece of meat that he craved, but with Nathan she felt cherished and respected.

Yes, she had a lot of thinking to do.

Chapter Eight

A little while later, Sarah returned to the stable with Bible in hand, along with a few other books.

Shadow welcomed her with a soft whinny. She inhaled deeply of the hay and alfalfa scented air as she rubbed the horse's soft muzzle. Shadow lipped at her hand, hoping to find a sugar cube.

"Sorry, boy, no sugar today, just some books for me to read." Sarah scratched between his ears. The big animal nodded his head, enjoying the attention.

As she petted the horse a few more moments, Sarah's mind went back to the conversation she'd had with Pastor Jake earlier.

Ever since talking with the Martins on the way to the hospital she wanted to dig further into the Scriptures and figure out this gift that she had. On the way back they stopped by the church, and Pastor Jake grabbed some books from his office about well-known ministers who also possessed gifts of faith and healing for her to read.

She had already browsed through a few of those for a while before coming back out to the stable and was fascinated by what she read. She was especially interested to read more about Smith Wigglesworth, a healing preacher who ministered from 1913 to 1947, and had some of the most unusual—and violent—healing experiences she'd ever heard.

One account said that he had punched someone in the stomach, and they were healed of some condition! He was known to pray and bring dead people back to life. Once someone brought a dead child to him, and he kicked the child's body off the stage, shocking everyone when the baby came back to life! Another time he had gone to a funeral, picked up the dead body, thrown it against the wall several times, and the person came back to life!

Now *that* is what you call faith! She couldn't imagine doing anything like that.

Sitting cross-legged on a bale of hay, Sarah opened up her Bible app to a passage Pastor Jake had referred to earlier and read 1 Corinthians 12:7-10:

"A spiritual gift is given to each of us so we can help each other. To one person the Spirit gives the ability to give wise advice; to another the same Spirit gives a message of special knowledge. The same Spirit gives great faith to another, and to someone else the one Spirit gives the gift of healing. He gives one person the power to perform miracles, and another the ability to prophesy. He gives someone else the ability to discern whether a message is from the Spirit of God or from another spirit. Still another person is given the ability to speak in unknown languages, while another is given the ability to interpret what is being said."

As she continued to read through the rest of the chapter, her curiosity heightened as Paul told his readers in the final verse of chapter 12 that he would show them a better way. First Corinthians 13 had always been etched in her memory as the love chapter—one that was read at weddings and quoted between husbands and wives. What did that have to do with spiritual gifts? Starting with the first verse she read:

"If I could speak all the languages of earth and of angels, but didn't love others, I would only be a noisy gong or a clanging cymbal. If I had the gift of prophecy, and if I understood all of God's secret plans and possessed all knowledge, and if I had such faith that I could move mountains, but didn't love others, I would be nothing."

As she thought about that passage, the Holy Spirit pricked her heart.

Was she being selfish and not acting out of love when she tried to keep this gift a secret? After all, it did say in chapter 12 that the gifts were given to help each other. Sarah recalled another place in the Bible that her mom had mentioned recently that said if you knew to do right and you didn't do it, it was considered sin to God.

As she contemplated this passage, she found herself asking God to forgive her for being so selfish and thinking of her own reputation and feelings more than the well-being of people around her.

Standing up, she brushed off some pieces of hay from her jeans and walked over to Shadow's stall. The big horse lipped at her hand again as she rubbed his velvety muzzle.

Wrapping her arms around his strong neck, she rested her head on his silky coat. Playfully, Shadow stretched his head around and nipped at the back of her sweater.

"Hey you, quit that." Sarah chuckled as she stepped back.

Shadow snorted and nodded his head up and down, asking for a treat.

"You want a carrot, don't you?" She opened a bin that held several apples and carrots and chose a large carrot. "You're so spoiled" She watched while Shadow munched it down.

Returning to the hay bale, Sarah's thoughts went back to her study.

She really wanted to understand this healing gift more, which actually seemed to be several gifts mixed together, according to what Pastor Jake and the apostle Paul were saying. One flowed into the other; you had to have a special type of faith to work miracles, and many times those miracles ended up being healing.

Looking at a different passage, Sarah came to the story in Mark 9 of the desperate father whose child was possessed by demons. He pleaded with Jesus in verses 22-23, saying, "'The spirit often throws him into the fire or into water, trying to kill him. Have mercy on us and help us, if you can.' 'What do you mean, "If I can"?' Jesus asked. 'Anything is possible if a person believes.'"

Sarah lay back on the hay, looking at the rough wood on the stable ceiling as she thought about the words of Jesus.

Anything is possible. Wow!

Anything was a pretty broad word; obviously it meant anything within the will of God, but even she felt like her faith was small compared to that Scripture. She recalled another place where Jesus said that mustard seed-sized faith could cause someone to speak to a mountain and tell it to be thrown into the sea, and it would be done. Now that wasn't something you saw every day!

Picking up the books Pastor Jake had loaned to her, she spent the rest of the time reading about other people whom God had endowed with the same types of gifts that she knew He had given to her. The more Sarah read accounts of these other people who had special gifts of faith, the more she was inspired.

Finally, there were others she could relate to with the gift she had. Before this, she had wondered if anyone knew what she felt. It was clear in the interviews; the sensations and emotions the miracle workers articulated that about their experiences were very similar to what she had felt in her own healing encounters. These people were not afraid to walk in their gifts and the anointing of God, and look at what God did through them—it was amazing!

As Sarah thought about these things she felt the Holy Spirit pricking her heart, echoing the words that she had been hearing more and more lately: *Don't be ashamed of your gifts*. Something stirred inside of her, a confidence that told her that she was not strange for having these God-given abilities, but special.

She was not a freak; she was a daughter of the King of Kings, and she had been given a specific task, a purpose—a destiny.

In that moment, Sarah made a choice that she was not going to hide it anymore. It was time to let it shine, no matter what the outcome.

In fact, she planned to ask Charlotte if there was anyone else from the church whom she could visit and pray for.

Chapter Nine

You're coming to my game after school, right?" Nick asked as they walked down the hall a week later.

With everything else going on, she had totally forgotten about the game. It should have tipped her off that all the football players and cheerleaders were in uniform again, but she had been distracted, still thinking about the things she had been reading.

"Maybe...I'm not sure yet, I might have to be somewhere later."

Last week, Charlotte had said that maybe she could join them on some visitations today. She intended on touching base with them later.

"Probably church again," Nick sneered and shook his head. "I don't understand why you want to be at church all the time." He ran his hand through his short blond hair, looked away, and sighed sarcastically. "I can see how important I am to you."

Nick interlocked his fingers with hers and turned his dreamy blue eyes on her. "This is a big game tonight; if we win this one we go to regionals. I really hoped you would be there."

"You *are* important to me, Nick. And it's not church today, just some other stuff I have to do. I'll try to come if I can." Sarah fingered Nick's ring hanging around her neck with her free hand as they walked.

There was a constant nagging feeling that she should break things off with Nick, but when? How? She really did like him, and besides, she didn't want to upset him before the big game. It could cost the whole team, and she didn't want to be responsible for that.

It would have to wait for now.

"Well, I hope you can come," Nick said as they neared his locker.

Before she realized it, he had navigated her next to his locker, pulled her close, and pressed his lips on hers in a brief, yet heart-pounding, kiss.

How did Nick manage to melt her resolve every time he kissed her?

In a low voice he whispered in her ear, "I wish we were alone right now. I would show you how much I care about you."

Feeling her face redden, she averted her eyes from his and put some space between them. "Nick, stop. Not right in front of everyone." She looked around and adjusted the weight of her backpack on her shoulders. "I have to get to ELA. See you later."

She could feel his eyes on her as she walked down the crowded hall, trying to slow her heart rate and gain her composure. With the anticipation of the game tonight, the noise level seemed to be doubled all over the school.

Spotting Maria down the hall in her too-short black-and-orange cheerleading outfit, she thought she would try what her mom said and show some kindness to her. It seemed like Maria was trying her hardest to ignore Sarah as they neared each other.

"Hey, Maria," Sarah said to get her attention.

Maria flipped her long dark hair over her shoulder and stopped with a hand on her hip, sizing Sarah up with a look of disgust. "What do *you* want?"

With a quick internal prayer, Sarah hoped her smile looked sincere. "I just wanted to say good luck tonight."

A confused look flashed across Maria's eyes for a moment. "Whatever," she said flippantly before turning back to her friends and walking away.

Sarah reminded herself that it may take a long line of interactions like that before things changed. At least she hadn't said anything hateful; she would take that response over hate any day.

Taking a deep breath, she watched Maria walk away. Between the throng of students in the hallway she could see Maria stop a few classrooms down—right where Nick was still talking with his friends by his locker.

Curious, Sarah stood on her tiptoes and saw Nick pull Maria close to him and whisper something in her ear. Maria smacked his arm lightly and giggled. It might have looked like normal football player-cheerleader banter, except Sarah knew the look that passed between them.

It was the same look that Nick gave her when he was getting ready to make some romantic move on her—like when he had pulled her into the supply closet.

Sarah felt a knot form in her throat as a mixture of anger, betrayal, and jealousy swirled through her.

Was Nick cheating on her? She blinked away the tears that threatened to break free and continued to her ELA class. *Nick wouldn't do that, not after telling me how much he cared about me, would he? It had to be playful fun*, she rationalized.

Still, something didn't seem right about the whole thing.

As she sunk into her chair, she spotted Nathan smiling at her from his seat across the room, and she managed a weak smile in return.

His expression changed and his eyes asked what was wrong, so she mouthed back, "I'm okay."

It was nice to have a friend who knew you were hurting without having to say a word; funny how such thoughtfulness could make her feel better.

After class, Nathan waited for her to finish getting her books in her backpack and fell in step with her as she headed toward the lunch room. "Something's wrong, right? What's up?"

Not wanting to talk about Nick just yet, she replied, "I was trying to be nice to Maria, but so far she's not being nice back."

"Is that all? I mean, Maria has been awful to you for how many years, and now you're letting it get you down? Come on, what's *really* bothering you?"

"Well...right after I talked to Maria I saw Nick and her talking...or flirting...or something, but they seemed a little too close to me." She let out a frustrated breath, trying to keep her emotions in check. Not wanting to seem like a ranting jealous girlfriend, she added, "It was probably nothing. I mean, football players and cheerleaders are always messing around with each other, right? With the game tonight and all, everyone's so worked up about it."

She paused and heaved the weight of her backpack up, holding both straps at her shoulders. "Yeah...I'm sure it was nothing."

"If it was nothing, you wouldn't be trying so hard to convince yourself." Shaking his head, Nathan flicked his hair out of his eyes and sighed.

"What?" Sarah asked as they maneuvered around a group of students talking in the hallway.

"I wish you would listen to me, Sarah. Nick is bad news." He stopped walking and placed a hand on her arm, concerned etched on his forehead. He searched her eyes, "I don't want you to get hurt by him. What if he *is* cheating on you?"

Sarah looked down as they continued walking. Changing the subject slightly, she said, "It's already hard to be nice to Maria; it's even harder now after that."

"Give it time. She'll come around if you keep it up," Nathan reminded confidently. "The Bible says to love your enemies and pray for them, remember?"

"I know, and I hope she changes her attitude toward me some day." Sarah was glad that he wasn't pressing the issue about Nick any further for now.

The smell of greasy cheeseburgers reached her nose as they neared the cafeteria. Not very healthy, but they taste good nonetheless.

"Hey, I might go to the game later, will you be there?"

"I'm planning on it; not too often the big game is a home game too. Maybe I'll see you there." Nathan playfully tugged on a lock of her hair before heading down the crowded hallway.

She stood there watching him as he left and caught him looking back at her once or twice, his too-long hair concealing one of his eyes.

Turning, she entered the lunchroom and spotted Nick, who was involved in a conversation with his football buddies, his back facing her. With her emotions still mixed with what she had seen earlier, she changed course and got into the lunch line before he could notice her.

After grabbing a cheeseburger and a side salad with some Thousand Island dressing, she headed to the small cafeteria where students were allowed to eat their lunch in a quieter setting and study. She found an empty table, set her tray down, and pulled out her science book to study for a quiz later, even though she was already confident that she knew the material well.

As she ate her cheeseburger and salad, she kept several napkins handy so she could flip pages in the textbook without getting them greasy.

A myriad of thoughts bombarded her as she tried to keep her concentration on chemistry and molecular structures. She volleyed between worrying about Nick and Maria to contemplating what she had been studying about faith and miracles.

Why would God want to use her when she had so many issues and problems? She wasn't some spiritual superstar, not a minister or someone who was praying all the time. She wasn't like one of those people she read about whose lives seemed so spiritual. Was she even worthy to have this type of gift? Why did He pick her?

So many questions assaulted her.

As she thought about these things, some Scriptures came to mind that she had been studying. Taking out her phone, she tapped open her Bible app and brought up Luke 9:1-2 to reread it, "One day Jesus called together his twelve disciples and gave them power and authority to cast out all demons and to heal all diseases. Then he sent them out to tell everyone about the Kingdom of God and to heal the sick."

She sat back and pressed her knuckles to her lips as she thought about this. What Jesus said to the twelve disciples was what he intended for every believer. Another book brought out the humanity of each of the disciples. The simple truth was that most of the disciples were just normal, everyday people who had no religious training or "church" experience.

In fact, Peter, one of the most well-known and loved of the disciples, was a hothead who was often caught talking before thinking. Thomas doubted so much that he didn't believe Jesus was alive, even when the other eleven disciples told him they had seen Him with their own eyes. It wasn't until Thomas saw Jesus for himself that he believed. Embarrassingly, James and John talked their mom into asking Jesus to give them a high position in heaven. These were the types of guys to whom God entrusted the future of the church.

As she pondered these things, Sarah gained more confidence that God was truly with her. A slow smile spread across her face as this truth took a deep hold inside of her.

If He could give those guys special gifts and empower them to touch others, surely He could use her.

Popping the last bite of cheeseburger into her mouth, Sarah went back to her science book.

She was almost done studying with a few minutes left when Nick pulled up a chair backward and sat facing her.

"Hey, whatcha doing in here? Why didn't you eat with me?"

"I have a quiz later that I needed to make sure I was ready for." She wiped her mouth, hoping her eyes didn't give away that anything was wrong. Without really knowing what was going on between him and Maria, she didn't want to bring it up before the game.

He looked at her textbook. "Science? That's your best subject. You could ace that quiz without even studying for it. I think you're just avoiding me," he said in a low voice.

She knew that tone and decided it was time to get going before he pulled her into a closet again to sneak another smoldering kiss. Looking around the room, she realized that the few other students who had eaten their lunch were cleaning things up and preparing to leave. The bell would be ringing any minute now.

"No, I'm not avoiding you, I just wanted to be ready." She stood up and grabbed her tray. "I'll text you and let you know if I can come to the game, okay?" Maybe that would deter his mind.

"Okay." Nick stood too. "You better. By the way, you look great today." His blue eyes roamed over her body as she walked over to place her tray in the kitchen window.

Her black skinny jeans hugged her legs and the long teal tunic with the scooped neckline accentuated her features. Modest, but modern. She could feel his eyes examining her as she walked back to retrieve her backpack. She decided that she better get out of there quick before he found another closet.

Chapter Ten

The school's football field was crazy with noise, excitement, and faces and hair painted orange and black as people cheered on their team. It was a packed house. With this crowd it would be hard to spot Nathan, or to even catch up with Nick after the game.

Between homework, taking care of Shadow, calling the Martins, and eating dinner with her family, Sarah was pretty late getting to the game. She had changed into a bright orange hooded sweatshirt and kept the black skinny jeans on to support the team's colors. She also brought a small blanket in a backpack to keep warm because the forecast called for a chilly night. It served as a good way to pad the rock-hard bleachers.

Out on the field the game was well on its way, and the two rival mascots were working hard to raise the excitement level to a state of frenzy. The Highland Falls mascot, the cougar, ran along the sidelines to lead the crowd in the wave while the other mascot, an eagle, pretended to be part of the opposing team's cheerleading squad, and was currently entertaining the crowd by shaking his feathery behind.

The Highland Falls Cougars were playing against the Monroe High Eagles, whose school was about an hour away from Highland Falls, and they were a hard team to beat.

Sarah wound her way around the screaming fans and found a spot high in the bleachers with some of her friends. A few of the girls were from her church and the others were in several of her classes. They greeted her with waves, and those closest to where she sat gave her a quick hug before she settled down to watch the game.

Scanning the scoreboard she noticed that it was just before halftime and the score was 14 to 0 with the Eagles leading.

Sarah could tell that everyone was on edge, as there was a minute and 32 seconds left in the second quarter and the clock was still running. It was the third down, seven yards to go to the end zone.

Sarah was not a huge football fan, but when she started dating Nick, both he and her dad taught her about the rules and how the game was played so she could follow what was happening on the field—at least a little bit.

Looking at the field, she could easily spot Nick with the large 31 on his jersey. With everything else going on, she had forgotten to text Nick earlier, so he didn't know if she was there or not. In her hurry to get there she left her cellphone at home.

The teams got into formation on the seven yard line.

As the running back, Nick squatted down directly behind the quarterback with his hands ready to receive the ball at the snap, a typical eye formation.

The player directly in front of the quarterback, called the center, snapped the back ball to the quarterback, who dropped back for a pump fake to distract the other team, making them think he threw the ball. Then he quickly turned and pushed the ball into Nick's stomach instead.

Nick held the ball fast while running behind the left tackle, who was protecting him from oncoming Eagles as he ran. As Nick got closer and closer to the end zone, the crowd stood and cheered loudly and Sarah stood with them.

Two players from the Eagles, the linebacker and their safety, reached Nick and tackled him, falling in a mess of legs and helmets on the second yard line.

The Highland Falls coach called a time out and the clock stopped. Only 58 seconds were left until halftime.

As Nick and the other players pulled themselves up from the ground, Sarah noticed him clutching his right side from the hard hit. She watched with concern as Nick took his helmet off, his forehead bunched up in pain as he slowly walked over to where the team was joining up for the huddle.

The team gathered around the coach to get the next play. In a few seconds they all put their hands in the center of the huddle and yelled "break!" before returning to the second yard line.

Nick looked better now as he secured his helmet and jogged to his position.

Squatting down, the quarterback yelled "down," and all the Cougars arranged themselves. Then the quarterback moved up to the center and yelled, "42...53...hit!" At this, the center snapped the ball to the quarterback.

The quarterback dropped back and ran to the left as the receivers, ready to catch the ball if it was thrown, ran slant to the right, drawing the Eagle's defense off in that direction.

The Cougar's tailback came alongside the quarterback to guard, while the fullback ran around the line toward the left side of the end zone.

The quarterback got ready to throw the ball to a receiver on the right but realized that the receiver was being bombarded by the Eagle's defense.

With a quick glance, the quarterback noticed that Nick was open on the left and threw the ball to him instead.

The crowd went crazy as Nick caught the ball in midair while being hit by one of the Eagles and fell into the end zone for a touchdown!

The score was now 14 to 6, and Highland Falls was back in the game.

With 23 seconds left to the quarter, the kicking team came out.

This time when the ball snapped, the kicker launched the ball for a successful extra point, making the score 14 to 7, with 7 seven seconds left on the clock. The players set up again, and the Cougars kicked the ball off, only to have it intercepted by the Eagles, who ran about

12 yards before being tackled by the Cougars as the buzzer rang out for halftime.

The crowd yelled out encouragement to the players as the Cougars relaxed, taking off their helmets and smacking each other on the backs and occasionally on the rear. The cheerleaders were dancing and waving their pom-poms in synchronization with each other in a cheery chant.

Being the head cheerleader for Highland Falls, Maria led the group, her movements perfect and her voice commanding.

When leaving the field, the football players jogged through a tunnel created by the cheerleaders and their pom-poms.

Knowing that Nick and the team would be busy in the locker rooms, Sarah sat back and watched the marching band perform while chatting with her friends.

When the third quarter started up, it was fairly uneventful except toward the end when the Eagles' quarterback fumbled the ball after being sacked by the Cougars' defensive tackle. The Cougars' middle linebacker picked it up and ran it in for a touchdown.

A successful field goal set the score at 17 to 14 going into fourth quarter.

The crowd gasped as the Eagles' quarterback still lay on the ground where he had been tackled, holding his right shoulder, obviously injured. The Eagles' coach and a medic ran out on the field to see what was wrong. After a few minutes, the medic and coach helped the injured player slowly off the field, where he lay on the flatbed back of a six-wheeler and was driven off to get medical attention.

This was bad news for the Eagles, but great news for the Cougars. With the Eagles' star athlete out of the game, the Cougars had a much better chance to win.

Right at the start of the fourth quarter, the Cougars scored another touchdown and made the extra point, sending the Cougars into the lead 17 to 21.

Now the Highland Falls fans were ecstatic as the numbers changed on the scoreboard.

With only two minutes left in the game, the Cougars drove the ball down to try for another touchdown, but were unsuccessful so they ran the clock down, keeping possession of the ball and winning the game.

The atmosphere was electric; the Cougars were going to regionals!

People in the crowd slapped each other's backs and milled about while the players and coaches shook hands with each other and headed off to their locker rooms to shower and prepare for the after-game gala that was sure to follow.

Knowing it would take a while for the team to get their gear off, shower, and come back out from the locker room, Sarah turned back to her friends and talked a while more. After thirty minutes or so she packed the blanket back in her backpack, swung it up on her shoulders, and made her way down to find Nick. There were a few parents and students milling around outside the locker room area and in the stands.

Sarah caught a glimpse of Nick coming out of the locker room, but he didn't know she was there and turned to head in the opposite direction. By this time most of the crowd was gone but a lot of the team was hanging out around the locker room doors and talking excitedly about their after-game plans.

She tried calling out to him but her voice was lost in the noise. She saw him give some high fives to his friends as he walked and then ducked behind the bleachers.

Why would he be going under there? she wondered. *Is he cutting through to the other parking lot?*

With her curiosity raised, she followed him.

Sarah had to let her eyes adjust for a moment from the brightness of the stadium lights as she went into the darkness under the bleachers. She walked slowly and navigated around the metal posts that held up the bleachers, being careful not to stub her toes.

She heard giggling from further back in the bleachers and moved closer. In a small shaft of light she could see the silhouette of a couple making out.

Although she already knew in her heart who it was, she took another step closer and Nick's unmistakable blond hair and Maria's long, dark tresses came into focus.

Sarah covered her mouth and turned sharply, startling Nick and Maria from their embrace.

"Who's there?" Sarah heard Nick call out, but she was already out of sight.

Tears streamed down Sarah's face as she made her way through the crowd and out of the stadium as fast as she could. She needed to get out of there.

So much for waiting; things were definitely over between her and Nick. Tomorrow she would confront him and let him know what she saw.

***

Sarah was halfway to her car by the time Nathan caught up with her. He had only gotten a glimpse of her from behind as she fled from the stadium and could tell something was wrong just by the pace she was keeping.

"Sarah, slow down. Where are you going?" He came closer. "I wasn't sure if I would see you, there were so many people in there, but..."

Seeing her tear-streaked face, concern filled his eyes as he reached for her arm. "Hey, what's wrong?" he crouched a bit to look her in the eyes.

Not able to speak about it, Sarah covered her face in her hands, shoulders heaving as she wept.

"Shhhhh...hey come here." Nathan enfolded her in his arms, gently stroking her hair and resting his chin on the top of her head.

After a few minutes she pulled back and dug a wrinkled tissue out of her pocket to wipe her nose, then pressed the sleeves of her sweatshirt on her eyes, leaving two blotches of mascara, "I should have seen it coming…I feel so stupid," she said angrily.

"Let's come over here and talk." Nathan led her to a bench near the parking lot that was bathed in light by a bright street lamp overhead. There were still a few people trickling out of the stadium and making their way to their vehicles, but most paid no attention.

After they sat, he asked, "What happened?"

"I went to find Nick after the game because he didn't know I was coming and I saw him go under the bleachers. I tried to catch up to him…but when I got under the bleachers…I saw him and Maria making out." Pain flashed across her face. "It wasn't just a peck, and it didn't look like a first kiss either. I don't know how long this has been going on."

She breathed a frustrated sigh and looked down at her trembling hands, "I knew he wasn't right for me. I was planning to break up with him soon, but it still hurts." Her voice broke as a lone tear made its way down her cheek and her chin quivered. She covered her face with her hands again and tried to stifle a sob.

Anger burned in Nathan's chest and he forced himself to unclench his fists. *What a jerk!* In a way he was glad that this had happened and things would be ending between Nick and Sarah. He couldn't stand to see her hurt by Nick again.

Looking over at Sarah, who was wiping the tears from her face again, the blossoming feelings for her grew another notch. He wished he could protect her, keep her from any more pain, hold her, and tell her that she would be fine, kiss away the hurt...better stop there. The last thing she needed was the confusion of a new relationship on the heels of what happened tonight. And especially since she hadn't officially broken things off with Nick yet.

No, for now he had to hold his feelings at bay and be the friend she needed.

Without moving closer he placed a hand on her back, "I know it has to hurt, Sarah, but Nick was wrong for you. Eventually he would have hurt you, maybe even more than this. It's probably better that you found this out now and not later."

Standing up, Nathan jammed his hands in his pockets, kicking at the gravel with the toe of his sneakers, "You haven't been the same since you started going out with him. You don't stand up for what you believe in as much anymore. I miss that in you."

"I know, I have been doing a lot of soul searching lately." She stood up to face Nathan. "And I need to apologize. You've been trying to tell me Nick was wrong for me, and I wouldn't listen. You tried to tell me that it's okay to use the gift God gave me. I'm sorry I didn't listen to you." She looked up into his eyes. "Can you please forgive me?"

"Of course I can."

Without thinking, he reached up and used his thumb to brush a tear from her cheek that she had missed. Crying had made her eyes look even greener than usual and, framed by her long, dark lashes, they were irresistible. Her eyes had always been captivating, but especially now, he couldn't look away.

She seemed to search his eyes and then her gaze slid down to his mouth. Could she really have feelings for him? More than anything he wanted to kiss her, but he knew it wasn't the right timing, not after what she had been through tonight. He didn't want to start a relationship based her vulnerability.

He tore his gaze away from her eyes and stepped back, breaking the moment.

***

Sarah willed her heart to stop pounding. *What just happened?*

One minute she was upset about Nick kissing Maria, the next she was thinking about kissing Nathan. When she was looking into his eyes it was as if all her pain had melted away and been replaced

89

with an overwhelming desire for true love, the kind of love she saw reflected in Nathan's eyes.

When Nathan stepped back and her head cleared, it was like waking up from a dream.

Clearing her throat she changed subjects, trying to make her voice sound as normal as possible. "I…um, talked to Charlotte Martin today. I'm going to start visiting people in the hospital with them sometimes; you should come too."

Nathan's face lit up. "Really? That would be great! I would love to come along."

Smiling, she started walking in the direction of her car. "You know, I'm starting to realize that it doesn't matter if some people think I'm weird, it's probably because they don't understand God, and maybe they never will, but I can make a difference; I know I can, and I am okay with that now." She turned back to look at him and a brilliant smile broke out on her face.

"Now that's the Sarah I know."

Chapter Eleven

S arah, I need your help." Nathan's hazel eyes pleaded with her the next day at school.

She had just left homeroom when Nathan grabbed her arm.

"You know my friend Brad Thompson? He goes to our church...I saw him this morning and he has a really bad migraine. Said he can hardly think. I told him he should go home, but he has a test second period that he can't miss. Can you come pray for him?"

Sarah's immediate reaction was to say no. This would be the first time she would pray for someone at school in three years.

In just a moment's time, so many thoughts ran through her head. She was still nervous about letting people see her gift in action, but on the other hand, she knew that God truly wanted her light to shine. Brad was a Christian, so he wouldn't think her strange, but what about the other people around when she prayed? Then again, just yesterday she had told Nathan that she wasn't so worried about what people thought anymore.

As if reading her thoughts, Nathan said, "Look, I told him to go to the small cafeteria; there shouldn't be anyone in there right now. We only have a few minutes before first period, so if you will pray for him we have to go right now."

Sarah bit her lip and looked up into Nathan's eyes. Here was the test to see if she really meant what she had said.

Shaking off her anxiety, she said, "Okay, let's go." She was glad that Nathan was mindful of her uneasiness with using her gift publicly.

The small cafeteria was just around the corner and they could see Brad sitting at a table with his head in his hands, his fingers laced through his wavy dark brown hair, obviously in pain.

"Hey, Brad, I brought my friend Sarah with me. Can we pray for you?" Nathan placed a hand on Brad's shoulder.

Brad looked up slowly and forced a smile in spite of the pain they could see in his chocolate brown eyes hidden behind the dark-framed glasses. "Yeah, thanks guys." Then he lowered his head back down in his hands with a small groan.

Nathan looked over and nodded to Sarah.

Clearing her throat, she took off her backpack and stepped up to Brad, putting a hand on his back and closing her eyes. For a moment she was silent; there hadn't been any time to spiritually prepare for this one.

Exhaling, she started to feel God's presence as she focused on the Lord, and her spirit connected with the Holy Spirit's will and plan for the moment. Before she even started speaking, she could feel an energy building up inside of her, moving up and down through her body as she began to pray.

"Lord Jesus, I lift up Brad to You. I speak to this pain and tell it to leave in Jesus' name. Be gone now!"

Sarah felt a release of the energy from her body flowing through her hand and into Brad.

At that moment Brad's body jolted as God's healing power impacted him.

Feeling that the healing was done, Sarah retracted her hand.

Brad lifted his head, his face evidence that the pain had subsided. His eyes were now clear and bright and the muscles in his face and forehead were relaxed. A smile broke out on his face so large that it looked like he was glowing with God's presence.

"Wow, thank You, Lord! Thanks, Sarah and Nathan." He looked at Sarah incredulously. "What was that? I've never felt anything like that in my life; that was amazing!" He reached up and kneaded the back of his neck, "My head barely hurts at all. I've never had a migraine leave that fast. It usually takes hours for meds to kick in. Thank You, God!"

"That's what you call a true-blue miracle." Nathan's eyes were ignited by the whole experience. "Sarah doesn't like to tell people, but God does stuff when she prays, if you know what I mean."

Chuckling, Brad replied, "Yeah, I think I do now. That's incredible, Sarah; why would you hide something like that?"

"Well, I'm getting more and more okay with people knowing about it. Most people don't understand, that's all." Sarah shrugged.

With only a minute left to make it to class, they picked up their backpacks and headed out the door together.

Nathan asked Sarah as they walked, "Hey, Sarah, did you figure out when you're going back to the hospital with the Martins again? I would love to tag along. Stuff like this—like what just happened—I want to be a part of it. When you see God touch someone like that, it's just so cool."

"I'm going to call him later today, I have some free time tomorrow after dinner, so maybe then—if Pastor Jake and Charlotte are free then. I'll let you know if they say yes and what time."

"Sounds like a plan." Nathan swept his bangs out of his eyes in one movement of his head.

Brad, who was still amazed that his headache was healed so quickly, overheard their conversation and asked, "Can you ask them if I can come too? I'll see if my mom's cool with it."

"Sure," Nathan and Sarah said in unison.

Looking at each other, they all laughed and said good-bye as they parted ways to their classes with only a few seconds left to spare.

***

Sarah managed to avoid Nick and Maria for the rest of the day. She was still sorting out her feelings, wanting to approach the situation when she was a bit calmer about it all.

At home she was just putting Shadow out to pasture when Nathan and Brad stopped by.

"Hey, Sarah, I brought Brad with me, hope you don't mind. He was so excited about what happened this morning that he wanted to thank you again personally." Nathan's hazel eyes twinkled. They walked up to where she stood and Nathan stepped up on the lowest rail of the fence, the breeze tousling his hair.

Brad placed a hand on the fence and smiled.

"Not at all, how's your head?" she asked Brad, returning the smile.

"I feel great, thanks to you, well...I mean, thanks to God." Brad looked out over the field where Shadow had broken into a gallop on the far side of the pasture. "Nice horse!"

"Thanks. Do you ride?" Sarah glanced sideways at Brad.

"I took lessons for a while so I'm pretty good with horses, but I don't get to ride anymore."

They watched Shadow and chuckled as the large horse dropped down and rolled around in the grass, scratching his back.

"Looks like he is enjoying himself," Brad remarked.

"He loves this part of the day. Hey, if you ever want to take him out for a bit you can. Nathan's ridden him a few times over the years, although horses aren't his favorite thing."

She looked at Nathan, giggling at the memory of Nathan riding Shadow when they were twelve. Shadow had spooked a bit and was running and Nathan had dropped the reins and wrapped his arms around Shadow's neck, yelling, "How do you turn this thing off?" Sarah had been able to yell back some instructions and within a few minutes Shadow slowed down enough for a shaky-legged Nathan to slide down off his back. He had ridden a few times since then, but she could tell he wasn't comfortable at all.

Nathan nodded. "Yeah, they can tell when you feel uneasy. I'll stick to a bike or a car any day." he grinned.

"I would love to ride. Thanks, Sarah." Brad turned to face her, pushing his glasses up on his nose. "And thanks again for earlier today. I aced my test, by the way. It would have been much harder to think if I still had that migraine."

"No problem. Thank Nathan. He's the one who came to get me." She gave Nathan a warm smile. He seemed deep in thought. "Hey, Nathan, whatcha thinking about?"

Nathan's eyes focused on her and she could almost see gears whirling inside his head.

"What if...there's always someone in school who is sick or having some kind of problem...what if we had a way to pray for them?"

"What, like set up a booth or something?" she joked.

"No, not something cheesy, I don't know. I'm kind of thinking out loud...just, when we hear about someone who needs prayer, maybe somehow we can let each other know and find a time to pray—like today—not like in the middle of the hallway or something, but in a more private place. I know we all have different schedules and stuff going on, but maybe there would be a way to meet."

Brad interjected, "I know a few Christian teachers. Maybe one of them would let us use their classroom after school. That should be private enough."

Sarah remained silent for a moment. When she decided to not care if people knew about her gift, it seemed like God meant business, "Maybe..."

"We would just need to find a teacher who can be there and would let us do that, and make sure we follow all the rules and stuff like that," Nathan added.

"Oh yeah, speaking of prayer," Sarah brightened, "Pastor Jake said we can all join him tomorrow night at six-thirty to go pray for people at the hospital. He said he can even pick us up on the way and take us home after."

"Nice!" Nathan and Brad said together.

They looked up as Shadow sauntered over to where the trio was standing. He sniffed at Nathan and Brad, who took turns rubbing his velvety muzzle, and stepped up to Sarah, lowering his head so she could rub the white star under his forelock.

"Hey, Shadow, you ready for your ride?" Sarah peeked over and gave Brad's outfit a once-over. He wasn't exactly dressed for riding, but it would do. "You want to take him out now, Brad?"

A big smile lit up Brad's face. "Sure!"

Grabbing the reins, Sarah patted Shadow's neck. "Okay, Big Guy, let's get your saddle on. You're gonna make a new friend today."

Chapter Twelve

Why are you avoiding me?" Nick asked the next day on the phone after school. "I barely saw you since school the day of the big game. You haven't even eaten lunch with me. What's going on?"

Sarah breathed a prayer as she flopped down on her bed. She had been avoiding this conversation, but being that it was the third time Nick had called, she figured she'd better pick it up.

As much as she wanted to put things off, it seemed she would have to face it head on.

Nick continued, "I miss you, Baby, I wish you had seen the game. It was great."

"I know...I was there..." She was starting to get upset as she remembered seeing him with Maria under the bleachers.

"You were? You never texted me...I didn't see you there." His voice sounded shocked.

Not that you were looking for me. She tried to keep her voice controlled. "I didn't get a chance to text you, wasn't sure if I would even make it. But I finally got there a few minutes before halftime." She bit her lip, praying for the courage to confront him on what she saw without getting emotional. Sarah wore her heart on her sleeve, and it didn't take much to make her laugh or cry.

"So you saw my awesome play then." She could hear the smile in his voice and could picture his face, so proud that he had helped bring his team to victory.

Normally it would make her smile, but today it just added to her aggravation toward him.

"Yeah, I did." Sarah took a deep breath, irritation evident in her tone.

"What's wrong? Aren't you glad we won the game? You sound upset."

It was now or never. "Nick...I have to talk to you about something." She paused to swallow, her stomach clenching. "After the game, I waited for you to come out of the locker room. When you came out, I tried to get your attention, but it was so loud you didn't hear me." She took a deep breath and closed her eyes. "I followed you. Then I saw you...under the bleachers...with Maria."

"What? I wasn't under the bleachers with Maria. What are you talking about?"

She stood and paced the room as she fought back the tears. It had to have been him. She knew it! How could he deny it?

"Nick, I *followed* you. I saw you kissing her." A lone tear made its way down her cheek.

"If you saw someone under the bleachers, at *night*, I don't think you would be able to tell who it was; it's pitch black under there."

Sarah stopped pacing in front of her window and placed her hand on the windowsill. "There was some light coming through the cracks between the seats. I saw your hair. I know it was you, Nick. And I heard Maria giggling, I know her voice. She used to be my best friend, remember?"

Sarah clenched the windowsill so hard that her knuckles were white. She let go and went back to pacing. She had to calm herself down.

"Yeah, like eight years ago. And Sarah, there's like four other guys on the team who have the same haircut as me; it could have been Trent or Gabe...or Connor, his hair is practically the same color as mine. And Maria flirts with everybody. They were probably was just celebrating after the game."

Sarah closed her eyes, fuming. Even if he denied it, she still had to break it off. "Well…whether it was you or not, I can't be with you anymore. Nick…we're like two different people. I don't know if I can trust you."

"Come on, Sarah, it *wasn't* me." She could hear the exasperation in his voice. "Look, I need to see you, please. Let's not talk about this over the phone. Let's talk this out in person, then…if you still feel that way…then we'll agree to take a break from each other."

"No way, Nick. I don't want to see you again. Good-bye." Sarah pulled the phone away from her ear to turn it off when she heard Nick pleading, a sound she couldn't remember hearing before. It caught her off guard and she slowly brought the cell phone back to her ear.

"Sarah, don't hang up on me, please! I can't talk on the phone about stuff like this. Please, Sarah, I'm begging you. Let me just see you."

For a moment she hesitated.

Her wounded heart said to hang up and be done with Nick forever, but she did agree that confrontation was more effective in person. She closed her eyes and weighed the options.

Against her better judgment, she heard herself say, "Okay, but it has to be now."

She could hear Nick breathe a sigh of relief. "I'll come pick you up. We can talk here at my house. Be there in five." He paused a moment. "Thanks, Sarah."

"Okay." She clicked the phone off. This wasn't exactly how she had planned for it to go.

She looked at the clock, almost four o'clock, still plenty of time to meet with Nick, break up with him, and get back in time to eat dinner before six thirty.

***

Exactly five minutes later Nick pulled up in his black sports car, smiling at her as she came down the walkway. She zipped up her jacket and crossed her arms over her chest, not returning his smile.

She still didn't know why she agreed to see him while she was so mad at him. She should have just broken up with him over the phone like she had originally planned.

It was now the middle of October and the day had become breezy and cool, evidence that winter was on its way. The smell of burning wood from a fireplace hung in the air and a few stray leaves danced across the driveway in front of her.

Nick jumped out and hurried around to the passenger side, opening the door for her, something he rarely did.

Boy, he was really trying hard to change her mind.

They drove for a few minutes without speaking before pulling up to Nick's impressive home in an upscale neighborhood. Between all of her activities and football practice, she had only been there a few times since they started dating, and each time she marveled at its expansiveness.

In spite of her anger she leaned forward to take in the sight of it. Her family's house would be considered large to some people, but Nick's house looked like a mansion compared to hers. She knew his family employed housekeepers just to keep everything clean and tidy.

He killed the engine, and she opened her door and got out before he could try to sway her again with manners she knew he didn't normally possess. They walked up the sidewalk to the massive double doors nestled between two large white pillars.

"Are your parents home?" Sarah asked nervously.

"Hmm, my mom is out shopping, and I think my dad is still at work." He punched the code into the keypad to unlock the door and motioned her into the grand entryway. An elegant staircase lined one curved wall to the second level.

"Story of my life." He set his keyfob onto a decorative accent table along the wall by the door.

"Maybe we can talk outside. My parents don't want me alone with a guy. You know their rules."

Like any teenager, she thought most of the rules her parents set were unfair, but right now she was thankful she could use this rule to get her out of there sooner.

"We aren't alone. Our housekeeper, Maria, is cleaning upstairs today and I'm sure my brother is around here somewhere."

Nick's younger brother, Tony, was eleven years old and was probably playing video games in his room, she guessed from past interactions with him. She was sure they wouldn't see Tony at all.

"Come on. Let's sit in the living room and talk." He placed his hand on the small of her back, trying to direct her to the next room.

Arms still crossed, Sarah stiffened and stayed put. "Nick, you can't talk me out of breaking up with you. It's going to happen whether we stand here and talk or go in there."

"Come on, Sarah. I just want to warm up by the fire. It's so cold outside. Let's just talk in the living room. Please?"

He sure was saying that word a lot today, which was way out of character for him.

Reluctantly, she moved toward the enormous living room.

The high cathedral ceiling made the room look even bigger than it already was. An expensive black leather corner couch with theater seats that recline sat along one wall facing a huge 70-inch flat screen TV mounted to the opposite wall with surround sound speakers in various places around the room. On one of the other walls an impressive fireplace with beautiful slate stonework warmed the room with a crackling fire. A smaller love seat sat in front of the fireplace with a fluffy, soft alpaca wool throw draped over the back of it, accented with decorative pillows. Modern black-and-glass side tables sat on either side of the love seat and a high-backed chair upholstered in deep red velvet sat next to one of the side tables.

They sat on the love seat in front of the fireplace as she started, "Nick, I can't be with you anymore. It's more than what I saw at the game..."

"I'm telling you, that *wasn't* me you saw; there's always people making out under the bleachers."

"Then where did you go when you left the locker room? I saw you duck behind the bleachers." Anger flared again at his denial of what she knew she saw.

"I went under part of the bleachers to meet my friends in the west parking lot," he insisted. "It was a shortcut. I wasn't kissing anyone under there." He moved closer to her.

This was possible, because the west side exit was on the other side of the bleachers. She could see that she was getting nowhere with this angle.

"Well, the day before that I saw you hug Maria and whisper something to her. I saw the way you looked at her." A mix of jealousy and fury pulsed through her and she started losing control of her emotions, tears threatening to break loose.

Nick took her hands and sat on the edge of the couch to face her, "Sarah, please don't cry. You know I don't like Maria like that. It was nothing. You should know how much I care about you." He studied her for a moment and smirked a bit. "I think you're jealous."

"No, it's not like that." She closed her eyes, frustrated. *Why wasn't this going right?*

Nick reached up and wiped the tears away with his fingers and before she could fight it, Nick was inches from her face, so close she could feel his warm breath and smell the expensive cologne he wore. For a moment the anger melted and she forgot why she was angry as he brushed his lips on hers.

Desire and warning welled up at the same time, and for just a moment, desire won.

Nick tilted his head to deepen the kiss, his tongue making entrance into her mouth and sending a tingling sensation through her body.

As her resolve slipped, she felt his hands run up her arms and down her back, pulling her on his lap as she gave in to the kiss.

After a few minutes, Nick lowered her onto the couch and was pulling the bottom of her shirt up a few inches, caressing the bare skin around her waist. The sensations were almost like a drug, intoxicating her and making her mind fuzzy.

He breathed in her ear, "Sarah, I want to be with you. Please don't break up with me. Let me show you how much I care."

Suddenly, neon lights flashed in her head and she realized what was happening.

Sarah could hear the faint noise of the housekeeper shuffling around somewhere on the second floor, a subtle reminder that they were not alone. A fresh surge of determination rose inside of her as she pushed him back, breathing hard. "Nick, stop it!"

She squeezed out from under his chest and stood up, pulling her shirt back down, shaking off the fuzziness in her head.

"This is another reason why I can't be with you anymore. I can't be pressured to do things I don't believe in. You know where I stand on it. If you really cared about me, you wouldn't try to take advantage of me." She echoed the phrase her mother had taught her when it came to dating and relationships. "Every time we're alone, you're trying to get me to compromise my beliefs."

Nick stood, running his hand through his hair. "Seemed like you liked it a minute ago. You're so confusing. You like it when I kiss you, but then you push me away."

"I just can't be with you the way you want me to, Nick." She grabbed her purse that she had put down next to the couch and yanked it up on her shoulder. "Look, I need a guy who has the same beliefs that I do, and you don't. I know it doesn't make sense to you, and it probably never will, but I just can't be with you, Nick."

Reaching behind her neck she unclasped the necklace with Nick's class ring on it. With shaky hands she took the ring off of the chain and held it out to Nick. "This is yours...please take it."

Reluctantly he met her eyes and took the ring. "If that's really what you want."

"Yes, it is. I need to call my mom to come and get me, I have to be somewhere later." Sarah fished her phone out of her pocket and dialed her mom, asking her to come pick her up right away.

"I can drive you home."

"No, I'm not getting in any car with you." Sarah shook her head, trying to keep her anger under control. She stood next to the front door so she could see when her mom was pulling up. If it wasn't so cold out she would have stood outside.

Nick turned. "There's someone else, right? I bet it's that Nathan guy you hang out with all the time. Are you meeting him tonight? No, let me guess. You're going to church again." His expression turned cold.

"No, there's not someone else. Nathan is a good friend, I keep telling you that. And I'm not going to church; it's something else." Why did he have to pry so much?

He would think she had flipped if she told him she was going to the hospital to pray for people.

They had walked back to the front foyer and were about to step outside. Nick put his hand on the knob but instead of opening it, he turned and looked her in the eye. "Are you meeting Nathan tonight?" He was clearly aggravated.

"I'm meeting a few friends, not just Nathan. It's sort of a community service project." She hoped he would leave it alone.

Shaking his head, Nick saw her mom's car pull up and threw the door open. "I knew it. I should have seen it all along. Have a nice life, Sarah. Have fun with your church boy."

She noticed his jaw clench as she turned to leave. The door slammed behind her as she walked to her mom's car. *I'm glad that's over.*

Sarah watched his house disappear in the distance as they pulled out of the driveway and drove away. She drew in a deep breath, exhaling slowly.

"You okay?" Stephanie glanced at her with concern on her face. "Nick seemed a little upset when you left."

Sarah turned to her mom and managed a smile. "Yeah, I'll be okay. I need to talk to you about some stuff before I leave tonight, though."

"No problem, sweetie." Her mom reached over to put a comforting hand on her arm as she drove the short distance home. Her mom was always good about letting Sarah talk things out when she was ready, and at the moment she needed a few minutes to gather herself back up before she got home.

One chapter in her life was ending and she felt a freedom, a newness of things to come.

Sarah pulled her phone out of her pocket and swiped the screen up to check the time. Just after five o'clock. Pastor Jake was supposed to pick up Nathan and Brad at Nathan's house and then pick her up at about six thirty. He had said that Charlotte was tied up with helping out with a school event so she wouldn't be able to be there tonight, but because the other guys were coming along, the car would be pretty full anyway.

This left just enough time to grab some dinner and talk with her mom about Nick and his overreactions.

Chapter Thirteen

So that's the whole story, Mom. I know I did the right thing, but it still hurts." Sarah's voice broke over the lump in her throat.

As difficult as it had been to tell it all, it felt good to get it off her chest.

While her mom peeled potatoes and cut up chicken for dinner, Sarah had relayed everything: seeing Nick with Maria, how Maria had been treating her, finally getting to the place where she wanted to stand out for God, as well as alluding to Nick moving too fast in their relationship—without giving too much detail. There's just some things she didn't feel like sharing with her mom yet. She found herself blushing even though she didn't fill her mom in completely about what he had tried. She ended with her breakup with Nick.

A single tear trickled down Sarah's cheek and she swiped it away, closing her eyes tightly.

Stephanie covered the pot of potatoes to boil, wiped her hands on a dish towel, and came around the counter to where Sarah sat on a stool. She wrapped her arms around her daughter and held her as Sarah cried, burying her head in her mom's chest.

"I know it hurts, sweetie. It's hard to do the right thing sometimes." She squeezed a bit tighter before releasing her. As Sarah's tears subsided, she ran her hand down the length of Sarah's brown hair before sitting down on the stool next to her for a moment.

"For what it's worth, your dad and I had been talking about your relationship with Nick recently. We've not been as involved as we should have been. And we were going to talk to you soon because we were concerned. He's just not the type of guy we feel God has for you long term. Does he even go to church? Does he have a relationship with God?"

Standing up, Stephanie rubbed a hand on Sarah's back before returning to the kitchen counter to start breading the chicken for the fryer. Her fried chicken tenders were better than any found in a restaurant. She mixed just the right combination of salt, pepper, paprika, and a few other spices in the flour to make them flavorful with a little extra kick.

"His family is Catholic. I think he goes to Mass sometimes. He says he's a Christian but I don't think he's really committed to God, not with the way he talks and acts—I don't think a true Christian would do those things." Sarah took a breath. "I tried to talk to him about the Lord, but he always found a way to change the subject."

"So why did you date him anyway? If you knew he wasn't right, then there had to be other reasons to stay with Nick besides wanting to fit in. You could have done that without a guy like him." She looked Sarah squarely in the face. "You have to look at someone you would want to date and ask yourself: Could I be married for the rest of my life to him? Will he help me grow to my full potential and help me fulfill my purpose in life?"

Sarah looked down and thought for a moment. "I guess I stayed with him because...well, part of me liked the way he made me feel—being wanted, having someone admire me, tell me how good I looked."

She looked up at her mom sheepishly. "That's bad, isn't it?"

"Honey, it's perfectly normal to want to be loved, but you need to find the right source for that love."

As they talked, Stephanie worked on breading the strips of chicken: first patting them dry with a paper towel and rolling them in flour so the mixture would stick better, then dunking them in some whisked eggs, and finally covering them generously with a mixture of flour and a variety of seasonings before gently placing them into an awaiting fryer at just the right temperature.

The familiar sound of bubbling and crackling oil made Sarah's mouth water in anticipation.

"It's really important right now that you make a firm decision to save yourself for your future husband. I know you said Nick moved too fast, and I don't know what that means exactly, but when you get caught up in a moment, even a casual kiss can be taken too far. Once you give that part of yourself away, you can *never* get it back and you are emotionally bonded with that person for the rest of your life. That's why God says in Genesis that the two become one flesh when a couple gets married. It really refers to the sexual connection they have."

Sarah leaned back and put up her hands for her mom to stop there. "Okay, Mom, you don't have to get into details. I've heard about the birds and bees before..."

"No, Sarah," Stephanie interrupted, "this is important." She put a lid on the fryer and turned to face her. "I want you to know beyond a shadow of a doubt where I stand on this, and I want you to know in your heart where your true love source comes from," she insisted.

"I think I know what you're going to say. God should be my source for love."

"Well, that's the bottom line, but it's much deeper than just that."

Stephanie set the timer for the first batch of the chicken strips so they didn't overcook and sat back down next to Sarah.

"Until Jesus becomes your first true love, you will search for that love in other places, but it will never really complete you. No guy can complete you. I had to learn that *after* your dad and I got married."

Sarah scrunched up her nose, "What do you mean? I thought you were a Christian when you and dad got married."

"You know that I grew up in a Christian home, my mom and dad took us to church every week when we were young. But I really didn't have my own relationship with God until right before I met your father. I made some bad decisions up until that point, and it was mainly because I was searching for love, and what I really was searching for was God. I don't want to see you make the same mistakes I did."

Sarah hadn't really heard her mom talk much about her life before she was saved so she listened as her mom continued.

"I found the Lord right before I met your dad. I walked closely with Him for a while but soon after we got married I focused so much on my marriage that I drifted from my closeness to God. I tried to complete myself through my relationship with your dad instead of God. Your dad loves me a lot, but it's still a human love, and no human can love someone else as completely as God can. Human love will always disappoint. So when your dad couldn't supply the perfect love I was longing for, I found myself getting upset with him. I tried to fill that longing with other things. It even strained our marriage for a while until one day about five years ago when God got a hold of my heart and showed me that I needed to fall in love with Him all over again."

She got up to check on the chicken, turning a few pieces in the hot oil. "Who knows where we would be if I hadn't gotten my priorities straight." She shook her head.

"Wow, I didn't know any of that was going on." Sarah watched her mom as she worked her way around the kitchen.

"That's why it is *so* important for you to make Jesus your first love now. Don't wait until later when you may have less time to give. You might think you have a lot of worries now, but it just gets harder when you have a job, a husband, a family of your own, and bills to pay— believe me. It can still be a struggle to keep things in check sometimes. We're all tempted in our weaknesses, no matter how strong of a Christian someone may be. I still struggle with it sometimes."

Stephanie lifted the lid off the steaming pot of potatoes and pushed a fork through a large chunk, testing it to see if it was ready for mashing. The fork slid through easily and the potato fell into two pieces.

"Just right." She grabbed a colander to drain the water from the potatoes. Next she set to work combining the potatoes with butter, milk, salt and pepper, as well as a bit of garlic powder, and parsley for color. Stephanie favored using a hand-masher to keep a few small chunks of potato in the creamy mixture without leaving them too lumpy.

As she worked at mashing the potatoes, the room filled with the aroma of garlic and spices.

A comfortable silence fell between the two of them as the final preparations for dinner were made. The aroma of fried chicken, a little spicy, reached Sarah's nose, making her glad that it was almost time to eat.

Dinner time was always a family occasion in the Wright household. While some families were content to watch television while they ate or grabbed dinner at different times with each doing what their schedules allowed, Sarah's mom and dad insisted that their family eat together with all distractions turned off or put aside while they ate. Stephanie and David had set a firm rule in place when the kids were small about the family dinner. They always said that "the family that stays together not only prays together, but eats at least one meal a day together."

Sarah rose to set the table without being asked, this being her usual contribution to dinner preparations. When she was seven, her mom had shown her the right way to set a table, down to the proper placement of each utensil. She made her rounds around the table, placing a folded napkin next to each of the square burgundy dinner plates.

As Sarah was mechanically fixing the table setting, her mind pored over her mom's words.

It was time for some serious changes in her life. Just talking about everything had brought a deep cleansing and Sarah felt she was ready to put the past—and Nick—behind her.

Grabbing a handful of silverware, Sarah proceeded to set a fork to the left of each plate, followed by a steak knife and spoon to the right, being careful to make sure the knife edge pointed inward as her mother had trained her.

With new anticipation she thought about the evening ahead of her—going to the hospital with Pastor Jake, Nathan, and Brad. She was learning a lot about healing and faith from the books she had been reading and from the Bible itself.

As she continued her musing, she filled glasses with ice and filtered water from the dispenser in the stainless steel fridge door and set them by each place setting to complete the dinner table.

Her mom and dad kept up their normal conversation during dinner with only a few questions directed toward her or Jordan about school or church, and Sarah was grateful for the opportunity to continue pondering the conversation she previously had with her mom.

What kind of guy did she want to end up with for the rest of her life? One thing was for sure, it was definitely *not* someone like Nick. No, the person she would share her life with would be a strong Christian, someone who would build her up, not try to get her to compromise her convictions. He would love her for who she was on the inside, not for her outward looks. Someone kind, caring, gentle, and respectful.

As she thought about these things, the image of one person kept coming to her mind: Nathan.

Sarah frowned and shook her head. Sure, she had felt things for him lately that had both surprised her and made her feel lightheaded, but that was probably on the heels of not being treated right by Nick. She didn't want to jeopardize the deep friendship she had with Nathan because of some misunderstood feelings.

"You okay, sweetie?" David asked, noting her expression. "You look troubled. Everything all right at school?"

Sarah quickly looked up at her dad and smiled. "Yeah, I'm okay, just thinking about some stuff Mom and I were talking about."

She glanced at her mom with a hopeful expression. She didn't want to rehash everything to her dad, especially personal things. She knew she could talk openly with her father, but she would rather have that discussion stay between her and her mom.

Stephanie gave Sarah a knowing glance before directing her attention to David. "Just some girl stuff. It's all okay. Your little girl is growing up into a young lady." she winked at Sarah.

"Well, I'll be glad to let you ladies handle the girl stuff." He ate his last bite of chicken, wiped his mouth on a napkin, and stood up to rinse his plate off. "Thanks for dinner, honey, that was really good." He rubbed his full stomach. "I'm gonna catch the last part of the game."

David retreated to the living room and Jordan stood to rinse his plate and clean up after dinner, his usual job.

"Thanks for dinner, Mom. It was good. Got a lot of homework to do tonight after I get the dishes in the dishwasher." He patted Stephanie on the back after depositing his plate in the dishwasher.

"Okay, glad you liked it." Stephanie smiled before Jordan returned to the dining room to bring more pans and dishes to the kitchen.

After he left, Sarah gave her mom an appreciative look for saving her during the dinner conversation. "Thanks, Mom."

"No problem, that's what moms are for."

Chapter Fourteen

After eating dinner, Sarah had a few minutes to spare before she got picked up. She quickly fixed her makeup and hair, brushed her teeth, and grabbed her coat as the car pulled into the driveway.

The guys had sat in the back, giving her the preferred seat. As she hopped in the car, Pastor Jake gave her a hello and a big smile as the familiar scent of his mint gum reached her nose.

Sarah twisted around in the seat to say hi to the guys, and Nathan and Brad greeted her in unison, looking excited to be on a new adventure.

"Are you ready?" Pastor Jake raised an eyebrow and glanced over at her as he backed out of the driveway.

Sarah smiled confidently. "Yup, who're we going to pray for tonight?"

"Well, there are two people we're going to see tonight. One is a lady from the church named Brooke Roberts, who has been having complications with her pregnancy. She almost had a premature delivery a few days ago so the doctor is keeping her under observation for a while. If the baby is born this early, there is only a ten percent chance it would survive. The other is a friend of someone in the church who has spinal meningitis, the bacterial type, and is under quarantine. We'll have to wear some protective things like gloves, a gown, and a mask when we go in to pray for him."

Sarah turned a bit and exchanged a worried glance with Nathan and Brad. *Quarantined?* "Is it contagious? Is that why we have to wear all that?"

"I asked about that. They said that he is on antibiotics right now, but that it's still contagious. We will be fine if we wear the protective stuff while we pray," Pastor Jake responded. "He still has an extremely high fever, 104 degrees I think is what they said."

"Wow." Brad frowned in the back seat. "That's really high."

"It is high…too high. I just heard about this guy today. His name is Joseph Santiago. The doctors are concerned that if they can't get the fever down soon, he might have permanent brain damage." Pastor Jake shook his head. "It was Randy Woods who told me about Joseph. He works with him. Randy said he doesn't think Joseph is a Christian so there is a lot more at stake. I've been praying that we will be able to share God's love with him as well as pray for his healing."

"Sounds like we have our work cut out for us then," Nathan added.

A solemn quiet took over the vehicle as they drove, each person silently praying as they came closer to the hospital.

Once they parked, Pastor Jake led the small group in prayer. "Lord God, I know we are just dirt and clay—earthen vessels—but we know that You want us to reach out to the world around us and share Your love. We ask You, God, to increase our faith tonight. Use us to help these people who desperately need a touch from You. Bring Your power, and flow through us. Let us be Your instruments of healing and love. We pray for favor, wisdom, and guidance, in Jesus' name. Amen."

They each added an "amen" before getting out of the warm car and crossing the parking lot to the hospital entrance.

They decided to visit Joseph's room first, his being the most critical situation.

Once again Pastor Jake led the way through the winding hallways, the heels of Sarah's boots clacking on the shiny tile floors as they walked.

In a few minutes they reached Joseph's room. A large sign that read "QUARANTINE" in red letters was posted across the doorway with a notice in smaller letters about checking with the nurse's desk before entering.

Pastor Jake told the trio to wait there while he went to the nurse's station.

Sarah recognized this as the same wing that they had come to when they had prayed for Anna. She looked around but didn't see Deanne anywhere.

After being approved to go in, they all suited up in gloves, light blue polka-dot gowns, and blue medical masks covering their noses and mouths.

Pastor Jake knocked on the door and a petite Italian-looking woman with short dark hair, also wearing the same protective gear, opened the door a crack and eyed the group warily as the nurse explained that a pastor and some friends had come to say a prayer for Joseph.

Although she still seemed hesitant to let strangers in to see her husband, the woman introduced herself as Joseph's wife, Isabella, and opened the door to let them file in around the hospital bed. Pastor Jake explained to Isabella their connection with Randy Woods and she seemed a little less apprehensive.

A dark-haired man who looked to be in his late forties lay in the bed, his dark skin flushed from the high fever and his eyes a bit glazed over. He wore a mask and had an IV hooked up, replenishing the fluids in his feverish body. He looked to his wife, unsure of why so many unfamiliar people were suddenly in his room.

"Joseph, your friend from work, Randy, asked his pastor to come and say a prayer for you," Isabella explained.

Joseph's eyes reflected a smile hidden under the mask, and Pastor Jake moved closer and introduced them all, his voice a bit muffled under his own mask.

"Hi there, Joseph. I'm Pastor Jake, and these are some young people from our church who love to pray for people; this is Sarah, Nathan, and Brad." He motioned to each of them as he said their names.

Joseph slowly reached out his IV-free hand and shook Pastor Jake's hand lightly. "Thank you. I appreciate it. I'm not a church-going guy." He looked up sheepishly as he spoke in his rich, Italian accent, "but you can pray for me all you want."

Isabella interjected, "The doctor tells us this fever has to go down soon, and they've been doing all they can to lower it."

"Well, let's pray about that fever. Let me explain a little bit about prayer. We believe God hears us when we pray and we also believe that there are certain actions that make prayer more effective. The Bible says to lay hands on people when they are sick and they will get better. What this means is that we will just lightly touch your shoulder or arm, nothing weird. There is something about physical contact that allows God's healing to flow into the sick person. Would it be okay if we prayed for you like that?"

Joseph looked a little unsure at first, but slowly nodded his head in agreement. "It sounds a little different than how we pray at Mass, but anything that might help this fever go down would be okay with me."

"All right." Pastor Jake placed his hand on Joseph's shoulder. "Sarah, why don't you and Nathan go around to the other side of Joseph's bed there and join me. Brad, you can come by me."

Sarah knew Pastor Jake was letting her be in position to be able to lay hands on the sick man as they prayed.

It seemed a bit awkward with everyone wearing all the protective gear. If Nick saw her now, he would think she was crazy for sure! Sarah held back a chuckle at the thought and laid her gloved hand lightly on Joseph's other shoulder as Pastor Jake started to pray. She could tell Joseph wasn't sure what to do, first looking around at them before closing his eyes tightly and folding his hands together on his lap.

Isabella crossed herself in typical Catholic style and folded her hands on her lap as well.

Pastor Jake ended his prayer without saying amen, waiting to see if someone else might lift up a prayer as well.

Nathan and Brad both were praying quietly so Sarah took the opportunity to pray. Feeling a surge of new faith, she started to pray, not only for healing, but also that God would send His angels into the situation and help Joseph.

When she said amen and they opened their eyes, both Joseph and his wife had tears in their eyes. But this time was different; there was no instant healing, even though Sarah really felt God's presence as she prayed.

In a way, she had hoped that Nathan and Brad would experience an instant healing tonight to help build their faith.

Was it something I said, or didn't say? she thought. *Is my faith too small? Why didn't he get healed right away? Does God not want him to get healed?* She had prayed the same as other times, and even had more time to spiritually prepare than on other occasions. *What went wrong?*

As these thoughts assaulted her, she looked over at Nathan and Brad, who smiled in spite of the absence of a miracle.

A little disappointed, she turned her attention to Pastor Jake as he was explaining to Joseph and his wife that Jesus had come to die on the cross as their Savior and that He rose again to give them the opportunity to live a changed life. In the precious moments that followed, the couple gave their hearts to the Lord.

Isabella embraced each of them as they stood to leave, commenting that she felt clean and new.

"Thank you again, all of you." Joseph motioned from the bed. "I've never before felt God so close as when you were praying for me. Please come back again, and I want to come to church when I get better." He smiled at the visitors.

He still looked flushed, but the glow on his countenance was proof enough that God was at work on the inside, though his body was still sick.

"I'll check back with you guys later." Pastor Jake's eyes twinkled under his dark rimmed glasses. "Those angels that Sarah prayed about are on the way to help, probably doing a little jig now to welcome you into God's family." Sarah, Nathan, and Brad chuckled in agreement as they exited the room, taking off their masks and discarding them in the wastebasket near the nurse's desk.

As they walked, they passed a nurse with short, spiky blonde hair pushing a large, industrial-sized fan as they left the intensive care wing. She smiled at them and said hello as if she knew them as they passed.

They worked their way to the maternity ward, which was on the opposite end of the hospital from where they were now. All the while, Sarah wondered why there hadn't been an instant healing for Joseph like in times past.

Not able to get rid of the nagging question, Sarah asked, "Pastor Jake, I know God doesn't always answer prayer the way we think He should, but I thought something more would have happened back there. I mean, like Joseph getting healed, or the fever going down right away or something."

Pastor Jake thought for a moment, "Well, Sarah, I really believe the greatest miracle of all *did* happen. That lovely couple gave their hearts to Christ, and whether Joseph's body—his shell—gets healed or not, the most important thing is that his heart has been healed. Besides, healing is not always instant, as much as we would like it to be; sometimes God has a plan that we don't see yet."

Sarah thought about this for a moment as the elevator reached the destination and the door opened.

They exited on the fifth floor and arrived at Brooke's room within a few moments.

Pastor Jake knocked softly on the door, opening it when they heard a male voice say, "Come in!"

Brooke's husband, Alex, rose to greet them. "Thanks for coming by, Pastor Jake." He reached out to give the pastor a firm handshake, looking over Pastor Jake's shoulder to the rest of them. "I see you brought some friends."

"I did. We have a little prayer group forming. You know Stephanie and David Wright, don't you? This is their daughter, Sarah, and Nathan's and Brad's families go to the church too."

"Yeah, I think I might have seen you all a few times. Thanks for coming."

Brooke's mom and dad were there in the room as well. They also attended the church and greeted them all warmly.

Pastor Jake looked over at Brooke, who looked like she was sleeping. Her wavy auburn hair fanned out over the pillow, and an IV was attached to the back of her hand. Various monitors checked the vitals of both mom and baby at all times. "How is she doing?" he asked Alex.

"She's still in a lot of pain, and the nurses say that her vitals need to get closer to normal before she can be released. She's only twenty-two weeks along so if the baby came now...he would be too little... he might not survive." Alex ran his hand over his black crew cut and shook his head.

Brooke stirred, wincing as she turned over a bit, reaching her hand down to her slightly enlarged belly, pain on her face.

She opened her eyes and looked a bit confused when she saw all the people in the room; then, spotting Pastor Jake, she managed a strained smile. "Hi, Pastor Jake."

"Hi there, Brooke. We came to pray with you. Would that be all right?"

"Sure. I think the pain meds are wearing off, so I could use it. I just want my baby to be all right."

"Well, we don't want to keep you too long, but we believe God wants to touch you. Sarah, why don't you come over here and lead us in prayer? Brooke, this is Sarah Wright; her mom and dad are Stephanie and David."

"Oh, I know your mom and dad." Brooke smiled through the pain. "Your mom is so sweet."

"Yeah, she's the best." Sarah grinned and took a position next to Brooke, placing her hand on her arm. She closed her eyes and began to pray, "Lord, thank You for Brooke, and for this baby. God, we ask that You would touch Brooke's body and heal her. We ask protection for this baby, that it would grow and develop like it should."

Sarah moved her hand cautiously to lightly touch the small bump where the baby was growing. She could feel God's power moving and her hand was trembling slightly as the Holy Spirit stirred more and more.

Nathan and Brad were praying quietly, pacing around the room a bit, probably because it would be awkward to lay hands on a pregnant woman. The intensity and volume of all of their prayers increased as the moments ticked by.

Suddenly Sarah felt a bolt of energy shoot through her hand and into Brooke's body.

Brooke gave a surprised cry and her hand went to her belly.

Alex stepped forward and took Brooke's other hand. "Are you okay, honey?"

Brooke paused, mentally taking note of how she was feeling. "Actually," she said slowly, "the pain is totally gone!" She looked at her husband incredulously, her eyes now brimming with tears. "I felt it. I felt God's power go into my body!"

Several minutes passed as they praised God and chatted excitedly about what God had done.

After a while, a tall, slender nurse wearing brown thin-rimmed glasses and dark hair pulled back in a bun came in the room, squeezing around everyone to get to Brooke's charts and the monitors. "Hi, Brooke, how are we doing?" she asked as she looked over the charts.

Brooke responded with a tearful but happy, "Really good!"

The nurse looked up over the top of her glasses, a bit confused. "Are you sure? You're crying. I bet those pain meds wore off a while ago. Do you need some more?"

Brooke shook her head. "No, I don't. Actually, the pain is totally gone! My pastor and some friends here just prayed for me, and I really believe God healed me! One second the pain was there, and then it just left!"

The nurse looked at Brooke, taking mental note of her condition. With a frown she looked at the charts again then moved to the monitors and compared what she read with what the machines were now saying.

"Huh...vitals are looking better too; what do you know about that? Very unusual, but great news for that baby." She smiled.

After a few minutes of checking the baby and mother, the nurse left to leave a message for the on-call doctor to let him know about the change in Brooke's condition. When she came back she said that it was likely that as long as things still looked good in the morning when the doctor did his rounds she could probably go home—taking it easy until she came to full term.

The youth and the pastor talked for a bit more and hugged Brooke and Alex and Brooke's parents before they left, leaving the happy family to marvel at God's goodness and faithfulness.

The little prayer team was full of excitement as they stepped back into the elevator and pushed the button for the lobby. It was so amazing to see God touch Brooke in the way He had.

As the elevator doors opened and they walked out, Deanne Campbell spotted them from down the hallway and rushed up to them, looking like she was about to jump out of her skin for joy.

"Pastor Jake! Sarah! I was hoping y'all hadn't left yet. You'll never believe what just happened!" she squealed, her Southern drawl even more pronounced in her excitement.

"Whoa there, Deanne, what is it?" Pastor Jake grabbed her elbow to calm her down.

Hardly able to contain herself, she gushed, "I started my shift just a little while ago and the first patient I needed to check on was Joseph. When I got to the room and checked his temperature, it was normal! I asked him what the doctor did to bring it down and he said the doctor hadn't been in, but a nurse came in with a huge fan and said, 'Still got that fever? We'll take care of that.' She turned on the fan and left and after a few minutes, he said he started feeling much better. The crazy thing is that we don't even allow those types of fans in this part of the hospital. I asked him what the nurse looked like and he said she had short, spiky blonde hair."

Deanne's eyes glistened with unshed tears and she brought her hands up to her chest. "There's not a nurse on this shift who looks anything like he described!" She leaned in closer. "Pastor Jake, I think it was an angel!"

Nathan elbowed Sarah lightly. "Your prayer. Sarah, you prayed that God would send His angels to help Joseph."

"Oh my gosh!" Sarah's eyes widened. "I did, and I don't normally pray things like that!" she thought for a second and her eyes lit up, "You know what? I remember passing that nurse pushing a big fan on wheels when we left Joseph's room! That's so cool!"

Deanne bounced up and down a bit. "And Joseph told me that he and his wife gave their hearts to the Lord when y'all were there. How exciting! Wow, God is so good, it just never ceases to amaze me!"

Pastor Jake nodded at Sarah. "I told you He had a plan."

They said good-bye to Deanne and continued to the entrance of the building. As they neared the automatic sliding doors, Pastor Jake got a call and took it. After hanging up he said, "That was Brooke's husband, Alex. Brooke's dad got called to come in to work right away and her mom needs a ride home. I told her we could drop her off. Alex didn't want to leave Brooke yet.

They waited near the elevators and after a few minutes Brooke's mother came off the elevator. "Thank you so much for giving me a ride home." Her expression was grateful.

"No problem. You three can fit in the back, right?" He turned to Sarah, Nathan, and Brad.

They all nodded and Nathan spoke up, "Sure, it will probably be warmer that way, as cold as it is outside." He shot a quick glance at Sarah.

They piled in the back of Pastor Jake's car and Nathan sat in the middle, straddling the humped floorboard, his leg resting against Sarah's in the cramped quarters.

Sitting this close to Nathan was unnerving.

In spite of her decision earlier that day to not view Nathan as more than a friend, she couldn't stop thinking about how close they were sitting. Every turn of the car, bump in the road, or change in acceleration caused their legs to rub against each other.

As they drove to drop off Brooke's mom, the backseat trio was quiet while the adults engaged in friendly banter up front. Brad hummed along with the music on the Christian station, seemingly lost in his own thoughts and worship.

Sarah was content not to be talking right now as she worked on calming her rapidly beating heart. She cast a sideward glance at Nathan, wondering what he was feeling. *Was he aware that his leg was rubbing against hers? Was it making his heart beat any faster?*

He caught her eye and smiled, which only served to make her heart start pounding in her ears. She was glad that it was dark because she could feel heat moving up her neck, reddening her cheeks.

***

Nathan could have moved his leg a little further inward so it wasn't flush against Sarah's, but honestly he didn't want to. The close contact with her was something he enjoyed.

Things had been a little strange lately. Sarah seemed distracted ever since they had talked after the football game. He was pretty sure that by now she would have broken things off with Nick, even though she hadn't come right out and said it. She would tell him eventually.

For now he would just savor the heat he could feel emanating from her jean-clad leg.

123

He looked over and smiled, hoping the ride would last as long as possible.

After a few moments, he leaned closer to Sarah. "That was really cool tonight." He resisted the urge to tuck a loose lock of hair behind her ear.

"Yeah, it was. God is so amazing, right?" Reaching up, she corralled the rebellious hair safely back in place. "It makes you think that there may be an angel sitting right next to you and you don't even realize it."

Nathan regarded her statement. In the darkness he was able to search her face, he hoped, without her realizing how long his eyes lingered on her. The passing street lights gave him brief glimpses of her face, illuminating her features in a soft glow.

Here was an angel, indeed, sitting right next to him. His eyes focused on her lips for a long moment and flicked back to her eyes.

"I agree. I bet there are more angels around than we realize."

***

Sarah noticed the way Nathan looked at her, the way his eyes held her, and she decided that it would be very easy to become more than just friends with him if she allowed it. Or was she just vulnerable on the heels of breaking up with Nick?

It had been a very emotional day, in addition to the heightened spiritual moments they had shared in the hospital. But after the conversation she had earlier with her mom, she needed to get her emotions under control and fall in love with Jesus before letting herself fall in love with anyone else. She also needed to set her own boundaries for future relationships and make a firm decision to keep those boundaries in place—no matter how she felt.

The car slowed to a stop in front of Brooke's mother's home, and she gave them all a cheery good-bye before heading up the walkway to the front door.

Pastor Jake twisted around in his seat. "Sarah, you want to come back up front? Give the guys a little more leg room?"

"Sure," Sarah said reluctantly, actually wanting to stay in the back, but deciding that she needed a little space between her and Nathan to help calm her heart rate.

She slid out of the back and waved to Brooke's mom, who had just opened her door and turned for a final good-bye before disappearing inside.

Pastor Jake was still turned around in his seat. "Are you guys hungry? Want to grab some pizza?" he offered. "My treat."

"Sure," they replied in unison.

There was a great little pizzeria just down the street where they stopped. As they opened the door of the pizzeria, the combined smells of garlic, spicy pepperoni, and baked mozzarella cheese engulfed them, making Sarah's stomach rumble.

They each ordered their slices—pepperoni for Brad, Buffalo chicken for both Nathan and Sarah, and a green pepper and mushroom slice for Pastor Jake. Then the pastor added enough garlic knots to the order so they could each have two.

The pizza shop employee slid the slices in a big oven and put the garlic knots on a plate. As Pastor Jake paid for the food, he handed a paper cup to each of them.

They filled their cups, found a table in the corner, and started in on the garlic knots while they waited for their pizza.

As Pastor Jake sat down he said a quick prayer for the food before grabbing a garlic knot.

Brad picked up a garlic knot too, and took a big bite, chewing a bit before saying, "I can't wait to tell my parents about what happened tonight; that was awesome!"

Nathan swallowed a swig of soda. "I know. I can't stop thinking about how happy those people looked after God touched them."

Sarah smiled, chewing on her garlic knot, enjoying the buttery but strong flavor. She reflected on how it was truly amazing the way God worked. Every instance in which God displayed His healing power that evening had been different.

After taking a long drink of his raspberry iced tea, Pastor Jake said, "You know, if every believer realized the power they have available to them, there wouldn't be as many people in hospitals today—not that God doesn't use doctors. I firmly believe that God gave wisdom to doctors and even calls some people to be doctors to bring healing in that way. But there are so many Christians who don't realize that they have access to the same life-giving power that raised Jesus from the dead!"

It was evident to everyone at the table that Pastor Jake was so ignited by the night's events that it was flowing out of him.

"I think people don't realize it because they never really see it happening," Brad interjected. "I mean, I've been a Christian for a long time and I know that God heals, but I didn't really think it could happen to me, or around me, because I had never experienced it before. But the other day when Sarah and Nathan prayed for me and my headache left, it was like a light bulb turned on."

Brad leaned forward. "For the first time in my life I knew that God was really real because He touched me. It gave me so much more faith."

"Yeah, me too," Nathan said as their pizza slices were delivered to the table. "Actually, the first time anything like that ever happened to me was when Sarah and I were ten. I had the flu, and she insisted on coming to my house to pray for me. I was back in school the next day."

He looked down at the pizza in front of him, a sad look on his face. "You'd think I would have more faith than I do now, being that God healed me like that so long ago." Nathan looked up and smiled. "But tonight helped me remember…remember that God's power is real."

They all dug in, cheese stringing from pizza to mouths as they ate. Sarah loved the pizza from this place. The crust was so crisp and their homemade sauce rivaled any found in a New York City establishment.

They continued to talk as they ate—the main subjects being faith, miracles, and angels. Pastor Jake, along with the events of the evening, gave them a lot to think about, study, and search out.

They left the pizzeria and piled back into the car, dropping off Brad before returning Sarah to her house. Nathan didn't live too far from Pastor Jake, so he would be dropped off last.

"See you tomorrow, Nathan. Bye, Pastor Jake!" Sarah said.

Nathan got out of the back to move up front, not wanting to make Pastor Jake feel like a taxi driver or a chauffeur. He gave Sarah a quick hug, breathing in the scent of her hair and closing his eyes for a second.

"See you tomorrow." He stepped back with his arm on the car door, grinning at her as she walked backward a few steps, then turned to prance up the walkway and into the house.

Chapter Fifteen

I'm getting sick of it!" Rachel Turner threw down the patient files she had been holding with a loud slap, turning the heads of the other nurses at the station.

Deanne looked up from the monitor in front of her. "What's the matter?"

"What's the matter?" Rachael mimicked in a squeaky tone. She rolled her eyes. "Like you don't know."

"No...I don't know, actually," Deanne drawled, wondering what in the world could have gotten Rachel so flustered.

They had never truly gotten along when working together, and Rachel had made it clear from the beginning that she didn't like Deanne. They had been able to tolerate working the same shift for a long time, although Deanne tried hard not to get in Rachel's way.

Rachel threw up her hands. "All this God-stuff. It seems like the only thing these patients talk about lately is Jesus-this, and God-did-that." She turned to face Deanne directly and pointed at her with narrowed eyes. "Ever since your friends came to visit people, it's just gotten out of control, especially since last night!"

"Come on, Rachel, it's not out of control. Haven't you noticed how much happier and healthier those patients are? Some of them have even gone home way before we thought they would be!"

Deanne couldn't believe she had to argue this idea. Why would Rachel have a problem with patients getting better more quickly? She should be happy for them!

"Oh sure, I'm glad they are feeling better, but now all they want to talk about when I come into the room is God, God, God. I can't even take someone's blood pressure without them asking me if I would go to heaven if I died. It's just crazy! It has to stop."

"They just care about you, Rachel, that's all. What's so bad about that?"

"*We're* the ones supposed to be caring for *them*, not them caring about my 'eternal security' or whatever it is they call it." Rachel held up her fingers and wiggled them to make quote symbols as she spoke.

Deanne thought she would step out on a limb, not sure how Rachael would react to her next question. "Well...what do you tell them?"

"Excuse me?" The question seemed to take Rachel by surprise. "What do you mean?"

"When they ask you if you would go to heaven if you died, what do you tell them?" She raised an eyebrow.

Rachel threw her hands up in the air again. "Oh, please! Really, Deanne, I thought you and I were done with this conversation years ago." She leaned forward with her hands on the high countertop and said sharply, "I tell them to mind their own freaking business! But in a nice way, of course," she added with a tilt of her head.

When Deanne had first been hired, she and Rachel had many discussions about the Bible and God, none of which Rachel had initiated. After getting so many snide remarks and heated answers back, Deanne stopped trying to reach out to Rachel, figuring by now she had shared enough that Rachel should know the truth and was responsible to God for her own choice to accept or reject Him. This was the first time in years that the topic had come up again.

Now Deanne prayed silently for new wisdom and strength once again to help her show His love to Rachel. There had to be a reason that God put her here in Rachel's path along with all these patients who were so excited about their newfound faith.

Wanting to reply to Rachel that she didn't have a right to be rude to people, she bit her tongue and instead looked Rachel in the eyes and responded softly, "Well, I hope someday that God becomes as real to you as He is to those patients."

Rachel looked taken back.

In years past, Deanne had been quick to quote a Scripture or retaliate in God's defense. A soft answer was not what Rachel had expected, but after a moment she quickly recovered, her face hardening.

"That will happen when hell...I mean heaven, freezes over." Rachel grabbed another stack of charts and stormed off to the filing room to put them away.

As she left, Deanne could hear her muttering, "If this keeps up, I'm gonna have to go talk to someone about it."

Deanne released the breath she hadn't realized she was holding. Somehow, someway, she would get through to Rachel.

How long that would take, she wasn't sure.

***

Sarah hoisted her backpack up higher on her back and greeted some friends as she inched her way down the noisy, crowded hallway at school.

Her mind was full of thoughts from yesterday as she walked mechanically to her study hall the next period. She smiled as she remembered the joy she saw emanating from both Joseph and Brooke when God had touched them. God was so amazing!

Lost in her contemplations, Sarah hardly realized where she was walking until she found herself near Nick's locker. She had intended to walk a different way for a few days to avoid seeing him until things calmed down a bit, but had totally forgotten.

She blinked, focusing her eyes on what she saw right in front of her, her eyebrows scrunching in disbelief.

Nick and Maria were in the middle of a passionate, tongue-twisting kiss, his body pressed as closely to hers as possible against his locker, and his hands roving almost to places they shouldn't, right there in the hallway!

Sarah's eyes widened and mouth dropped, her hand instinctively coming up to cover it. Tears sprung to her eyes, unbidden.

It hadn't even been twenty-four hours since she had broken up with him! Even though it was over, the feeling of betrayal cut deeply. From the looks of it, she was right about what she had seen under the bleachers at the football game, but even that truth didn't ease the pain of what she was now witnessing.

As much as she wanted to run away, crawl under a rock, and hide for the next month or so, she heard herself start talking.

"It was you, both of you, under the bleachers." Sarah's voice was shaky. Tears streamed down her face and she balled up her fists, trying to control the anger she was feeling.

Nick and Maria parted, at least their lips did, and they looked at her, obviously annoyed at the distraction.

A satisfied grin took over Maria's face, knowing that she had hurt Sarah.

Nick gave Sarah a disgusted look. "You and I are over, remember? *You* broke up with me, so don't be so shocked when I find someone who can give me what you wouldn't."

"I have morals, Nick, something you obviously don't have, and every time you were around me you wanted me to break them," Sarah replied through clenched teeth. She wasn't really surprised at what he was wanting, that he was now using Maria to fill his void.

Maria, happy to take full advantage of the moment, spoke up, "Well, you don't have to worry about your precious morals now. I can give Nick *everything* he needs." She turned Nick's face back to hers and pulled his body back into the position they were in before Sarah interrupted them.

With their lips back in motion, they ignored Sarah, not wanting to waste the few seconds left before the bell rang.

At their clear dismissal of her, Sarah turned with shock and frustration and quickly retraced her steps. Seeking some quiet reprieve, she let loose the emotions she was trying to hold at bay.

The school courtyard should be empty as the bell was about to ring for fourth period. Even though she had a study hall next, Sarah knew she couldn't possibly sit in a classroom and do anything constructive in this mental state. And she didn't want the embarrassment of crying in front of everyone—especially Nathan, who was in her study hall too.

She had to pull it together so she could operate for the rest of the day. She would go straight there as soon as she composed herself enough.

Opening the door to the courtyard, she was met with a blast of cool air just as the bell sounded. The temperature was about forty-five degrees right now and was forecasted to reach the mid-fifties today, normal weather in New York for October.

As she expected, the courtyard was vacant.

In the spring and fall the courtyard was a beautiful place. Being that it was the size of four classrooms put together, there was a lot of room for the trees that were carefully positioned and a cement walkway that wound around to different areas. Some teachers and students had started a gardening club and took it upon themselves to care for and nurture the beautiful flowers and bushes. The courtyard was positioned in the center of the school building and walled in on three sides by glass, giving teachers and passersby the ability to see almost everything going on. Several curved stone benches were situated in different areas, some facing the windows, others not.

She was taking a chance of a teacher telling her to get to where she was supposed to be, but she needed a few moments to gather her emotions back and calm her spirit.

Sarah picked a bench not facing any windows that had a few evergreen bushes to each side and a colorful maple tree right behind to allow for a bit of privacy. She sat down, the cold from the stone penetrating quickly through her jeans to her skin. At the moment she didn't care, lowering her head into her hands to release the pent-up sobs and finding relief. Having a "good cry," as her mom always called it, was like a healing balm in times like these.

After just a few minutes she heard the glass door to the courtyard squeal open, alerting her that someone was coming.

Sarah breathed in sharply, whirling around to see who was there.

To her relief, Nathan poked his head around a cone-shaped evergreen bush.

"Sarah, are you okay? I was on my way to study hall and saw you crying so I followed you to make sure you're all right."

Quickly wiping the tears from her face, Sarah was suddenly glad she had decided not to put on much makeup today, but had wished she'd skipped the mascara. Even the light coat she'd applied probably made her look like a raccoon now.

"Hey, Nathan, you scared me for a second." She stood up, pulling a tissue from her pocket to wipe her nose and eyes, rubbing the tip under her bottom lashes to hopefully remove the black smudges before stuffing it back into her pocket, "I'll be okay, I guess."

Nathan came over to where she stood, searching her glossy green eyes with concern. "What happened? Is your family okay?"

"Yeah...no, it's nothing like that; nobody's hurt." She exhaled slowly and hugged herself to ward off the cold, looking down at her shoes. "I just happened to see Nick with his new girlfriend, Maria, swallowing each other's faces by his locker. We just broke up yesterday, and he's already with someone else."

"Oh...well that explains it." Nathan turned, looking like he wanted to punch something but instead shoved his hands through his hair. "What a jerk! I knew he was bad news." Nathan said as a new wave of tears came over Sarah.

She pressed her hands over her eyes. "I'm pretty sure they didn't know I was there until I interrupted them. I should have broken up with him a lot sooner." Her voice caught in her throat.

She swiped at the tears again, shaking her head. "I knew he was wrong for me; you told me too. So it shouldn't bother me. I just didn't think he would be with someone else so soon. It's like he didn't really like me for me...I was so easily replaced," she managed between sobs.

Nathan reached to touch her arm. "Shhhh...hey, come here."

He pulled her closer, wrapping his arms around her and gently rubbing her back. "It's gonna be okay. Let them do whatever they want. You made the right decision."

"I know." Her voice sounded muffled as she spoke into his chest.

She let her muscles relax as Nathan held her. It felt right, pure. She knew that Nathan truly cared about her.

***

Nathan rested his chin on Sarah's head, closed his eyes, and breathed in deep through his nose, savoring her fragrance. He knew it wouldn't look right to others to be holding her, but he told himself he was comforting her; she needed him.

He had never felt this way about anyone else before, and right now he knew without a shadow of a doubt that he was falling in love with Sarah Wright.

At the same time, he knew he had to keep his head; guys in love could do—and say—stupid things. He had seen that firsthand with some of his friends when they fell for a girl.

Sarah calmed and he felt her relax, but he kept holding her.

When he first saw her in the courtyard today, his heart had gone out to her. He had watched her from the window for a few moments before going into the courtyard. The red around her eyes, coupled with smudged makeup, proved that she had been crying. It was like he could feel the pain she was experiencing. He wanted to make sure that she felt loved and appreciated, to take away the pain she was feeling.

As they stood there, she moved her hands away from her face and leaned her head against his chest, stirring up emotions and feelings stronger than ever.

"Thanks, Nate. I can always count on you."

Nathan glanced down; her eyes were closed, framed by long, dark lashes. Her cheeks were pink from the cold, her face so close.

More than ever he wanted to kiss her, and he wondered for the thousandth time what it would be like. He moistened his lips, wondering if she could hear his rapidly beating heart with her head on his chest.

Sarah lifted her head slightly off his chest and opened her eyes, tilting her chin up slowly until their noses barely touched.

Their breath mingled together in a cloud of translucent white between them as their eyes locked for a moment.

He lifted his hand up to her face and gently rubbed the baby-soft skin on her jawline with his thumb.

Her eyes slid closed and he inched his face closer to hers and closed his eyes too.

Then when it seemed their lips would finally touch, Sarah suddenly breathed in sharply and dropped her head, stepping back from him.

***

It had happened so fast. Nathan hugged her, and suddenly they were almost kissing.

What was going on?

In a rush, all the conversations she'd had recently with her mom and the Lord came swirling back through her mind and she stepped back. If she were ever to start a relationship with Nathan, it needed to be right.

Today was all wrong—the timing, the moment. She needed time for God to become her true love or Nathan might end up becoming another casualty of a half-devoted passion.

"I'm sorry. I really want to kiss you...but I...I just can't right now. There are some things I need to work out in my own heart first."

She lowered herself back down to the cold stone bench and motioned for him to sit next to her. "I need to tell you something."

He sat obediently, making sure not to touch her, a bit confused, and said, "Okay."

She lifted her eyes to meet his. "After I broke up with Nick yesterday, I had a long talk with my mom. She told me that before I give my heart to another guy, I really need to give my heart fully to God, to really fall in love with Him first." She looked down and rubbed at something on her jeans. "I think I went out with Nick because, even though I was a Christian, I wasn't letting God be my first love."

Nathan swallowed. "So...what happens now? I really care about you, Sarah. I think by now you know that." He grinned sheepishly. His face turned serious again. "But I can't hide the way I feel about you."

Sarah blushed at his admission, wanting to say more, to tell him how she felt about him too. But right now that probably would not be good.

She put her hand over his on the bench. "I need some time, Nate. I need to make sure that Jesus is first in my heart before I share it with anyone else. I hope you understand." Her eyes pleaded and searched his.

Nathan looked down at their hands and slowly moved his fingers to intertwine with hers, then he slowly lifted her hand to his lips and gave it a soft kiss before releasing it.

"I do, and I'll be waiting for you when you're ready."

Just then the door opened and they both turned to see one of the school's security guards stepping out.

"You two supposed to be somewhere?" the guard asked firmly.

Nathan released her hand and spoke up first. "Yeah, sorry. We both have study hall but I saw my friend here was upset about something and wanted to make sure she was okay." He glanced at Sarah, "Think we can head to study hall now?"

Sarah nodded, giving a final blow to her nose in the last tissue she held.

The officer eyed Sarah with concern. "You okay, Young Lady?"

Nodding again, Sarah replied, "I'm fine, just some personal stuff I'm dealing with right now. I know I was going to be late but I couldn't go to study hall like that. Nate saw me and stopped to help."

"Don't make it a habit. Too many tardies, and penalties start coming," he reminded.

"I don't plan on it." Sarah rose.

Nathan rose too and lifted his backpack onto his shoulder, his bangs fanning over one eye in typical Nathan fashion.

The officer held the door open for them as they left the chill of the courtyard behind and met with the warmth of the hallway.

"Have a good day," the security officer said as he closed the door behind them and continued on his rounds.

They started in the direction of the study hall.

Sarah took a deep breath. "Thanks, Nathan…for everything." She smiled.

"You're welcome." His eyes held hers tenderly before looking ahead.

In just a few moments they arrived at the classroom and explained the situation to the study hall monitor. Because they were so late, the only available seats were across the classroom from each other.

After they were seated, Nathan's eyes met hers for a moment across the room. He winked and then got to work. It was his reminder to her of the conversation they had in the courtyard. He wanted to honor her wishes.

Sarah took another deep breath and exhaled slowly, lifting her eyes upward. *Well, Lord, it's just You and me for now.*

Strangely, she felt at peace.

She was looking forward to getting home later and spending extra time in her personal sanctuary with nobody else to listen in but Shadow. She smiled to herself as she pulled out a textbook from her backpack.

***

"Guess what, Sarah?" Brad's voice sounded excited on the other end of the phone.

She had barely walked through the door when her cell phone rang.

"I talked to Mr. Roberts, my science teacher. He is a Christian, you know. Anyway, he said that there are no after-school programs going on in his classroom on Tuesdays so it would be empty and we could pray there for people once a week as long as there's a monitor in the room," he rattled on, "and if I remember right, you and Nathan and I are free that day, right?"

"Yes, I know I am. That's so great, Brad!" Sarah responded enthusiastically.

"So he said that as long as we are the ones doing the praying and setting it all up, it should be fine. I have a few friends from other churches who've been sick or going through stuff and could use some prayer. Maybe it won't be non-Christian kids who come yet, but hopefully they will eventually."

Sarah could tell that Brad was really pumped about the whole idea. It made her a little nervous, but knowing all the good things God would do through it was calming that nervousness.

"That's great, Brad! When do we start?"

"Next Tuesday, right after school in Mr. Roberts' room. I already told Nathan about it, and he will be there too."

Sarah felt her stomach do a little flip thinking about seeing Nathan after their encounter today, but she mentally stuffed her feelings down and reminded herself about her decision to let God have her heart first.

"Count me in."

Chapter Sixteen

After dinner, Sarah excused herself from the table and quickly gathered some books and her phone and headed out to the stable. She shivered as she stepped into the cold air and zipped her jacket up the last few inches while snuggling her chin down into its warmth. It was a blustery evening, and a few dead leaves swirled past as Sarah opened the stable door, holding tightly to the handle so it didn't blow out of her hands. The stable was warmer than it was outside; it felt good to get out of the cutting wind.

Shadow gave a low whinny from his stall and stretched his head down over his gate to greet her. Sarah turned on a space heater before crossing over to rub the big horse's velvety muzzle, smiling as he playfully lipped at her hand.

She pulled a sugar cube out of her jacket pocket with her other hand and held it up. "Looking for this, boy?" She cupped her hand down for Shadow to get the sweet treat and rubbed the spot between his ears.

She gave him a kiss and wiped her hands on a nearby towel, finishing up with a bit of hand sanitizer before pulling her cell phone out of her pocket.

Sarah had been faithfully using a daily reading plan on her favorite Bible app that allowed her to read through the whole Bible in a year. The Scripture version she used had an audio option, so sometimes she would sit back and listen to the Bible being read while she stroked or braided Shadow's mane and tail. If it was a shorter reading, she would sometimes start it over again and catch things she didn't pick up the first time. This is what she did today, mechanically brushing the horse's mane until it had a fine sheen while she absorbed the scriptures she heard.

After a few chapters she switched it over to the Song of Solomon. Being that it was only eight chapters long, Sarah intended to listen to most, if not all of it today, and planned to reread it every day for a week. She had heard someone at church talking about the Song of Solomon, explaining that it was much more than a love letter between a bride and groom; it was God's love letter to all His children. She figured this was a good place to start in her journey of making Jesus her first love.

Sarah started listening. When she got to chapter 1 verse 15, she paused the audio and read it out loud:

"How beautiful you are, my darling, how beautiful! Your eyes are like doves."

She thought about this for a moment. This was Jesus talking to her, saying that she is beautiful! She closed her eyes and lifted her face upward at the thought. Nick had told her she was beautiful, but it had felt fleshly compared to this revelation. She prayed that God would give her a yearning for Him more than for the physical love of any guy.

Time flew by as she continued to listen to the Word and pray intermittently as the Lord dealt with different areas of her heart. The Song of Solomon came alive in a way she had never experienced before. She felt her heart fill with love as she followed the story of the Bridegroom and His true love. When she got to the place in chapter 4 when the woman, longing for her lover, opened the door and found He wasn't there, she could feel the emptiness that the Shulamite experienced. In fact, it was a similar feeling to what she had felt before she had really committed her heart to the Lord—something had been missing.

Sarah continued listening, and as the last chapter finished, she lay back on the hay bales and thought about the ending. The two lovers ran away together; they couldn't wait to be with each other.

Sarah sighed, contented. Her heart was so full of love and affection for her Jesus. Her mom was totally right. How could she really give her heart to a guy if God was not first in her life? She could see how that in itself could create all sorts of issues and problems.

Sarah lay there for a while, just resting in the fact that God loved her and wanted to be a huge part of her life, even more than a best friend. He wanted to be intricately involved—even in the details that she had earlier thought He wouldn't be concerned about. Actually, it was getting Him involved in those details that would help the big things in life run smoothly.

Eventually, Sarah's mom knocked on the stable door before opening it slowly. "Sarah, are you all right? You've been out here a long time!"

Sarah sat up and smiled. "Yeah, Mom, I'm great." She held up her phone. "I listened to the whole book of Song of Solomon. I'm gonna go through it every day for a while."

Stephanie came over and sat down by Sarah on the hay bale. "That's great, Sweetie! Isn't it beautiful?"

Sarah hugged her mom. "Thanks for talking to me earlier. I really needed this time alone with God." Sarah gathered her books and phone, looking to see the time. "Wow, I guess I *was* out here a long time; it's already after nine!" She stood and brushed a few stray pieces of straw off her pants.

Stephanie stood too. "Well, time flies when you're having fun, right?"

"Exactly." Sarah chuckled. They walked to the door but before Sarah opened it, she turned to her mom. "I told the Lord tonight that I won't date anyone for a while, at least until I know for sure that a guy won't come before Him again."

Stephanie rubbed her daughter's back lovingly. "I'm really proud of you, Sarah. And when that time comes, He will give you just the right guy—someone who will encourage you to reach higher and to be the best version of you that you can be."

***

Sarah couldn't wait until it was time to go home after school every day. That was when she would escape to the stable and pray, worship, and read, getting to know more about her Lord, best Friend, and Lover. She made sure to keep up with homework and studies after dinner, but she was beginning to feel like the Shulamite, longing to go and be with Him anytime she could. At school she kept herself busy, trying to see the needs of people around her. It was a good distraction because she could feel the attraction in her heart for Nathan growing steadily, but there wasn't much time left in the day to dwell on it.

In just two weeks, the little prayer group on Tuesday afternoon had gained some publicity by word of mouth. That first day several students came and two of the three had been instantly healed by the time they left, with the other having a confirmed healing later that week. Some of them thought the group needed a name instead of just being "the prayer group" and after some ideas were brought up they decided the best name was "Impact," being that the purpose of their prayer ministry was to impact people's lives for God. Sarah thought back to that starting day of Impact when the first student had walked in.

***

The first day of the prayer group had been wonderful and exciting for everyone. Before anyone showed up, the little group was talking excitedly with each other about what God was doing. Mr. Roberts leaned casually against his heavy wooden desk while Nathan, Brad, Sarah, and a few other students sat on desk tops or stood around.

At a soft knock on the door they stopped talking and turned to welcome the visitor.

Samantha Peck was a tall, skinny girl with long, straight red hair and vibrant green eyes. She stepped in the room cautiously, not really knowing what to expect. From what Sarah knew, her family had a very conservative religious background, and Samantha was very quiet and proper in how she presented herself.

"Hi, I'm Samantha," she said as she walked closer.

Sarah smiled and stepped over to meet her. "Hi, Samantha, come on in!"

"Thanks. Brad heard me talking to my friends this morning about this rash on my arm that I can't get to go away and said I should stop by." She pulled up the sleeve of her shirt so the group could see the bright red rash.

"Wow, that looks like a pain…no pun intended." Nathan grinned and leaned in a bit to see it better. "Have you gone to a doctor yet?"

"Not yet. I was hoping it would go away on its own. I'll go next week if it's not gone by then. I've been using different creams and stuff trying to get rid of it." Samantha shrugged.

"Well, we can pray for you," Sarah offered. "Come on over." She pulled a chair over and patted the seat with her hand.

Samantha sat down and situated herself, the arm with the rash on her lap in front of her.

Nathan, Brad, and Sarah looked at Mr. Roberts, who motioned with his head for them to go ahead with the prayer. Then Nathan and Brad both looked at Sarah and smiled, waiting for her to begin.

Sarah smiled back at the guys. She didn't want to freak Samantha out by their style of prayer if she was coming from a really conservative church. She figured she better explain what was about to happen. She put her hand on Samantha's shoulder and Samantha looked up.

"I'm not sure how people normally pray for things in your church," Sarah stated, "but in the one I go to, we believe in making prayer personal. I know that the power of God sometimes works greater when I put my hand on the person. That is what people mean when they say they are 'laying hands' on someone. Is that okay?"

"Sure, I guess," Samantha said. "If it helps it heal, I don't care," she added with a grin.

"Okay, well, let's pray." Sarah moved her hand from Samantha's shoulder to lightly touch her arm near the rash. She closed her eyes and the rest did the same as she started to pray.

"Lord God, we're here to lift up Samantha to You and ask that You bring healing into her arm. Thank You that You love her and want to do awesome things in her life. Touch this rash and cause it to disappear, in Jesus' name."

"Oh, my gosh," Nathan whispered. Then Samantha gasped.

"Did you see that?" Brad asked. "There was a flash of light just a second ago. I saw it out of the corner of my eye!"

"I think I saw it too!" another student exclaimed, while a few others nodded.

Sarah opened her eyes. Nathan and Brad stood there with their mouths hanging open, staring at Samantha's arm. Her eyes widened as the rash, once bright red, was now a pinkish color that was fading as she watched it.

Within just a few seconds, the skin looked as normal as the rest of her arm!

Samantha ran her hand over the spot where the rash used to be. "I can't believe that! I saw it go away, I…wow! I've never seen anything like that in my life. It was like what you see in a movie or something!" Her eyes were wide and then a big grin came over her face.

Mr. Roberts looked totally amazed at what God had done as well. He fumbled and almost fell away from the desk he had been leaning against as he stepped over to inspect Samantha's arm too. Coming from a more traditional church, he had never seen a healing or miracle firsthand and was as amazed as the rest of the group.

Samantha stayed a few more minutes and talked with the group, saying she might come back sometime to hang out with them and pray for other kids too. As she was leaving, another student, Timothy Maine, was coming in for prayer and she excitedly showed him where her rash had been and explained how bad it used to be before God touched it. Timothy shared her excitement and this ignited his faith to believe for his own miracle. Timothy had come in with a wart on his hand.

As they prayed, they watched with wonder as it turned black and popped off right before their eyes and the skin became normal.

Another student who came in that first day of the prayer group was a girl with chronic allergies who had been taking medicine daily for the past three years to control it. After seeing Timothy healed instantly, she decided that God was big enough to heal her through prayer too, and stopped taking the medication after talking to her doctor. She wanted to make sure he was okay with her doing that. The following week she wasn't having any allergy problems and reported back to the group that God had, in fact, healed her! She said in the past if she was off the meds for a week, she would go into coughing fits and her sinuses would get all stuffed up, but she was perfectly fine.

***

The miracles continued every week, with students asking for prayer here and there during the school day who could not make it to Impact. By the third week, there were around six or seven students who would come in with various issues ranging from physical problems to emotional and family problems. A few teachers even stopped by with prayer requests.

More students joined Impact, making about five or six students available to pray for those who came in. They would normally gather in a circle around the student to pray. Sometimes there was a need that was more personal and a pair of either guys or girls would pray with the student.

As the faith in all the students increased, it was no longer just Sarah who saw healing and miracles when she prayed; it was becoming a regular thing with all of the core people in the prayer group. They were becoming bolder as they realized that they had what others needed, and it was available to them just by asking.

145

Although many students were cured of colds, sicknesses, or emotional problems like depression, not all of them were healed. Sometimes they came back more than once for prayer. One student came to Nathan and Sarah three days in a row during lunch for prayer before her leg stopped hurting. She had fractured it and needed complete healing right away because she played basketball and wanted to contribute to the team.

Another guy named Brent who was having a rough time at home talked and prayed with Nathan and Brad several times each week before he started seeing the situation get better. Brent's father was an alcoholic and abused the family. Over the last few weeks since Brent had gotten closer to Nathan and Brad, his dad had realized how much damage he was doing to his family and began attending a support group.

The persistent prayer was paying off!

The success of Impact was not always met with kindness, however, from the school population. Those who had been touched by God were happy about it and told other students about what God had done for them, but there were many students who thought there was some type of mystical or cultish thing going on.

An awkward moment came yesterday when Maria actually showed up for a few minutes. She didn't say a word, just stood by the door with her arms crossed and a frown on her face and left a few minutes later.

Sarah wondered why she had come. *Did Maria want prayer or was she spying on the group? Was it with good or bad intention?*

Chapter Seventeen

y now there was so much interest stirred about Impact that their numbers were growing steadily, and a few students pulled Sarah aside to ask if they could meet every day. Sarah planned to bring it up to Nathan and Brad when she got a chance. What was even more encouraging was that there were times when someone would catch Sarah or one of the other leaders in the hall or at lunch for a quick prayer over a need they had.

Whenever possible, it seemed like Maria tried to interrupt or disturb these spontaneous prayer times, and Sarah wondered if this was a personal vendetta or if Maria had just flipped out. She already had Nick as her boyfriend now, and the rumors of what went on between Nick and Maria flew all over the school, most of which Sarah assumed were true.

Today was no different when it came to Maria's persistence in disturbing ministry time. Sarah was just getting ready to pray with another girl who found Sarah at her locker and asked to be prayed for about some family problems she was having.

The girl's name was Taylor Lewis, a junior at Highland Falls and a very smart girl with long, dirty blonde hair and glasses. She had a very sweet spirit in spite of her plain appearance, and the issues she was dealing with at home seemed to weigh heavily on her, coming out in her expression and countenance. She walked with slumped shoulders and too many creases on her forehead for someone so young. Sarah could tell that Taylor felt awkward about praying in the hallway, but her situation must have been desperate enough that it caused her to push aside the uneasiness.

"Last night he came home drunk again, my stepdad." Taylor looked down at her worn sneakers and sniffed. "He beat my mom up pretty bad…I think he wanted to hurt me too, but I went in my room and locked the door. Then I hid in my closet until he passed out." Taylor bit her lip and looked up at Sarah, hoping that her admission wouldn't cause Sarah to reject her.

Sarah couldn't imagine having that type of abuse at home, a place that was supposed to be safe, but she kept her face from showing any shock she felt. She reached out and hugged Taylor with compassion.

Taylor continued, wringing her hands in front of her. "I'm really worried about my mom. I told her she should kick him out, but she keeps saying that he'll change…that she loves him and needs him." She drew in a deep breath, her eyes glistening from unshed tears. "I know we need the money he gives us, but to me it's not worth it. I don't know what to do. Can you please pray for me and my family?" Her soft blue eyes pleaded with Sarah.

Sarah's heart went out to Taylor. How many other students were dealing with similar home situations and she was so oblivious to it all, having grown up in the bubble of her peaceful home and church?

"Of course I will, Taylor. Let's pray right now."

Sarah closed her locker and put her hand on Taylor's shoulder and was about to begin praying when suddenly she was hit hard in the back, causing her to lose her balance and bump into Taylor in the process.

Sarah turned sharply to see what hit her and realized that Maria had walked by, way too closely. She knew immediately that it had been intentional because the hallway wasn't very crowed at the moment. As Maria walked by she must have shifted her backpack to slam into Sarah's back.

Maria turned with a satisfied smirk and said smugly, "Oh, sorry. I didn't see you there." Then she flipped her long, dark hair triumphantly over her shoulder and continued down the hallway.

Sarah turned back to Taylor. "Are you okay? Sorry about that." She tried not to let her annoyance at Maria destroy the chance for her to reach out to Taylor.

Taylor, who had been bumped back against the lockers, righted herself and pushed her glasses up on the bridge of her nose. "I'm fine. What's her problem? Does she not like you or something?"

"I'm not exactly sure." Sarah looked down the hallway at Maria's retreating figure. She didn't want to go into the details, especially because she didn't even know what happened to make Maria hate her so much.

She turned her attention back to Taylor. "Anyway, I really want to pray for you before we run out of time."

"Okay." Taylor smiled and bowed her head as Sarah placed her hand on her shoulder where it had been before the interruption.

Sarah closed her eyes, focusing on the Lord and what He wanted to do in Taylor's life.

In the past, something like what Maria had done would have made her frustrated and distracted, but since she had been spending so much time in prayer and reading the Bible, she found the strength to push those distractions aside quickly and tap into the presence of the Lord. Sometimes all she had to do was whisper His name or close her eyes, and it felt like He was right there standing next to her, ready to move and answer her prayers.

Today was the same, a powerful sense of God's presence hung over the girls as Sarah drew in a deep breath and began to pray with an intensity and boldness she had only recently experienced.

"God, I sense Your presence here right now. I know You see Taylor and You have not left her alone. Your love for her is so strong. Lord, send angels to protect her and her mother, and give them supernatural wisdom to know how to be free from this abuse. Fill their home and lives with Your love and presence so strongly that the enemy can't stay. Satan, in Jesus' name, we tell you to leave Taylor and her family alone; you are not welcome there anymore. And, Jesus, wrap Your arms around Taylor and her mom and bring breakthrough in their lives. In Jesus' name. Amen."

Sarah looked to see tears streaming down Taylor's face, and hope illuminated the girl's blue eyes as she opened them and looked at Sarah.

"Thank you," she whispered.

Sarah remembered that she had a clean tissue in her pocket and pulled it out, holding it out to Taylor. "It's wrinkled, but clean."

"Thanks." Taylor took it, dabbing at her eyes and nose. She didn't have to worry about mascara running because she didn't wear makeup. She gave Sarah a big hug and thanked her again and they parted, barely making it to second period before the bell rang.

***

Maria smirked to herself as she walked to her second period class. The bewildered look on Sarah Wright's face had been totally worth it.

She had overheard that nerd-girl, Taylor, talking with a friend right after homeroom and saying she was going to talk to Sarah. Maria had a feeling Taylor was going for prayer; she had been close to tears when she saw her. She followed the girl from a distance until she saw the two about to pray. Then she put her plan into action—to get Sarah so flustered that she couldn't focus on praying for anyone—and it looked like it might have worked, even though she didn't stick around to see what happened next. She knew Sarah and a few of her friends started that stupid prayer group, and she wanted to put an end to it.

Prayer—even the thought of it made Maria's insides coil and the hatred burn anew.

She had given up on God and prayer long ago. When her dad left, she had prayed earnestly that her family would be restored to the bliss it had once been, which, now that she thought about it, hadn't been that blissful at all. Her parents had fought a lot, but at least they had been together.

After months of praying she just gave up—gave up on prayer, gave up on God, and gave up on Sarah. Every time she had seen Sarah with her family, so happy, it cut deeply—like a knife. Oh sure, Sarah still tried to be a friend to her, but every time she was around Sarah, it was just another reminder about how much her life sucked.

It was so easy to take Nick away. She knew Sarah wouldn't fulfill Nick's wants and needs the way she was willing to. She wasn't sure why Sarah even went out with Nick in the first place when they were from such different worlds. She could tell that Nick wanted Sarah in a way she wouldn't give. At first it made her jealous, but when she realized that Nick wasn't getting much more than a kiss from Sarah, it was easy for Maria to step in and show Nick that she could please him the way he wanted.

But even that truth made her hate her life even more. Now Sarah had something else that Maria could never get back—her purity.

Maria thought about how much her life had worsened over the years. After her dad left, her mom couldn't make the mortgage, and they'd been forced to move into a tiny apartment. It was a huge step down from where they used to live, but at least they had a roof over their heads. Her mom worked two jobs—one cleaning rooms at a local motel and the other waitressing at a truck stop, neither of which brought in a lot of money.

Last year, Maria had to get a part-time job at the mall to help out with the cell phone bill and to buy the expensive clothes she wore to cover up her poverty. Only a few people at school really knew how she lived, and the rest didn't need to know.

Just a few days ago she had found out that her mom had cancer and would have to stop working to begin treatments right away. The cancer was stage four. Her mom had been ignoring the symptoms and signs, hoping that it was something that would go away on its own. She finally went to the doctor earlier that week because she was losing the strength to get up and go to work. That's when their whole world changed.

Maria's thoughts turned back again to Sarah and the prayer group. *All that God-crap has to stop. It isn't real anyway. If God cared so much, why did my dad leave? Why am I stuck in the hell I have to live in every day? Why does my mom have cancer? If He is really real, why doesn't anyone care about me, the real me?* Anger welled up inside of her, threatening to come out, and she willed herself to calm down.

Shaking herself from her reverie, Maria spotted Nick coming up the hall toward her. At least Nick could make her feel good, even though his lustful advances toward her never really filled up the void she felt. She pushed the thoughts out of her mind as he got closer.

"Hey, you," she purred seductively, "I missed you." She wrapped herself around him and received a hot kiss in response.

"Where have you been all my life?" Nick said after he finished kissing her.

"Oh, I just *'ran into'* your ex, Sarah. She's a fool for letting you slip out of her hands," Maria said triumphantly.

"Believe me, I was never really in her hands. She barely let me touch her, but you, on the other hand, are like putty, babe." He pressed in with another kiss and a squeeze to her backside.

The gesture gave her mixed feelings, making her feel wanted but at the same time sleazy. She pushed the latter feeling aside and smacked him back on the bottom.

"Gotta run to class. See you later." Nick winked at her.

The tone of his voice gave her a clue of what he wanted later, along with the way he appraised her body as he left, walking backward a few steps before he turned and jogged down the hall as the bell rang.

Fortunately, her social studies class was a few steps away. She joined the other students who were filing into the classroom as the bell finished ringing.

***

Sarah thought back to the incident with Maria several times that day. She could see how her time with the Lord was really strengthening

152

her and giving her prayers a boldness and power that she had not been able to tap into before. But she couldn't let these distractions from Maria continue. If it kept up, she would need to confront Maria and try, once again, to resolve their issues.

She wondered for the millionth time what it was that drove Maria in the relentless tirade to upset her life.

She's looking for Me, and she doesn't even know it.

The voice was almost audible. She knew this voice well now, heard it every day. God was giving her a piece of Maria's puzzle.

But why me? Why is she so against me?

A passage of Scripture came to her mind that she had been reading lately in John 17. It said that the world hates believers because they do not belong to this world, just as Jesus did not belong to this world. She heard the Lord speak to her heart again.

Your family represents everything she lost that she tried so hard to hold on to. It looks like she hates you, but it is Me she is trying to push away.

As the class started, Sarah continued her silent dialogue with the Lord.

Will we ever be friends again, Lord? I know she hates me, but I still miss her. A pang deep inside hit her. It was not just a desire for Maria's friendship to be restored, but it was like Sarah could feel the Lord's heart—longing to be reunited with Maria. The feeling was so powerful that she almost groaned out loud, but kept it inside.

Soon, was the reply.

Feeling hope for Maria, Sarah grabbed her textbook out of her backpack, placing it on her desk and opening to the page number written on the multi-media Promethium board at the front of the room. She knew from experience that whenever God planned to do something great, like what she sensed He was about to do for Maria, things would get worse before they got better. The devil would try anything he could to stop what God was planning, so she mentally prepared herself as she started taking notes.

Toward the end of class, Sarah thought again about Taylor; at least she got her phone number and e-mail address so she could keep in touch with her. Taylor's story made her want to reach out to the girl. Maybe she would invite her over sometime. She wondered if Taylor liked horses at all; if so, she could have her come ride Shadow.

While she was thinking about it, she sent Taylor a quick text asking how her day went today.

On the way to Spanish she saw Nathan walking in the other direction. Her heart flip-flopped as he smiled and waved, tossing his head to the side to swipe the bangs out of his eyes.

"Hi, Sarah." he stopped and stepped over to her. "Oh hey, the Martins asked me if we can go to the hospital again tonight and to someone's house who needs prayer. You wanna come?"

They hadn't been back to the hospital for a few weeks so Sarah was excited to go back. "Sure, what time?"

"He said it would be a bit earlier if possible. Is five okay? They said we can grab dinner while we are out—on them."

"I'll have to double check with my mom, but I'm sure it will be okay. Is Brad coming too?"

"He's not sure yet, but probably." Nathan grinned.

"I'll text you after I get home to let you know if I can, but plan on me going."

The thought of spending the evening around Nathan sent her heart soaring but she kept her emotions in check. She took a deep breath. She still needed more time before letting him know how she really felt.

She wouldn't be in the stable very long tonight reading and praying, but she had been making a lot of headway with getting God first in her life. The more she read the Bible and spent time with God, the more she realized that He had created her for a purpose—mainly to be His child, free to love Him back. She had started reading through the Psalms, and God was showing her how much the psalmist was just like her, a real person with troubles and hardships who chose to praise God in spite of every horrible thing happening in his life.

These truths were drawing her heart closer and closer to the Lord.

Chapter Eighteen

Just as she expected, Sarah's mom and dad were fine with her going to pray for people, as long as she got her homework done first. She headed straight to her room to finish up her English and science homework so nothing would cause her to miss tonight.

A few minutes before five o'clock, the Martin's car rolled to a stop in front of Sarah's house. She was surprised to see Pastor Jake's son, Colton, in the front seat instead of Charlotte, while Nathan and Brad sat in the back. Colton didn't strike her as one to go praying for people; he didn't seem to be very close to God.

As she neared the car, Nathan leaned to the middle of the back seat and moved over to open the door for her to get in next to him. Blushing, she greeted everyone, glad that the chilly outside temperatures could be blamed for the redness in her cheeks instead of her proximity to Nathan.

"Hi there, Sarah," Pastor Jake said. "Charlotte stayed home today because we have a full car already and she was meeting up with a friend. I will be dropping Colton off at a friend's house on the way to the hospital."

"You sure you don't want to come with us, Colton?" Nathan asked.

"Yeah, I'm sure," Colton responded. He turned to look out the window and muttered, "That place freaks me out."

Sarah noticed Pastor Jake raise his eyebrows and take a sideways glance at Colton, wondering why he would say that.

Within a few minutes they dropped off Colton, and Sarah reluctantly moved up to the front seat at Pastor Jake's offer. Then they continued on to the hospital, talking about school and what was happening lately with Impact.

They had specifically come to pray for a man named Charlie Murphy. Pastor Jake had filled them in ahead of time on his story.

Charlie had become very depressed and admitted himself into the psych ward of the hospital at the urging of his family when they discovered that he had been contemplating suicide. His mother attended the church and was very concerned for her son, and for good reason. Her husband had killed himself when Charlie was just eight years old, leaving the family devastated and full of questions that were never answered. While he was alive, Charlie's father was very abusive, and although his mother had found solace and restoration in the Lord and in her church family, Charlie had never really come to terms with the whole situation. Pastor Jake said that he believed God showed him that the depression developed because Charlie had unresolved feelings toward his father. Knowing some of the history of Charlie's past, he suspected that certain issues were coming back to haunt him in ways that were making him feel hopeless and depressed.

They entered the hospital and greeted the staff as usual, who now recognized them by name. After making small talk for a few moments, they found the psych ward and Charlie's room fairly easily, now that they were familiar with the hospital and its layout.

Pastor Jake requested that he talk with Charlie alone before the rest of the them came in the room. He felt that Charlie might feel more comfortable talking one-on-one with another man, so the teens found a waiting room down the hall and prayed quietly. Pastor Jake said he would text Nathan when he was ready for the rest of them to come in.

***

Pastor Jake entered the room. The curtains were drawn and a small light was just bright enough to see. On such a sunny day it was a shame not to have the windows open, but he didn't want to impose on Charlie or upset him. Charlie was a tall, broad-shouldered guy with brown hair, brown eyes, and the scruffy beginnings of a beard, whether it was intentional or just from lack of motivation, he wasn't sure.

"Hi there, Charlie," Pastor Jake began. "I'm Pastor Jake Martin. Your mom told me you haven't been feeling so great lately. I hoped to come by and talk for a while. Is that okay?"

Charlie shook Pastor Jake's hand and seemed to consider saying no, but just shrugged and mumbled, "Sure, I guess."

They sat down across from each other in a few chairs in the room. Pastor Jake could tell that Charlie was feeling a bit uneasy, so he broke the ice. "So, have you had many visitors?"

Charlie nodded and his eyes went from sad to cold. "Yeah, my mom told a lot of her friends why I'm in here, so some of them have come. I know they mean well, but to be honest, I get tired of people telling me that I would get better if I would pray more, read the Bible more, or just have more faith. I really don't want to see anyone unless they actually care about me, not try to give me some pat answer to my 'big problem.'" His voice was bitter.

Pastor Jake reached out and patted Charlie's knee. "Well, let me reassure you that I'm not here to tell you what you need to do. I just want to listen and pray with you."

Charlie looked visibly relieved and sat back, scratching his stubbly chin, his eyes returning to their sadness. "Okay then, Pastor."

They made small talk for a few minutes, talking mostly about the weather or things that interested them both, like fishing and hunting.

Once Charlie seemed more comfortable with him, Pastor Jake moved on to more serious topics.

"Charlie, you might think this is a bit strange, and that's okay, but I was praying for you this morning, and I felt like God shared with me that your current condition is a direct result of some things that happened to you as a child, something to do with your family." Pastor Jake hesitated a moment then tilted his head. "Does that make any sense, or am I way off?"

Charlie blew his breath out, looked down, and ran his hands through his hair. When he looked back up, his eyes were glassy with emotion. "No, you're right on the money." For a moment he was silent, then he continued, "It was my dad. He had an explosive temper and took it out on me and my mom."

Even as he spoke, Charlie's eyes hardened and he set his jaw. His mouth turned down in disgust. "He would beat her until she passed out. Sometimes I thought she was dead! And then when he was done with her, he would come for me. I hid in the closet or under the bed, thinking maybe, just maybe, he would leave me alone." Charlie shook his head, anger and pain flashing across his features. "But he always found me. He was careful not to leave marks on me where people would see them. Then he threatened to kill my mom if I ever told my teachers, friends, or anyone else about it." Charlie looked Pastor Jake in the eyes; with his face contorted in bitterness and his voice shaky. "I was glad when he killed himself. He didn't deserve to live."

Pastor Jake looked Charlie straight in the eyes. "Charlie, I can't even begin to imagine what you have been through." And he sincerely meant it.

They sat in silence for a moment and Charlie's face relaxed.

Pastor Jake remarked. "Your mom is a real blessing to the church. I'm glad that she has come to peace with it."

"I don't know how she does it, you know…forgive him." Charlie looked down at his hands in his lap for a moment then looked up, tears starting to run down his cheeks. "Do you know what he told me the night he shot himself? He said I would end up just like him, a loser. Said I would never amount to anything worth anything." He clenched his jaw tight. "Guess he was right…look at me now."

Pastor Jake interjected, shaking his head, "No, Charlie, he was wrong about you. You're more valuable than you realize. Your mom mentioned that she reads the Bible to you, so I know that you've heard how much God loves you, Charlie, and He wants to be involved in your life."

"Yeah, right. All of a sudden God wants to be my friend. Why now, after all these years?"

"He's always wanted to be your friend, and much more than that. He wants to be the one you lean on when you're sad, or when you think you can't make it anymore. He has always been waiting for you to come to Him." Pastor Jake scooted a bit closer. "You mentioned that your mom has forgiven your dad. What about you, can you forgive him?"

Charlie looked away, pain evident on his face. His Adam's apple bobbed as he swallowed. "I can't. I tried to a few times, but I just couldn't stop thinking about how badly he treated me."

"I don't have a doctorate in science or psychology but I read a lot and stay up on medical findings because it is so closely tied to what I do as a pastor, dealing with people every day. Lately there have been findings that link sicknesses, especially mental illness, with people who are not able to forgive someone."

"Really?" Charlie turned back to Pastor Jake, his eyes widening. "I never realized that."

"That's why God is so big on forgiveness. God even goes so far to say in Matthew 6 that if you can't forgive other people from things they have done to you, than God can't forgive you of your sins. You see, unforgiveness is also a sin. But the great news is what we find in First John 1:9 where it says, 'If we confess our sins to him, he is faithful and just to forgive us our sins and cleanse us from all unrighteousness.'"

Charlie chuckled. "My mom has been saying that to me for many years, but it never really clicked until the way you just said it now." He paused for a moment. "So…there's a chance that if I forgive my dad…I won't be this way anymore?"

"I'm not a medical doctor, but I know God's Word is true and forgiveness is part of healing. Yes, there is a good chance of that. I brought a few friends with me who love to pray for people. If it's okay, I will have them come in so we can pray with you. I had them wait down the hall while we talked. They may seem young, but God has given these kids some really powerful gifts in prayer. Things happen when they pray. Is that okay?"

Charlie nodded. "Yeah, I guess I could give it another shot."

"Great!" Pastor Jake pulled out his cell phone and texted Nathan.

In just a few moments there was a light knock on the door, announcing their entrance, and the door squeaked open.

"Come on in," Pastor Jake said.

***

Pastor Jake introduced them. "Charlie, this is Sarah, Nathan, and Brad." He smiled as they filed into the room.

Charlie nodded a greeting to them. Having had a mom who raised him to respect women, he stood up and offered his chair to Sarah before sitting down on the side of the bed. Nathan pulled up another chair and Brad stood, seemingly too energized to sit.

The first impression Sarah got of Charlie was that he looked like he would fit in well at a rodeo. When he stood up as they came in, she noted that he was at least six feet tall, maybe a few inches more. He had brown hair and hadn't shaved in a few days, so his face was a bit scruffy. He had on faded blue jeans with a few dirt stains and a button-down shirt with fancy emblems—the kind a cowboy would wear. Her suspicions proved true when she glanced over and saw a cowboy hat hanging on the back of the chair in the corner. He looked to be in his late twenties and she imagined that when he was all cleaned up, he would be a good-looking guy, in a rugged way.

Charlie's sad brown eyes greeted them as they stepped further into the room.

"Pastor Jake," Brad said excitedly, "can I share something before we pray?"

"Sure."

Brad directed his attention to Charlie, who eyed him a little suspiciously—not sure of what would follow. "Charlie, when we were down the hall we were praying for you, and God told me something to tell you. Pastor Jake told us a little bit about your past, but not much. A few minutes ago I felt that God told me to pass on to you that if you're willing to forgive your dad, God will heal your heart and your mind and make you whole."

Tears sprung to Charlie's eyes at the revelation. "He said that? Pastor Jake and I were just talking about the same thing."

Brad nodded. "Yeah; He can do it too. I know He can. We see miracles every day, man."

"Well, let's pray. Brad, go ahead and lead us." Pastor Jake knew this was an area in which God had been giving Brad more and more authority.

Charlie lowered his head and closed his eyes, but looked back up when Brad stepped closer to him.

"Hey, Charlie, when we pray is it okay if I put my hands on your shoulders? I don't want you to think I'm trying to be weird, but it's like electrical power—you have to have a connection for the energy to flow. God's power flows easier through a conductor. Does that make sense?"

"Yeah, it does, I used to do some electrical work, so it makes perfect sense, actually."

"Great." Brad reached up to place both hands on Charlie's shoulders and drew in a deep breath before he began. "Lord, we're here with Charlie today. You know what he's been through; You know his heart. Lord, help Charlie as he forgives his dad for the bad things he did to him. Help him let go of the pain and let Your love fill his heart."

Charlie leaned forward with his elbows on his knees and his shoulders began to heave as he began to let go of the bitterness and anger that had been stored up for all those years. His sobs continued for a few minutes, then he prayed through his tears, "God, I forgive my dad…I forgive him…please forgive me too." He continued to pray, releasing years of pent-up emotions until his voice broke off into more tears. Pastor Jake got down next to Charlie and led him in a prayer of forgiveness and repentance. Another lost sheep was home.

The group continued to pray as a sweet presence filled the room and clashed with the darkness that was there. A spiritual tenseness rose in the room and Brad spoke up again.

"Satan, you have tried and tried to keep Charlie depressed and down. You want him dead and you even tried to get him to do the same thing his dad did, to end his life. But he is not your property. He belongs to God now and we tell you to get your hands off him and leave now, in the name of Jesus!"

Like a snap in the air, the physical heaviness—which had been present in the room when they entered—lifted. They could feel it rising higher and higher until it seemed to go right through the ceiling and vanish, replaced by a warm, light atmosphere.

They opened their eyes and Sarah squinted. A physical golden fog, a mist, hung in the room, and as she breathed in, she smelled a sweet fragrance that wasn't there before. Brad lifted his face upward and closed his eyes, breathing a prayer of thanks for what God had done.

When they opened their eyes again, the fog was gone.

Charlie wiped at his eyes with his sleeve while Sarah grabbed a few tissues from a side table by his bed and handed them to him.

"Thanks." He directed his attention to Brad. "How did you know? I kept hearing a voice telling me to end my life the same way my dad did, that I would be better off that way because I was like him already. I didn't even tell my mom about that; thought it would really freak her out, you know. How did you know?"

"I didn't. It just came out while I was praying. Sometimes God shares stuff with us that we have no way of knowing. I guess it's His way of letting you know that He's the one touching your life, not us."

Pastor Jake was all smiles. "Charlie, you look different."

Sarah took a closer look at Charlie; he *did* look different. His whole face was glowing with the presence of the Lord. Where there was once despair, peace was evident. Where sadness ruled, joy abounded. A new creation in Christ!

"I feel different, lighter…I feel…happy. My mind feels clear. It used to be so jumbled that I could barely keep my thoughts straight, but not anymore. That's amazing…I don't even know how to thank you!"

"Don't thank us, thank God. He's the One who did it. We're just the conductors, remember?" Brad grinned.

"Yeah, I remember," Charlie said with a chuckle that quickly turned into a full-bellied laugh, one that came from deep down inside. It wasn't that anyone said anything funny; joy had replaced the sorrow and was now bubbling up, a spring that overflowed the new vessel.

Contagious joy spread to every person in the room and a hilarious uproar continued for several minutes, drawing a few curious nurses to peek in the room and leave shaking their heads, wondering what in the world was so funny.

When at last the laughter died down, Charlie wiped his eyes once again, this time from tears of joy. "I can't even tell you how long it has been since I laughed like that; probably since I was a kid. Oh, I needed that."

"It's the joy of the Lord, Charlie." Pastor Jake grinned from ear to ear. "We all needed that. Laughter is a medicine, Proverbs says. Science proves that it's true too!"

They chatted for a few more minutes with Charlie before saying their good-byes, with Pastor Jake promising to come back and visit again soon if Charlie was still there, which he doubted given the present condition of his mind. Pastor Jake assured Charlie that he would not be alone to walk into his new life and that he would set Charlie up with a few guys who could help teach and guide him in his new adventure of being a Christian. He also warned Charlie that the devil might try to come back and persuede him into his old ways of thinking. He explained that it may take some time to be totally free from those old thoughts or habits. Although Charlie's mind was instantly changed and renewed and his spirit was saved, he still lived in an earthly body with years and years of habits that would need time to change.

Before leaving, Nathan gave Charlie a Bible, one that would be easy for a new Christian to understand.

After leaving Charlie's room they met up with Deanne, who pointed them to a few patients who had asked specifically for them to come once they heard about the other people who had experienced healing. They must have prayed for five to six different people in different situations before they left, two of which were other patients in Deanne's unit.

The increase in God's presence and power flowing through all of them was clearly seen as people were touched and sicknesses were healed—both physical and emotional. Pastor Jake was operating now in both healing, in words of knowledge, and prophecy on a regular basis, as God was revealing personal things to him about the people they were praying for. The confirming and encouraging words meant much to those they prayed with, as well as the family members who were in the room.

Sarah also noticed that Nathan and Brad were stepping out more and praying with an increased level of faith and authority. It seemed that the more they worked together in prayer, the more their own personal gifts flowed and combined together. Nathan was an encourager and brought life and light to the room whenever he entered it, and Brad seemed ignited when he would pray for people to be set free from oppression and things that they were bound by. When Brad prayed for people like that, the atmosphere became electric with the presence of God.

After leaving the hospital they grabbed a quick dinner at a burger joint, then stopped at another congregation member's home, seeing yet another miraculous intervention.

They were amazed at what God was doing!

***

Back at the hospital, Deanne was glowing as she returned to the nurse's station, so excited to see how God was changing people and working in their lives.

As usual, Rachel was there to squelch the moment.

"Saw your friends here again tonight." Her sassy remark was paired with tight-lips and narrowed eyes. "That's just great. Now I have to deal with 'Jesus this' and 'God that' again for the rest of the week!"

Deanne prayed silently, asking the Lord how she was to respond to Rachel's bitterness in a way that would draw her closer to Him. She was also determined not to let Rachel's bad attitude destroy the good that was happening in the hospital.

At least, until her next statement.

"I went to talk to someone in HR about it all yesterday though, and your little cult friends won't be coming back much longer." Her expression was smug as she turned her eyes sharply at Deanne.

"Cult? What are you talking about? We're not in a cult, we just love God and are trying to let people know that God cares about them and that they don't have to be sick and defeated." Deanne couldn't believe what she was hearing.

"Sure you are. Try explaining that to those people. Besides, I know for a fact that a few of those people they visited didn't even ask for prayer. Your buddies just went right on in, pushing their beliefs on that poor person. There are laws against that, you know."

"They might not have asked personally, but a relative or friend did because they were not able to ask for themselves."

"And how do you know that those people aren't getting sick again when they go home? Do you personally go and follow up on them?" Rachel spat.

"Well, no…I'm sure if they got sick again they would come back—"

Rachel cut her off. "Right, and let everyone know their precious 'Jesus' didn't really heal them? Come on, Deanne," she snapped. "I'm gonna have a talk with Doctor Kramer about it soon."

Wow, she is really going off the deep end. "There's no need to include Doctor Kramer in this. He will probably be happy that people are feeling better. It is good for the reputation of the hospital."

"Well, I can't work under these conditions, and there's other nurses who agree with me, so I'm still going to talk to him and file a complaint." Rachel's tone dared Deanne to say anything otherwise. Grabbing a patient's chart, she stormed off.

Lord, help us! Deanne prayed.

Chapter Nineteen

Sarah breathed in the sweet fragrance of hay mixed with alfalfa as she entered the stable the next afternoon. She was eager, as usual, to spend time with the Lord today. As she brushed down Shadow she made it a point to pray for Taylor and her mom, declaring out loud from Psalm 91 that Taylor was covered with God's feathers and sheltered in His wings. She also prayed for Maria, asking God to restore their friendship somehow.

Shortly after, she started singing, lifting up her favorite worship songs to the Lord. As she sang, Shadow whinnied softly and twisted his ears all around as he listened to her worship time. After a while she fell into a comfortable silence, combing the snarls out of Shadow's tail. There was such a sweet atmosphere that she could almost feel a tangible presence of God.

A few moments later she heard a knock on the stable door and it creaked open, letting in cold air and a bright shaft of light into the not-so-well-lit stable.

"Sarah? You in here?" Nathan poked his head in. Looking around a bit and seeing Sarah, he stepped in and closed the door behind him.

Sarah felt her pulse quicken and she tried not to sound over-exuberant to see him. "Hey, Nate, what's up?"

"Oh, I was just passing by, and I thought I would pop in to see if you were going to church early tonight. Remember Pastor Thomas asked for the student leaders to be there earlier?"

Sarah tipped her head to the side and smiled. "Of course, silly. Why wouldn't I be there?" she asked playfully.

"I figured you were; just asking."

Nathan stepped up cautiously to Shadow as Sarah continued brushing his tail. For as many times as Nathan had been around the big horse, he still seemed a bit nervous to be close to him. He reached out his hand and gently stroked Shadow's soft back, "You would think I would be used to him, but he seems so big when you're standing right next to him."

"So that starts at 6:30, right?"

"Yup."

Nathan kept stroking Shadow's back and watching her; she could feel his eyes on her. She glanced up and their eyes locked for a moment. Not knowing what to do, Sarah diverted her gaze back to Shadow's tail, now combing out the ends to a fine sheen and trying to keep her rapidly beating heart under control.

Nathan cleared his throat. "You look like you could do that with your eyes closed."

Sarah chuckled. "Actually I have, many times. This is my sanctuary out here, the place where I meet with God. I have my eyes closed a lot out here," she looked around. All at once, an image of her and Nathan kissing with their eyes closed flashed across her mind, and heat rose up her neck and face at the thought. She quickly dismissed it. This setting was such an intimate place with Jesus that tender moments felt natural here.

Knowing that Nathan could see her blushing, she figured she better change the subject before he could ask her about it. There was no way she was telling him what she just pictured; as much as she wanted it to happen, it still wasn't time yet.

Fortunately, he hadn't been staring at her but was lost in his own thoughts. Their eyes met once more and he said, reluctantly, "Well, I better get home. See you later."

"Okay, see ya."

***

"Later" came quickly. Sarah found a place to sit for the student leaders' meeting and hung her coat over her chair. As she chatted with some of her friends, Nathan came in and claimed the vacant seat next to hers. It was normal for them to sit next to each other, most people expected it, but now that she knew how he felt about her it was unnerving to be so close to him every week, and she had to admit there were a few Wednesdays that she had no idea what Pastor Thomas had talked about when she left because her mind had been distracted with Nathan's nearness. She would need to keep focused tonight.

The student leader meeting started and Pastor Thomas presented a new plan of action where the older students in the youth group would be assigned to a younger student, as well as a group that had three older and three younger students in it. The purpose was to help the newer members of the youth group feel welcome and have someone to look up to, someone who had a solid relationship with the Lord and could mentor the younger one. He took his text from Titus 2 where Paul exhorted Titus to encourage those younger than him, and to have older women teach and train up the younger women.

The plan seemed great, and Sarah could definitely see how it would benefit everyone. Sometimes the older students slacked off in their walk with Christ; and being accountable and responsible for another person's view of the Lord would help them have a purpose for building their personal relationship with Him. Younger students tended to look up to the wrong examples or drop out of youth group for lack of relationships, feeling like nobody really cared about them. This seemed like a great solution for both of those issues.

As Pastor Thomas closed out the meeting, he asked everyone to grab the hand of the person next to them.

Sarah had held hands like this with Nathan in a meeting, but not since she started having feelings for him. She felt her heart start to pound, and immediately her hands began to sweat. She wiped her palms on her jeans before reaching both hands out to either side.

"Sorry, my hands are sweaty," she said to her friend, Jenna, who was sitting on the other side of her.

She felt Nathan's warm hand envelop her left hand while Jenna's small cold hand grasped her right.

Jenna smiled. "That's okay. Mine are cold. Maybe yours will warm mine up."

Sarah returned her smile before glancing at Nathan, who was grinning back at her. He was enjoying this way too much.

They all bowed their heads and closed their eyes as Pastor Thomas began to pray, not that Sarah heard a bit of what he was praying. She swallowed, trying to get her mind back on the prayer but all she could think about was Nathan's thumb that was now gently stroking the back of her hand.

As the prayer continued, not seeming to stop anytime soon, Nathan slowly moved his fingers to interlock with Sarah's.

Heat flushed her face and she cracked her eyes open, looking down at their fingers entwined together. It felt good and brought a rush of emotions she had been trying to stuff away ever since she broke up with Nick.

Hesitantly, she glanced over at Nathan and realized that he was peeking at her too. She tilted her head and lifted her eyes to meet Nathan's as he searched her face, his eyes moving slowly from her eyes to her mouth and back again. With her heart pounding, Sarah held his gaze until she heard Pastor Thomas winding the prayer down, then she forced her eyes back down again, looking again at their hands.

Respectfully, Nathan unlocked their fingers and held her hand normally before anyone opened their eyes at the end of the prayer. It seemed he didn't want others thinking they were dating if there wasn't anything "official" yet. She noticed he couldn't help giving her hand a gentle squeeze before he reluctantly released it.

She glanced at him again and couldn't help but return the big, goofy grin that was plastered on his face.

When Brad came in, Nathan said he was going to go sit by him, which was fine with Sarah. Maybe she would get something out of the service yet.

Pastor Thomas tied in what the student leaders had just met about with the whole group and at the end the students were paired off, student leaders with a younger student to take under their wing. A few student leaders had two younger students assigned to them as there were more young youth group members.

Sarah was paired off with a thirteen-year-old red-haired, brown-eyed girl with braces named Casey. Nathan was paired up with Pastor Jake's son, Colton. Colton was only about a year younger than Nathan, so she figured there must be a reason why Pastor Thomas had paired them up that way. She prayed that Nate would have a positive influence on him.

They took the last fifteen minutes of youth group to get to know each other. Before they all split off, Pastor Thomas assured them that first thing next week they would be in small groups of six to eight, keeping the student/mentor groups together.

Sarah liked Casey immediately. She had spunk and her eyes held a slightly mischievous light, proving that having someone to look up to and learn from would probably be a good thing. Casey also seemed boy-crazy, ogling every guy in the room, including Nathan…especially Nathan. It seemed that Casey must have known that Sarah was good friends with Nathan. She fired off question after question about him.

Yeah, Sarah was pretty sure there were some things about life and relationships she could teach and model for Casey as they got to know each other in the coming weeks.

Chapter Twenty

Colton Martin stared into the mirror at his reflection, his hands gripping the edge of the sink like a vise. He closed his eyes and tried to control his breathing, only opening his eyes when he felt that his heart rate had returned to normal.

He had been combing his hair when the apparition had returned. *I've got to get it together.*

Colton glanced at his reflection again, looking at the wall behind his head for any sign of the dark figure that had appeared for a moment and vanished just as quickly as it had come. Nothing now. He breathed out a sigh of relief, but knew it was temporary; it would be back.

And at what moment, he didn't know.

Straightening his dark gray button-down shirt over his black jeans, Colton wondered for the millionth time if anyone else saw the things he did. *If they do, they sure have a way of hiding it.*

In the back of his mind he remembered what a traveling evangelist said to his dad when he was five. "Colton is special. He is set apart for a very specific purpose." It's amazing what a five-year-old can remember. There were other things that the evangelist said to his dad about him that his little mind couldn't comprehend, so he didn't remember what those things were, but he was pretty sure his dad did.

Being a pastor's kid hadn't been easy or fun for Colton in any way. His family had been here in Highland Falls for about ten years now, and before that his dad was an associate pastor in a town a few hours away. All he had known was being a pastor's kid—and he hated it. He felt like people were watching him all the time, just waiting for him to mess up so they could talk about it.

That was why he dressed like he did now, just to irritate those people in the church who had scrutinized him all those years. If ten kids were running through the church hallway, the only one everyone had actually seen was him—and his dad heard about it the next day on the phone. In spite of his dad telling the congregation that his family was just like everyone else's, for some reason, people in the church always tried to hold Colton to a higher standard than the other kids, and he got sick of it.

Checking his reflection one more time, Colton smoothed his fingers over the dark eyebrows above his steely gray eyes and removed the earring from his left ear before leaving the bathroom.

He knew the black stud earring drove his parents crazy—he could tell by the looks on their faces when he wore it—but he didn't care. Maybe he wore it *because* it drove them crazy. Being in a private school meant that he wasn't allowed to wear it to school, so the first thing he did when he got home each day was to put the earring back in. Fortunately, he didn't have to wear his school uniform today because Fridays had been deemed "casual day."

As he walked out of the house and headed to the bus stop, Colton thought back to when he was a kid.

Not long after that evangelist had spoken over him, Colton started having visitations from spiritual beings—some good, some bad. No matter which one it was, it always startled him. Anyone would be freaked out if all of a sudden you saw something that wasn't there just a second before. He'd told his parents about some of the encounters, and his mom thought he was having nightmares because most of the visitations occurred at night. He wondered why that was. Probably because that was when his mind was the most idle. Maybe that was why he tried to keep busy—to try to keep the visions at bay. It seemed to help, until recently. Now it seemed something would pop into his peripheral vision at any moment no matter what he was doing.

It was worse at certain places or locations—especially at the hospital.

When Colton was eleven, his dad tried to get him to tag along when he went to visit people. Most of the people he saw in the hospital had some sort of spirit or demon close to them, even some of the staff. Many times the evil spirit would be sitting on the person's shoulder or digging its transparent claws deep into the person's skull. This was especially true in the mental health wing. Once, they had passed a room and he saw a demon pounding on a lady's head as she cried, telling someone else in the room how lonely she felt.

It became so overwhelming that he would cry all the way to the hospital. Eventually his father just stopped making Colton go with him. What pastor wanted to bring along a sniveling, whimpering kid when they were trying to pray for someone in pain?

His dad asked him why he didn't want to come, but Colton hadn't been able to process what he had been seeing. He would never believe him anyway. It seemed like something out of a horror movie, the ones he wasn't allowed to watch but did when he stayed over at a friend's house. There was even a time when he watched a horror flick and the scenes were so familiar to something he saw and experienced in real life that he had to leave the room.

Colton arrived at the bus stop and shook his head, trying to rid his mind of some of the memories from the past. He was glad in a way that he didn't go to the same school as Nathan, Brad, and Sarah. He could only imagine all the spirit-world stuff they were stirring up over there with their prayer group and all. The private school he went to was not really into supernatural things and the teachers and administration seemed to shy away from talking about that part of the Christian life.

On the other hand, he would like to be around Christians who believed in the supernatural, which he knew to be the case with Nate and the others. He was glad that he had gotten paired up with him in youth group the other night. But any whim to go to the same school as Nathan was easily squelched by the desire to avoid the hellish visions and apparitions that seemed to perpetually haunt him.

He had almost panicked when Nathan had asked him to come along with them to pray for people the other day. It was all he could do to keep his composure and decline.

No way that's happening again. He shuddered as he watched the bus turn the corner and head his direction.

***

Sarah greeted Nathan and Brad as they joined her in the small cafeteria before school. They sat down at a table in a corner of the room. There were a few students eating breakfast or talking here and there but it was generally quiet as the buses had not arrived yet.

They were dropped off early by their parents today by Sarah's request. She wanted to talk to Nathan and Brad alone about expanding the prayer group to meet every day before asking the whole group. She had checked with Mr. Roberts, who he said that would be fine because he was normally there grading papers.

Sarah pulled her gray knit fly-away sweater tighter around her, trying to ward off the morning chill. November in New York was hit or miss with weather. It could either be snowing or mild and in the sixties as was forecasted for today. This morning there was a slight layer of icy frost covering the ground as she left the house, but she dressed in layers, prepared for the warm up later today.

Today she wore a white short-sleeved shirt paired with her dark skinny jeans and the gray long-sleeved fly away, her favorite sweater, which came down to about the middle of her thighs.

Nathan had dressed in layers too, a gray T-shirt visible under a black button-down shirt with a slight gray pin-stripe design running vertically, the first few buttons unbuttoned. He looked good, and Sarah couldn't help admiring. They dressed to match today and hadn't even planned it. She noted that he started wearing the skinnier style jeans for guys and it complemented his style.

Her gaze moved to Nathan's face. His features had become more chiseled over the last few months as he was changing into a man and not a child anymore.

He looked over at her and caught her staring at him, and she blushed, averting her gaze.

Brad, who looked like he had just woken up, took off his glasses and rubbed his eyes, stretching his arms behind his head before replacing his glasses on his nose and speaking. "Hey Sarah, that girl you know came to prayer yesterday, but she just stood there and left a few minutes later. Didn't seem happy."

"What girl?"

"What's her name again?" Brad said to himself. "Oh, Maria…the one who doesn't like you."

Sarah had missed Impact yesterday because of a quiz she had to make up in one of her classes. "Did she say anything mean or nasty?"

"No." Brad thought back. "She didn't say anything, but she wasn't smiling either. She probably stood there like two minutes and then left pretty quick."

Sarah didn't respond, just thought about it for a minute. Again she offered up a silent prayer for Maria. Maybe she had honestly come for prayer, or maybe she just wanted to spite Sarah and left because she wasn't there yesterday. Only the Lord knew.

Not wanting to change the subject, but because they didn't have much time, Sarah spoke up. "Well, the reason I wanted to talk to you both is because a few people asked me if Impact can meet every day. I checked with Mr. Roberts and he is okay with it. I think we have enough people to maybe work out a schedule so a few people can be there to pray. I can usually do Tuesdays, Thursdays, and Fridays," Sarah said excitedly.

"You know, someone asked me the same thing last week," Nathan said. "I think it's a great idea. I can still do Tuesdays, plus Wednesday and Friday. Thursday gets busy for my family though."

"Well, I'm free on Mondays and Thursday, and I can still come Tuesday too," Brad reported, looking more awake now.

"Great! Then it's settled, we can announce it next Tuesday and get people signed up for different days," Sarah said triumphantly. "We can make an online schedule so people can sign up there."

Other students were now preparing to head to homeroom so they stood and left the cafeteria together.

Brad had to go the opposite direction of Sarah and Nathan because homeroom classes were located in different areas of the school by grade. Sarah and Nathan continued on together, the crowd in the hallway forcing them to walk so closely to each other that their arms and hands touched.

As her fingers brushed his, Nathan captured them between his own, causing her heart to flip-flop. She glanced up at him and held his gaze for a moment.

Just then someone pushed through the crowd behind Sarah, bumping her into Nathan and pushing them both against a locker, their faces just inches apart. Nathan reached out instinctively to steady her but made no move to put any space in between them.

"You okay?" His voice was almost lost in the din of the crowd behind her.

Sarah swallowed. She wanted him to kiss her, but not here, not right now. She was confident now that Jesus was securely her first love, a place that neither Nathan nor any other guy would be able to even come close to. At the same time, she recognized that God created men and women to be together, not alone, and that there was a God-created place for romance and love as long as it was pure and didn't take His place in her heart.

She was also sure now that Nathan was more than a friend to her, much more. In due time she would let him know, but not right now.

She took a step back and smiled, willing her heart to stop pounding. "Yeah, I'm fine."

Their fingers were still interlocked and Nathan brought their hands up to kiss the back of hers. "I have to go." He released her hand and grabbed his backpack's straps to reposition them better. "I'll see you later." He turned to go and walked away.

Sarah caught him glancing back at her with a smile at least twice before she moved to head to class.

Chapter Twenty-One

Maria's hands shook as she waited, forever it seemed, for the image to appear.

She should have started her cycle three weeks ago but it was late. Her body normally functioned like clockwork and she could usually predict—to the day—when it would come.

It was never late…until now.

After a few moments, two lines became plainly visible, sealing her future like the final nail in a coffin. This was the third over-the-counter pregnancy test that she had taken today, all showing that she was pregnant.

Pregnant.

The reality of her whole life gone wrong began to swirl through her mind and Maria muffled a sob. First her dad left, then they lost their home, her mom was dying, and now she was pregnant. Could things get any worse?

At least her friends at school wouldn't think too much of it; they already assumed that she was easy. Honestly, it had all been a front until Nick.

There had been something about the sweet victory of giving him the things that Sarah wouldn't, at least at first. But as the days went on he expected more and more from her, making her feel like his own personal prostitute or human slave. She hated herself for it, for everything. She would do anything to reverse time and go back to the blissful days before her father left. If only she had been a better daughter maybe all of this wouldn't have happened.

Maria grabbed a makeup kit, shoved it into her backpack, and slipped out from the house early, being careful not to wake her mother. She had to find a place where she could deal with this new crisis alone before school started. There was a quiet place in the woods not too far from school, but far enough away from earshot that she could be alone.

Once she had cried and screamed it all out, she sucked up the rest, got to school, and slipped into a bathroom to apply her makeup, masking her grief. She quickly ran a brush through her long, black tresses and smoothed out the wrinkles from her miniskirt.

As she adjusted her white button-down shirt and checked to make sure she had matched the buttons up with the correct holes, she tried not to look at the flat material over her abdomen where new life was growing. She would figure out later how to deal with this issue. Maybe she would have one of her friends take her to the clinic sometime in the near future.

Just a few years ago she would never have stepped into a place like that, but things had changed, and desperate times called for desperate measures. She told herself that she could only deal with one tragedy at a time; she needed to be there for her mom, not getting ready to bring a child into the world. She was supposed to leave after fourth period today to go with her mom to her first chemo treatment, and neither one of them needed another crisis.

Taking a deep breath, Maria put on her perfect fake smile and pushed the bathroom door open. As she walked down the hall by the small cafeteria she overheard Sarah, Nathan, and Brad talking on the other side of the wall from where she was standing. If she had kept going, the edge of the wall gave way to full glass around the corner and they would have seen her walk by.

Cautiously, she peeked around the corner to confirm that it really was them she heard and retreated back to listen in on their conversation. She could faintly hear them talk about how their prayer group was expanding and how they were going to start meeting every day after school soon.

Anger began to boil up inside of Maria.

She wasn't even sure why she felt such a strong reaction about Sarah and her Jesus freaks praying for people. It just made her so angry.

She had gone several weeks and stood just outside the door during their prayer time when nobody was watching, wanting to tell them to stop and that it wouldn't do any good. But then a supposed miracle would happen and she obviously couldn't say anything then. Other times she felt drawn to step into the room to see what might happen for her, but something always reminded her that God didn't care one bit about her. Look at the mess her life was right now. If God were real, He wouldn't let all this happen to her, right?

What kind of craziness could happen if that group started meeting every day? Maria made up her mind to pay Sarah a visit today and turned to head the long way to her locker so the group wouldn't catch her snooping.

***

Sarah closed her locker and turned to start walking toward her third period Spanish class and found herself face-to-face with Maria Romano.

Maria's long, dark hair was pulled back in a ponytail, revealing silver looped earrings that shone against her naturally tanned skin, a gift from her Italian descent. With a hand on her hip she smirked at Sarah with narrowed eyes.

"A little birdie told me that you and your Jesus groupies are planning to start meeting every single day after school. What makes you think everyone wants your God?"

Sarah could literally feel the bitterness and hatred exuding from Maria as she spoke. She tried to keep her voice steady as she responded, "Oh, who did you hear that from?"

"I have my sources."

Maria took a step forward and pointed a finger in her face, her anger coming even more to the surface. "Why don't you just stop trying now before you get hurt? It's not like prayer really changes much of anything anyway. It's just a show to make people think that God is real and that He cares when He clearly doesn't."

Maria turned on her heel and started to storm off when Sarah found herself speaking up, "Actually, Maria, He does answer prayer. We've been seeing miracles happen every week. Just because a few people don't want us praying doesn't mean we will stop. We have to keep it going for the sake of all the people in this school who are hurting and need help…like you."

What had gotten into her? It's not like she was trying to pick a fight. The words just came out!

Wheeling around, Maria gave a flamboyant laugh. "And what in the world would make you think that I'm hurting, Sarah Wright? You don't even know what hurting even is…with your perfect little family and your perfect little grades and your perfect little religion." She spat out the words.

Sarah faltered for a moment. *Perfect*, she thought, *my life isn't perfect. Lord, show me what to do.*

Instantly the Lord put words in her mouth and she took a step forward and said softly, "God knows your pain, Maria. He saw you in your house this morning and He wants you to know that He has it all under control."

That was strange. She had no idea what it meant; it was as if God had taken over her mouth for a moment and spoke through her.

A look of panic crossed Maria's face and Sarah could tell that the words had hit something personal.

The vulnerable moment didn't last long as it was quickly replaced by the familiar coldness. "Are you stalking me? Just leave me alone."

Maria flipped her ponytail and turned suddenly, smacking right into a student two lockers over. Maria clenched her fists and screamed at the unsuspecting student, "Watch where you're going! Geez!" before storming off, red-faced.

Everyone around laughed, and even Sarah had to hold back a chuckle, but quickly recovered as she remembered Maria's wrath toward her.

A few girls whom Sarah knew, but was not really close to, were still giggling nearby and patted Sarah on the shoulder. One, whose name was Amie, said, "Don't pay any attention to her. She's going through a lot with her mom and all."

"Her mom? What's going on with her mom?"

Amie looked around and stepped closer.

"Maria doesn't think many people know, but her mom just got diagnosed with cancer. It's like stage four or something. I guess she didn't realize it until recently. I heard Maria tell her friends that she has to leave early today to go with her mom to get chemo." Amie shrugged. "I guess it's really bad. She told her friends that she doesn't know where she'll live if her mom dies."

"Oh…my gosh…that's really sad." Sarah shook her head slowly.

Amie and the other girls headed to their class, leaving Sarah with her thoughts as she tried to digest this new information.

Images of Maria's mom, Andrea Romano, popped into her head. She had always remembered Andrea as a beautiful woman; with her deep hazel eyes and jet black hair like Maria's, she had a striking beauty. She was always tanned, even in the winter, and was very dramatic in everything she did. It was fun at Maria's house when they used to play together as children. Andrea made a big production out of their sleepovers and had a whole agenda planned with everything from picnics on the floor in front of their fireplace to playing salon. One time she did their hair and makeup, and even painted their fingernails and toenails with special designs on their ring fingers and big toes.

As the memories flooded back, a deep sadness for Maria and what she must be facing hit Sarah and she clapped a hand over her mouth, tears springing to her eyes. What would it be like to know your mom was dying? Sarah was determined to find Maria later and try again to reach out to her.

***

After spending some time praying in the stable after school, Sarah walked the mile or so to Maria's apartment complex. The temperature had reached sixty-three, validating the weatherman's predictions, and she was glad it wasn't the bitter cold it had been the week before.

As she neared the building she could see Maria helping her mom into the door. Andrea looked a lot frailer than she remembered and was moving pretty slowly. Sarah had talked with her mom about Andrea, and her mom said, from her friend's experiences with chemo that the first treatment could be a long one, up to six hours even. It was about five o'clock now so it must have been long for Andrea as well. She wondered how she could talk to Maria without disturbing Andrea.

She didn't wonder for long as Maria came back out to grab some things from the car. It was now or never.

Sarah jogged closer. "Hey, Maria, can I talk to you a sec?"

Maria shut the car door and turned. "What are *you* doing here?" There was anger still in her voice, but she looked drained and her eyes were a bit puffy, evidence that she had been crying.

Sarah ignored the coldness coming from Maria. She was driven by a deep compassion she had been feeling all day for Maria and Andrea. "I heard about your mom. I'm so sorry."

"I see you're still stalking me." Maria's voice was bitter.

"Actually someone at school told me about it. Look, if there's anything I can do—"

Maria cut her off. "There's nothing you can do. There's nothing *anyone* can do. The doctors filled me in today, okay. She's having treatments, but even then they said she probably won't survive because the cancer has already spread too far." The tears that she had been crying all afternoon once again tumbled down her cheeks. "So no, there's nothing you can do, Sarah." It seemed the rage gave Maria new strength.

Sarah felt a boldness she didn't have a minute ago. "You're wrong, Maria, there is one thing I *can* do. I can pray for her. God does things when I pray. We have seen people healed from injuries, depression, cataracts, migraines, allergies, and so many other things in the last few months. I *know* He can heal your mom."

"Well, that's nice, but have you seen anyone healed of *stage four cancer*? Probably *not*." Maria spat as she turned to go, "So go away! Go pray to your God somewhere else. It won't do us any good. Just leave us alone!"

Maria disappeared through the apartment door, leaving Sarah standing on the sidewalk.

Sarah started home slowly. The air was now shifting colder as the sun was going down. She shoved her hands in her pockets and sighed.

What would it take to get through to her?

Chapter Twenty-two

Two weeks later

Deanne was quietly shutting the door of a sleeping patient's room when she noticed Rachel's purposeful stride in her direction. *Uh oh, this doesn't look good.*

"Is something wrong, Rachel?" She took note of Rachel's narrowed eyes and set jaw.

"You'd better believe there is," Rachel hissed. "You need to come with me."

Without a backward glance at Deanne, she headed toward the elevators.

Deanne hurried to catch up and tried to match Rachel's long steps. "Where are we going?"

"To Doctor Kramer's office," she answered coldly.

Deanne opened her mouth to ask why but closed it. She would find out soon enough, and it would probably be better to find out from the doctor and not Rachel, at least not with the way she was acting right now. Doctor Kramer was one of the newer doctors and had come to Highland Falls Memorial Hospital fresh out of medical school seven years ago. All the other doctors had been there twenty-plus years.

Rachel pushed the button for the elevator and they stood in silence as they waited. Rachel inspected her professionally manicured nails, obviously not wanting to have further conversation.

As they rode the elevator and walked to the doctor's office, Deanne thought back to the few interactions she had had over the years with Dr. Kramer. They all seemed genuine. He always had a warm smile when greeting her. When he talked with her, it didn't seem like they had a whole lot in common, but they were able to make small talk comfortably. She wondered what this meeting could possibly be about.

A glance at Rachel confirmed that her coworker still looked angry and Deanne's stomach twisted. *All the recent threats to stop the prayer group from coming to the hospital—is that what this could be about?*

Over the last few days Deanne had been sensing a warning in the Spirit that something was amiss. Could this have something to do with it? If that were the case, Deanne felt pretty sure that if Rachel was going to try and accuse her of something in front of Dr. Kramer that he would be on her side. He would have to be, right? People were getting better and that was the whole purpose for a hospital to begin with.

She breathed a silent prayer for strength.

Deanne's mind wandered to some of the more recent miracles that had happened over the last few weeks when the Martins and their young prayer team had come back. Most of them were not in her wing, but the one that was under her care had been amazing. She could picture it like it was yesterday.

***

Deanne had just met Mr. and Mrs. Applegate a few days before the Martins were coming for weekly visitations. They were a cute couple; both shorter, between five-two and five-five. Their height alone seemed made for each other. They both had reddish brown hair and Mrs. Applegate's was cut in a cute bob that came down longer in the front. Their two-year-old son, John, or Johnny, had a serious blood disorder that would cause the child's skin to have black and blue splotches. They had told her that one day the police had shown up, interrogating them with all kinds of questions. It seemed that some nosy neighbors thought they were abusing Johnny. As his condition quickly worsened, their doctor put the young boy in intensive care as they raced against time.

It had been almost two weeks ago when Deanne walked into the room to find Mr. Applegate comforting his wife, Tina, as she wept. Her heart immediately went out to the hurting woman. She glanced at the sleeping form of their small son, Johnny. He seemed the same as the last time she had come in.

"Do you want to talk about it, honey?" Deanne rubbed the woman's shoulder gently.

Tina looked up into Mr. Applegate's chocolate brown eyes, which were pooling with tears. She fought to gain her composure but was unable to speak, so her husband, Ted, spoke up.

"The doctor was just here a little while ago and said..." His voice faltered and he took a slow, deep breath. "He said they weren't sure what more they can do right now."

"Did Johnny take a turn for the worse?" She quickly scanned the machines hooked to the small boy's body but nothing looked very different from before.

"No, but he warned us that this type of sickness can continue to worsen over time, that sometimes the body rejects any natural healing that tries to happen…and he isn't responding to anything they are doing." He swallowed hard, his Adam's apple moving up and down. "He said to prepare for the worst." The tears he had been holding at bay spilled over and down his cheeks as he closed his eyes tightly.

Deanne remembered that the Martins said they would be returning that day; in fact, he might be here soon. "I'm not sure if you have a church or a pastor, but my pastor is going to be here soon if you would want him to stop by and pray for y'all." Her Southern accent hung in the air.

Tina glanced up. "We're not giving up yet. He doesn't need confession." She looked confused.

"Oh, no. Not that kind of prayer. You see, my pastor and some friends of his come to pray for people to get better, and lately we have been seeing many people getting healed—maybe not right away, but they get better much quicker."

Ted replied, "Sure, anything that might help our son."

Tina nodded her head in approval.

"Great, let me go give him a call and see if they can come by your room while y'all are here." She hurried to get her phone.

Within a few minutes she returned to Johnny's room. "They're actually on their way right now and will come here first."

She left to check on some other patients in the meantime and came back when she heard Pastor Jake's voice in the hallway. Sarah and Nathan were with him and Charlotte today. She gave them all a quick hug and led the way to Johnny's room.

They stepped into the room and she introduced everyone to the Applegates. Deanne could feel the presence of the Lord descending already, and it was so thick that it almost seemed heavy.

Pastor Jake briefly explained to the young couple why prayer was so important in healing, and then Sarah stepped forward to pray for the boy.

It was very different than what Deanne had expected. With such a strong presence of the Lord, she thought Sarah would be praying profound things over the child. Instead she gently laid her hands on the boy's head and prayed the most simple prayer imaginable. "Father, heal this child, and use him for Your glory, in Jesus' name. Amen."

Sarah kept her hands on Johnny's head for a few moments longer, her eyes shut, a smile on her face. Before they left, the Applegates expressed their appreciation to the group.

Pastor Jake explained that sometimes healing is not instantaneous, and to keep believing that God cares about them and is working even when they don't see it.

Deanne walked them to the elevators. She turned to Sarah. "That was different. Usually you pray more…um...longer."

Sarah chuckled. "I know. God gave me specific instructions to 'keep it simple' today. Believe me, I wanted to pray much differently back there, but He showed me that it's not about my prayer. It's all about Him."

"Well, it was definitely simple!"

***

It didn't seem like anything had happened immediately after the prayer, but then Johnny got better so quickly that he was allowed to go home only a few days later. She watched the doctor write on the chart, "No further need for treatment." It had been wonderful to see the little boy's character and personality blossom the better he felt. He had gotten so curious about all the machines in the room that he asked her all sorts of cute little two-year-old questions about them.

Johnny's parents were so happy that they hugged the doctors and all the nurses they came across, telling them of all the wonderful things God had done.

Deanne smiled at the memory of Johnny—happy, healthy Johnny, not a bruise in sight—running down the hallway before he left the hospital to go home.

You would think that all the staff would have been happy about it, especially because Thanksgiving was just days away. But the countenance on the nurses in her hall had changed. Rachel had stirred them up, and after the happy family went home, the tongues were wagging.

Deanne had steered clear of the other staff as much as possible, knowing she wouldn't be able to keep silent if she was in earshot of their negative conversations. Could this be what the meeting with Dr. Kramer was about? She knew that some of the patients who were healed recently were his patients. Was he upset about it too?

They arrived at Dr. Kramer's office, and Rachel knocked on the door.

Within a few seconds, Dr. Kramer opened the heavy oak door and smiled, his pristine white teeth standing out against his tanned skin.

191

Steel gray eyes and wavy black hair in combination with his height would classify the young doctor as tall, dark, and handsome.

It seemed that almost immediately Rachel's foul mood disappeared as she greeted Dr. Kramer.

"Hello there, Doctor." Rachel's smile was wide.

"Come on in, ladies, we were expecting you." Dr. Kramer motioned with his hand as he opened the door wider.

Expecting us? We? What's going on? As she walked in the room she noted that three other nurses were present, seated in the posh chairs situated in a semi-circle across from the wide expanse of Dr. Kramer's desk.

Rachel hurried to greet the other ladies, speaking to them in hushed tones as Deanne found an empty chair and sat down, feeling very much like an outsider.

Dr. Kramer closed the door and returned to his seat behind his desk. He cleared his throat and Rachel took her seat.

"It has been brought to my attention that there have been some recent...altercations concerning religious matters disrupting the workflow in certain sections of the hospital. As you all know well, our profession is one of great importance to many people here. Sometimes life and death are in our hands so we have to be very careful what we allow and don't allow to take place."

Dr. Kramer paused and Deanne stole a glance at the others in the room. They were nodding to one another and glancing coldly in her direction. It seemed as if she was the only one who didn't know for sure what was happening.

"Deanne, there's a certain group of people you are acquainted with who have been at the forefront of these altercations. I'm told that they come in whenever they want and visit with our patients, pushing their religious beliefs on them and somehow convincing them that the patients no longer need treatment. On top of that, I have been told that they get in the way of the nurses' duties and are even pushing their religion on the staff. We try hard to make this a peaceful place where natural healing can take place, but these people are causing all sorts of issues."

The doctor looked at Deanne as though waiting for some type of response.

Deanne looked at the others in the room for some support but was met with icy stares. "There must be some mistake, or you've been given misinformation. I believe the people you're talking about are my pastor and his wife along with a few young people who like to pray for people. How can that be disruptive? Didn't y'all hear about the patients who have been healed by God as a result of them being here? Why just recently little Johnny got to go home, the one who had the serious blood disorder and was black and blue all over! Y'all had practically given up hope that he could even recover. Didn't you see how healthy he was running down the hall before they left?"

Dr. Kramer scooted forward in his chair. "He may have shown great enough improvement to be sent home, but sometimes those conditions can relapse and come back even stronger. Who's to say that won't happen with any of those patients who have been, quote-unquote, healed?"

Deanne faltered, not knowing quite how to respond to this. "I guess that is where you trust that God healed them. If it does come back, the parents would certainly let their doctor know. This hospital has allowed pastors and people to come pray for patients from the time it began. I am not sure why it's such an issue now?"

Rachel spoke up, "The big issue is that we don't want other people's religion shoved down our throats every time we take someone's temperature!"

The other nurses in the room added their agreements with what Rachel said.

Deanne felt a new boldness take over as she opened her mouth.

"Really? I think I know exactly what the big issue is." She saw Rachel blink and sit back, shocked that Deanne was speaking up.

She laid her hand on Dr. Kramer's desk and continued, "The big issue for you, doctor, is that your patients are actually getting better more quickly and not requiring the follow up care that would bring more revenue to the hospital and your pockets. Let's face it. As much as we are in the business of making people well, if nobody is sick anymore, we are all out of a job. And with the insurance reimbursement cuts that have been going on, I believe the 'issue' really is your financial bottom line. Prayer wasn't a problem before now, not even prayer to Allah, Buddha, or a Tree God, or using Reiki healers. Why? Because it wasn't really helping people get better, at least not in a profound way. Now when my Christian friends come in and people *actually* start getting better and there are more vacant rooms, it's suddenly an issue!"

She took a breath and turned to the other nurses, Rachel specifically. "And I know what the big issue is for you ladies too. If you admit that it truly is God who healed these people then it means the Bible is true and suddenly you find yourself responsible for how y'all have lived your life. So instead of making a decision to accept or reject God, you reject the fact that He is alive and active, and that He wants to help people." She softened her voice. "And you also reject the fact that He loves you."

Rachel's face contorted with anger. "There it is again, that God-crap. Does it never stop?"

Dr. Kramer cleared his voice loudly. "At this point, it doesn't matter what *you* think the issue is. I have discussed the issue with the hospital board, and they have made a few adjustments to the way our visitor guidelines are handled. The board instructed each doctor to meet with the staff under their care to explain these new regulations. I wanted to meet with you before the rest of the staff in our section. I will explain these things to all of them later today."

He continued, "Other than Pastor Jake Martin and his wife, the only way your other friends, or anyone else who isn't immediate family or clergy for that matter, can come visit with a patient is by personal invitation, and if they are seen here otherwise, they will be escorted down to the lobby by security. If someone does ask that they come, they may only enter a patient's room one at a time. We just can't operate a hospital with the types of distractions that have been taking place. Everyone on our list for visitation pastors will be notified of the new guidelines for all visiting clergy, including rules restricting personal contact to ensure the health and sanitation for our patients."

He sat back, making it clear that this conversation was not a discussion. "I'm going to personally notify Pastor Martin of these changes this afternoon."

Deanne had a whole speech coming to mind, but she instantly felt the Lord tell her to not say another word. She knew this would change things, but strangely enough she felt a peace about it.

She glanced around the room before leaving and noticed Rachel had her arms crossed and a smug look on her face, as if daring her to challenge what Dr. Kramer had said.

Deanne looked at Dr. Kramer and forced a smile. "All right; if there's nothing else, I'll head back to work now."

Dr. Kramer stood with a smile and the others in the room stood as well. "That will be all, Deanne. Thank you for coming." Then he crossed the room to the door and held it open for everyone to exit. "If you'll excuse me, ladies, I have to check on some patients."

They all filed out of the room, most of the other nurses walking in a group and talking quietly. Deanne returned to work numbly, the exciting reminder of Johnny's healing totally taken from her with this new development.

A hospital restricting visitation for Christians and clergy when coming to pray for patients? Who would have ever thought?

Chapter Twenty-three

Maria reached for the tissue box next to her bed. She couldn't stop the tears from coming. She thought that telling Nick about the baby would help matters, but it just ended up making things worse. Now he wanted nothing to do with her and was already flirting with some of the other cheerleaders at school, probably to spite her.

On one hand, she would picture herself cradling a little blanketed bundle, someone she could love who would love her back with no biases or conditions. The thought warmed her heart. She ran a hand over her flat stomach, picturing herself as a mother.

But how will I be able to support a baby? What if my mom dies? What will I do then? Where will we live? I'll already have to get a job to support myself because mom can't work. How will I work while pregnant or if I keep the baby? Just the thought of it all made her sick to her stomach all over again. The last few days she had not been able to keep hardly anything down, both from stress and from morning sickness.

"Why is all of this happening to me?" Maria moaned aloud.

She knew there would be no answer.

Mom was in the hospital now, and God never answered her anyway. She would steel her emotions when she saw her mom later today. She hadn't told her mom about being pregnant, still not sure what she was going to do. Every day it seemed her mom got weaker; she was on so much medication that yesterday she wasn't even sure her mom knew she was there. If only she had a sister or brother with whom to share some of this pain, but she was an only child.

She was planning to spend Thanksgiving Day with her mom, being the only family around. Any aunts or uncles lived far away or just didn't care. It was less than two weeks before Thanksgiving, so she didn't have much time to plan something special for her mom. It looked like it would be the last Thanksgiving she would ever have with her. Tears spilled over her cheeks again.

She smoothed a hand over her abdomen. From what she had read Online it would only be a month or two before she would start showing, then she wouldn't be able to hide it anymore. A war of emotions swirled through her mind, wanting to keep the life that was growing inside of her, but a stronger force convincing her to just end it and be rid of the unwanted complications. Her life was already difficult enough, right? There was no need to make it any harder.

In the end, darkness won, and Maria decided that sometime before Thanksgiving she would put an end to this madness—at least she could control that part of her life.

***

Colton stilled as an image formed in front of him. It was happening again.

He had been getting the same vision over and over, especially when he was around Sarah Wright. What started out to be an enjoyable fundraiser for the youth group had turned into a visual nightmare for Colton. At any moment, the chain of events would play out in his mind's eye across the sky in front of him—an open vision, as his dad called them.

The girl with long black hair was back, lying in a fetal position on the ground, clutching her stomach and screaming, "I'm so sorry. Someone please help me!" Then he saw a doctor holding a bloody mass and dropping it into a trash can before everything faded to black.

Colton pressed his eyes shut and shook his head. If it kept up, he would have to say something to Sarah. Maybe it would make sense to her.

"Dude, you okay?"

Colton looked up and saw Nathan looking at him with concern, "Yeah, I'm all right, man. I just...uh...didn't get much sleep last night." Which was the truth. He didn't sleep well most nights, afraid he would open his eyes to be staring in the face of some demonic creature in a dream or vision.

The fundraiser, being about a week and-a-half before Thanksgiving, allowed parents to drop off their children for an afternoon of child-free shopping time or preparations that were desperately needed in most households. The families could donate whatever amount they thought fair for the childcare; some gave generously while others gave what they could.

Virtually every part of the church had been transformed to accommodate the event. The sanctuary was turned into a huge theater where one of the most recent popular kid's movie played across a huge screen. Colton, Nathan, and some others had been assigned to the gymnasium, where five big bouncy houses were filled with air, and the noise level was at the max with children bouncing and laughing.

Colton glanced over at Sarah again cautiously as she helped a few kids getting out of the bouncy house next to the one where he was stationed. She was currently tickling a little blonde-haired girl who had an infectious laugh. Nathan, who was also stationed at the big bouncy castle with him, noticed his gaze and looked puzzled.

Not wanting to appear as though he was looking at Nathan's girl, he said, "So my dad says that Sarah has some type of healing thing, like she prays for people and they get better."

Nathan smiled. "Yeah, it's really cool. Just last week we prayed for this guy who had a lump on his neck and it just shrunk, right in front of us. It was crazy!"

"That's cool." Maybe Nathan would know who this girl was in the vision. It was worth a try. "Does she have a friend with long black hair and a nice tan?"

Nathan tilted his head and looked at Colton curiously. "Why? You looking for a girlfriend?" He elbowed Colton playfully.

"No, I don't know. I think Sarah might know somebody I've seen," Colton responded seriously.

Nathan stopped teasing. "There's a girl who looks like that at our school, but she stopped being Sarah's friend a long time ago. In fact, Sarah found out her ex-boyfriend had been cheating on her with that girl."

"Ouch."

"How do you know Maria?"

"Who?"

"Maria Romano, the girl with the long black hair?"

Colton checked on the kids in the bouncy house; it was time for the next group to come in. He told the kids inside that their turn was over and got the next ten kids safely inside before answering. He stepped a bit closer to Nathan, not wanting to share with the whole gym by shouting. Nathan seemed pretty in tune with God, maybe he would understand.

"I keep seeing this girl...Maria...I guess, in a vision over and over, especially when I'm around Sarah. It's really freaky. I get the feeling that maybe I should tell Sarah about it."

"What's the vision about?"

After Colton shared the vision with him, Nathan asked, "So do you see stuff like that a lot?"

"Yeah, well, it's mostly like angels and demons and stuff, but I see visions, too, sometimes, like this one."

"I bet that gets freaky, like Halloween every day."

"That's why I can't go to the hospital with you guys—too much stuff goes on in there. It gives me the creeps!" Colton shuddered.

"Does your dad know what you see, or Pastor Thomas?" Nathan asked.

"I tried to tell my dad about it a long time ago, but he thought I was making imaginary friends when I told him there were angels hanging out in the backyard. I guess I never tried again after that; didn't think he would believe me."

"I bet he wouldn't think it so strange now. He's really open to supernatural stuff with all the miracles happening lately."

"Maybe I'll try again sometime." He paused. "So do you think I should I tell Sarah about that vision I keep seeing today?"

Nathan nodded. "Yeah, you should. Mind if I'm there too?"

"Not at all. Wouldn't want you to think I'm trying to take your girl away."

"What do you mean, Sarah and I aren't..."

Colton laughed, ribbing Nathan. "Yeah, right. I see how you look at her, and how she looks back at you. You can't hide that."

As if to accentuate what Colton had just said, Sarah looked in their direction and winked at Nathan, causing his face to turn several shades of red as he grinned back at her.

"Told you so."

***

The next day, Pastor Jake asked Sarah, Nathan, and Brad to meet him in his office after church. He said he had something important he needed to share with them. Pastor Jake's large office was separated into two areas: one side with his large mahogany desk and two black leather chairs in front of it, and on the other side a more informal setting that held a black leather love seat with two red captain's chairs across from it. The floor was blanketed by plush, deep red carpet.

The scent of cinnamon met them as they entered, which must have been coming from a red jar candle on his desk. Pastor Jake motioned for them to head to the area away from his desk where there would be enough seats for all of them.

Brad went in first, taking a captain's chair and forcing Sarah and Nathan to sit on the love seat together. Nathan grinned and nodded a thank you to Brad while Sarah tried to sit with at least a few inches between her and Nathan, not because she didn't want to sit closer, but she didn't want to be improper in her pastor's office.

Pastor Jake sat down heavily. "I'm afraid I have some bad news, guys. The hospital just informed me yesterday afternoon that all of us coming in together to pray for people is no longer allowed."

"What?" Nathan was shocked. "How can they tell people they can't come to pray for people in a *hospital*?"

"That's not right. We didn't do anything illegal or wrong!" Brad responded.

Pastor Jake took a deep breath. "They didn't exactly say we couldn't come in to pray for people, but the restrictions that they are imposing tell me they don't want us there. They said that our presence was distracting their staff from their duties and that we are pushing our religion on them, which is not allowable." He sat back. "Their words, not mine."

"But how were we distracting anyone, especially the workers?" Sarah asked.

"Honestly, I don't know. They said the only one they will allow to return is me, unless you guys have a personal invitation from the patient or their immediate family. They also have new rules for visiting clergy, like I can only visit people from a personal invitation or those in my own congregation or I could lose the privilege of visitation altogether, and they are minimizing any physical contact from non-family visitors down to a handshake for sanitary reasons, along with a bunch of other regulations. Oh, and they will only allow one visitor in the room at a time, unless, of course, they are family members. I know we are most effective together, but with these new guidelines, I don't see us being able to really minster to people the way we used to. I wish I knew why they're doing this, other than that we made an impact, and somebody didn't like it."

"Does Deanne know about it?" Sarah asked.

"I wondered the same thing so I called her. It seems she got called into one of the doctor's offices with a bunch of nurses there to back him up, and he spoke with her about it before they called me. She said there's a nurse she works with who doesn't like her and may have stirred up some of it. Apparently, the other nurse never seemed to like us being there or praying for people."

"I think I know who she's talking about. That nurse gave us dirty looks every time we went to Deanne's section." Nathan nodded.

"Well, you three are still welcome to come with me for home visitations. There are hurting people everywhere. Oh, that reminds me, how is your school prayer group coming along?"

Brad spoke up, now that he had been taking over more of the responsibility for the school prayer time. "Impact is meeting every day after school now. We announced it yesterday, and everyone was so excited that each day we have at least three core group members who will be there."

"Great! You guys will have to let me know how it goes." Pastor Jake smiled.

They talked for a few minutes more before leaving Pastor Jake's office. He said that he had a few things to do before he could leave and one other couple to talk with for a few minutes. Then he would drive them home because he had kept them after the service. Brad's parents were waiting for him, so they said their good-byes to him. Charlotte had already gone home to start dinner.

Nathan and Sarah sat down in some chairs in the foyer as Colton approached. The light gray shirt he wore this morning contrasted with his dark hair, and it appeared that he purposely left a little stubble on his face to give himself a rugged look. It seemed Colton never wore anything but shades of gray and black for as long as she could remember. At least he took out his black stud earring at church. She had noticed it in the car the other day.

"Hey, Colton, how's it going?" Nathan stood and gave Colton a fist bump. "That was fun yesterday, huh?"

"Yeah, it was." Colton chuckled. "I didn't realize how funny little kids could be."

Colton seemed to be acting a bit nervously, shuffling his feet and rubbing the stubble on his chin for a moment before he turned to Sarah. "Um, Sarah...I need to tell you something. I shared it with Nathan yesterday, and he thought I should tell you too."

"Okay." Sarah looked puzzled. This was the most Colton had spoken to her in several years combined. He was usually withdrawn, but she had started noticing some positive changes in him since being around Nate more. He seemed a bit more lighthearted and open than usual.

Colton sat down in the chair next to Sarah, "Well, let me start by saying that I know you have spiritual things happen to you, like the miracles that happen when you pray for people." He paused and looked down, then leaned forward and rested his elbows on his black jean-clad knees, his hands clasped together. He looked up again and took a deep breath. "I have spiritual things happen to me too...but it's really different, freaky even."

He ran a hand over his hair and scanned the hallway to make sure nobody was too close to listen and lowered his voice. "I see things all the time...demons...angels...visions...stuff like that. Well, yesterday I kept seeing the same vision every time I was anywhere near you. Then I saw it again this morning when I first saw you. It didn't make sense to me, but Nathan said it might to you."

"Really? What was it?"

"I saw this girl with long black hair and really tanned skin. She was holding her stomach and screaming, 'I'm so sorry. Someone please help me!' Then I saw a doctor holding something bloody and dropping it in a trash can." Colton sat back and shrugged. "That's it."

Nathan leaned closer to Sarah. "I thought it sounded like Maria."

Sarah nodded. "That's who came to my mind too." She paused and shook her head slowly. "Wow, she must be going through a lot of stuff right now."

"So do you know what it means?" Colton looked hopeful.

"I can't be totally sure yet, but if it means what I think it does, then I need to try to talk to her soon," Sarah said quietly. "Thanks, Colton."

"You're welcome." Colton smiled and then rose. "I'm gonna check and see how soon my dad will be ready to leave."

Chapter Twenty-four

Sarah had a hard time keeping her mind on school the next day. Ever since Colton had told her the vision about Maria she felt an urgency to talk to her. She had walked all the usual places that would take her past Maria at school, paths she normally avoided, but didn't see her at all.

It seemed Nick had found a new interest...or two; she saw him walking down the hall with cheerleaders pressed up against either side of him. As usual, he ignored Sarah as she passed, which was fine with her. The feelings of anger and betrayal over what he had done had long since left. She knew now that she should never have allowed herself a romantic interest with Nick to begin with; and now that her love for God was secure, she had recently sensed a release to pursue the deep feelings she had for Nathan. She hadn't had a chance to talk to Nathan about it yet but hoped the opportunity would present itself soon.

Seeing one of Maria's friends who wasn't normally too snooty, Sarah maneuvered her way through the crowded hallway and tapped the girl on the shoulder. "Hey, Jessica, have you seen Maria today?"

"No, I heard she was sick, but she's probably visiting her mom in the hospital." Jessica smoothed her long strawberry blonde hair with her hand, twisting the end of a lock between her thumb and forefinger.

"Her mom is in the hospital?"

"Yeah, I guess it was like a week ago. She's not doing too good... Maria's not handling it too well either. I can tell it's been really hard on her."

Jessica stopped and eyed Sarah suspiciously. "What do you care anyway? Aren't you guys like enemies or something?"

"I guess it would appear that way, but we used to be best friends a long time ago. Someday I hope she and I can be friends again," Sarah added wistfully. She took a breath and smiled. "Hey, thanks for the info."

"No problem," Jessica said before turning to go to her next class.

Sarah continued on slowly. She didn't dare ask anyone about what she thought the vision might mean. With the way Maria and Nick had been acting, her best bet was that Maria was pregnant and contemplating having an abortion. She only hoped that it wasn't too late. If Maria was out of school today she might even be getting an abortion today.

Sarah prayed silently for Maria, her mom, and for the possible new life growing inside Maria's body. *Lord, let it not be too late!*

***

Just after her last class Sarah caught up with Nathan at his locker to ask him what he thought about the plan she had come up with concerning Maria.

"Hi, Nathan, how was your day?"

He looked her direction as he was putting some books into the overhead compartment and smiled, causing her heart to feel faint. "Not too bad, except for a hard science test." Nathan closed his locker and made sure it was secure then leaned closer to her. "I wish I had your brains in that area."

Sarah caught herself breathing deeply of his familiar scent before he straightened. She tried to distract herself by shuffling the books she was holding. Her backpack was already full so she had to carry a few extras home today.

"Here, let me carry those for you."

Before she could agree or disagree, Nathan reached under the books, his hands making contact with hers, sending a wave of warmth that quickly reached her cheeks. Instead of taking the books right away, he slowly stroked her arm with his thumb for a moment before sliding the books from her grasp and stowing them under his arm.

"Thanks."

They began walking toward the buses. Nathan was walking close enough to her that their arms touched, sending warmth through Sarah in spite of the chilly November air.

Sarah forced her mind back to Maria. "Hey, I found something out about Maria."

"Oh, yeah?" Nathan tilted his head to the side and raised an eyebrow.

"I asked one of her friends why she was gone today, and they said she was sick, but that she might be visiting her mom in the hospital. It figures just when we can't go back without a personal invitation, which I know we wouldn't get from Maria or her mother, I find out that her mom is there. I feel like we need to pray for her, like be there with her and all. I'm not sure how we can do that now."

"We'll have to come up with a plan."

"I think I'm going to try to talk to Maria again this afternoon. That's what I wanted to talk to you about. I need to know that I have someone praying for me as I go over there, you know, like a prayer covering that Pastor Jake talked about. He said it could be like a shield when others are praying for someone they know is going into a hard situation. Do you remember when he talked about that?"

"Yeah, I do. A few weeks back, right?"

"Yup." Sarah lowered her voice. "I'm gonna try to talk to her about what Colton saw in the vision."

They exited the building, and it was much less crowded on the walkway leading to the buses. There were still a few minutes before their buses would leave.

Nathan turned to face her, a look of concern on his face, "What do you think he saw?"

Sarah peeked around to make sure nobody was close enough to be listening. "I think she's pregnant and is planning to have an abortion soon."

Nathan nodded slowly. "I was wondering if that's what it meant." They continued walking. "Well, you can count on me praying. Just be careful. People can do strange things when they're hurt." He pulled the books from under his arm and handed them to her. "Let me know when you get back from talking to her, okay?"

Sarah deliberately grabbed the books in a way that their fingers would touch again, and looked into his eyes to see if he felt it too. From the way his gaze shifted from her eyes to her mouth, she knew he had definitely felt the electricity from their touch. "I will." She smiled before she turned to get on her bus. She felt him watching her as she went up the stairs and down a few rows to take a vacant seat. When she looked out the window, he waved with a lopsided grin on his face before jogging to his own bus.

***

Sarah pulled her wool coat tighter around her as she walked the distance to Maria's apartment complex in the brisk November air. The few dead leaves that were still attached to the trees rustled loudly above her and several found their freedom, dancing their way to the ground ahead of her. Sarah breathed out, trailing white vapor behind her and growing more nervous as she got closer.

She rounded the corner to Maria's apartment building and noted that a car was in one of the parking spots assigned to Maria's apartment. Fidgeting with her necklace with one hand, Sarah pulled open the door that led to a hallway leading to various apartments. Maria lived on the bottom level to the right.

She breathed a quick prayer for God's guidance and knocked on the door.

"Coming!" Sarah heard Maria call from inside. After a few moments she heard the metallic sounds of the door and deadbolt being unlocked and the door opened a few inches, a security chain still fastened a few inches above Maria's head and preventing the door from opening all the way. In just moments, a flurry of mixed emotions ranging from surprise to panic to anger surged across Maria's face before she spoke again.

"Why are *you* here?" Maria asked, tight-lipped.

"I need to talk to you. Can I come in?" Sarah tried to keep her voice light.

"Whatever you have to say, you can say it right there."

Sarah's mind quickly scanned the many things she planned to talk to Maria about. There may only be one chance to say what was needed and it would have to count. She wanted to ask about the vision first, but decided that would not be the best topic to start with, considering how edgy she was. "I heard you were sick today and I was hoping you felt better," Sarah started lamely, inwardly kicking herself.

Maria answered back sarcastically, "Well, as you can see, I'm just fine, so you can go home now." She started to close the door.

Sarah put her hand on the door. "Maria, wait. I heard your mom is in the hospital. Is there anything I can do to help you guys?"

"Anything *you* can do..." Maria laughed coldly and looked up. With one movement she unlocked the chain and opened the door wide, stepping into the doorway and pointing her finger into Sarah's chest. "Why don't you and your little dorky friends go pray to your precious *Jesus* about it. That's the *only* thing you can do to help us."

Sarah bit her lip, "Actually that's what we want to do. I mean, we are already praying for you and your mom, but we want to come see her and pray for her in person in the hospital, except now we can't come unless we're invited by the patient or their family."

Maria scoffed, "Like that's ever gonna happen."

"Maria, I don't know what the doctors are saying, but I know God can heal her. I've seen Him heal so many people—"

Maria interrupted her, her voice rising. "I told you already. It's *not* gonna happen, so stay out of my life. Haven't you caused enough trouble yet?"

Maria stepped back and started to close the door.

Sarah took a deep breath; it was now or never to confront Maria about the vision. "I know about the baby, Maria," she said just as the door shut.

Just as quickly, it reopened and Maria leaned out, panic on her face.

***

Maria's heart dropped into her stomach. She didn't know why Sarah had come here.

One part of her wanted to pull Sarah into the apartment and tell her everything, knowing Sarah actually did care for her and most likely would support her and be there for her, but the other part raged. Who told her about the baby? The only other person who knew about it was Nick. Of course, by now the whole school might know if Nick blabbed about it to one of his friends. There was a small chance that he might not have told anyone, being that his friends would look at him differently knowing he had fathered a child. *How does she know about the baby?*

"What did you say?" Maria asked, scanning the hallway to make sure nobody else was around. Sarah opened her mouth to repeat what she had said, but Maria put her hand up. "Wait."

Knowing that she had nosy neighbors who could be listening through their doors, she grabbed Sarah by the sleeve and pulled her into the apartment and shut the door.

Sarah looked around briefly, a look of surprise on her face.

"Now, what did you say?" Maria repeated, her arms crossed in front of her.

Sarah's eyes softened. "Maria, I know about the baby, and I know you're thinking about...um...a way to get rid of the problem. But please, don't have an abortion. I know for a fact that you will regret it and want the baby back."

Maria struggled with her words, trying to hold her emotions at bay. "Who told you about this? The only person who knows is Nick, and he doesn't want anything to do with me or the...the baby."

Tears welled up in her eyes. Just saying the words out loud hit her like a freight train and she wondered again what she could do about it.

Sarah reached over and touched her arm sympathetically, but Maria remained stoic, not willing to release her emotions to this reminder of her once-happy life.

"I'm so sorry, Maria." She withdrew her hand and explained, "It might seem strange...well, I *know* it will sound strange, but I have a friend who saw you in a vision holding your stomach and screaming. You were saying something like, 'I'm so sorry! And you were asking for help. Then he saw a doctor throwing away something bloody into a trash can. When I asked God about it, I felt like He said you were pregnant and thinking about killing the baby by abortion."

Sarah continued, "Maria, you have a real, living person growing inside of you. God loves you so much, and loves that little baby too!"

Maria placed a hand over her mouth and closed her eyes, silent tears streaming down her cheeks. Deep in her heart she knew what Sarah was saying was true. There was a tiny person growing, living, alive inside of her—and to end it would be murder.

Sarah relaxed visibly. "Maria, if there's anything me or my family can do to help you, now or after the baby is born, we will be there for you." She reached again and gently placed a hand on Maria's arm.

Suddenly rage boiled up inside of Maria and all of the previous concerns came crashing to the forefront of her mind.

What if my mother dies? How could I care for a child alone? Sarah says she will be there for me, but eventually she would forget again. Everyone else does. The baby wouldn't even have a dad, and who would want me now with a baby? The best thing to do is put this whole problem behind me and focus on my mom. Why should I be caught up trying to prepare for having a baby when I might not have much time left with my mom?

Maria flicked Sarah's hand away and stepped back. The atmosphere in the room grew icy. "I told you before that we don't need your help—*now or ever*."

Stepping over to the door, she swung it open. "I want you to leave," she said through clenched teeth.

Sarah blinked, obviously taken aback by the turn of the conversation. "Please, Maria—"

"I asked you to leave. Now *go!*" Maria shouted, new tears streaming down her face.

Was that pity she saw in Sarah's eyes? Now she knew everything about her—what a lowlife she was to let someone like Nick take her most precious gift away from her—her purity. *She must think I'm the most shallow girl alive.*

Sarah hesitated another moment and Maria couldn't stand seeing her in the apartment any longer. Just like she pulled her in, she grabbed Sarah's sleeve and shoved her toward the door. *"Get out!"* she screamed, slamming the door and locking it through her tear-blurred vision.

She ran to her room, slammed the door, threw herself on the bed, and sobbed.

***

Sarah stood there forever it seemed. She heard a door slam further back in the apartment and listened as Maria wept. Covering her face with her hands, Sarah slid to a kneeling position on the floor in front of Maria's door and wept too—for Maria's mother, for her lost friend, and for the tiny person who may never have a chance to live.

Chapter Twenty-five

Sarah hummed to herself as she walked to Impact after school the next day. She spent a long time in prayer yesterday once she got home and felt more at peace. The issue with Maria and her mother was in the back of her mind, but she was still excited about the after school prayer group.

As she turned into the room, Sarah was happy to see fifteen to twenty students already gathered. She greeted Mr. Roberts as she came in and spotted Taylor sitting at the table closest to the door with a thin girl she never met before. The girl had hair about the same color as her own but wore it pulled back in a neat ponytail. She remembered seeing her in the hallway a few times, but because she was a freshman, they didn't have any classes or interaction.

Taylor and the new girl stood, and Taylor gave her a hug. "Hi, Sarah, I was so excited to see the flyer about the group. I hope you guys don't mind that I brought my friend, Mandy. She goes to my church."

Mandy smiled shyly and gave a small wave. "Hi."

Taylor turned to Mandy. "This is Sarah, the girl I told you about who prayed with me about my family, remember?"

"Yeah, I remember." Turning to Sarah, Mandy added, "Did Taylor tell you that her stepdad actually came to our church last Sunday? I couldn't believe it!" Her ponytail bobbed as she bounced a bit.

"Really? That's great, Taylor!" Sarah reached over and gave Taylor another quick hug.

Brad was welcoming all the students to Impact as Sarah sat down in the chair next to Mandy. She looked around the room, meeting the smiling faces of many students they had prayed for at different times over the last several weeks. Everyone looked as excited as she was to be here.

As she turned her attention back to Brad, she noticed Nathan watching her from his seat next to Brad. Their eyes locked for a moment and he smiled—the depth of his feelings for her evident in his face. She returned his smile and felt her heart pick up pace. Pulling her eyes away from his gaze, she figured she better get her attention back on the meeting and the reason they were gathered.

"Welcome everyone!" Brad was saying. "So a lot of you have prayed with us either on Tuesdays or at some point during the day, and several people asked us if the group can meet every day, which we thought would be a great idea, so here we are."

One student piped up, one they had not seen at their prayer times before. He introduced himself as Luke. He had fair skin and light blond hair. The bright blue, button-down shirt he wore brought out his light blue eyes. "Is it true that you guys see miracles happening? I heard someone talking about—like some rash or something just disappeared right in front of them when one of you prayed for them. I didn't know that stuff was real."

Nathan was the first to respond. "Yeah, man. We see stuff like that happen all the time." He nodded to Sarah. "Sarah, you remember that?"

"Yeah, that was Samantha." She looked around and saw Samantha sitting across the room. "You want to tell everyone about it, Samantha?"

Everyone turned to face Samantha, who looked a bit startled by the sudden attention, "Um, sure. Some of you already heard about it." She rolled up her sleeve to reveal her smooth ivory skin. "I had this really red rash on my arm. I don't know what it was, but it was itchy and painful. I tried everything I could for a few weeks to get it to go away 'cause I don't like going to the doctor." She looked up with a sheepish smile. "So then I asked Sarah, Nathan, and Brad to pray for me, and when Sarah was praying, I felt something hot on my arm, and the rash just disappeared as I was watching it!"

"Oh, yeah, I remember that now!" Brad exclaimed. "That was the first day we had the prayer meeting. That was amazing."

"See!" Samantha held her arm higher in the air. "It never came back." The group chatted quietly and a few girls closest to Samantha touched her arm as she pointed out where the rash had been.

"So what else have you guys seen happen?" Luke asked.

Nathan responded, "Here at school we have seen minor things from colds and stuff healed, to family problems getting solved, to headaches leaving instantly. Brad here had a migraine and it instantly left when Sarah and I prayed for him."

"And if you've ever had a migraine before, you know that's a miracle," Brad interjected. "They usually take hours to go away, even with meds."

A few students nodded their agreement, having had experience with migraines before.

"Sometimes Nathan, Brad, and I go pray for people in the hospital or at people's homes with our pastor," Sarah added. "Of course, their situations are very serious, being that they're in the hospital and all. One time we saw God touch a woman who was in a car accident, and by the time we left, she was already doing a lot better. One guy had spinal meningitis and had an angel visit him after we left, and he was totally healed not long after that. Another woman we prayed for was in the hospital because she was pregnant and the baby started coming too soon. She was having severe pain, but when we prayed, she said it was like a bolt of energy shot through her and the pain left."

The students were totally enraptured as the stories were shared; in fact, just recounting the past events of what God had done was stirring something in her. They were meeting to pray, but she felt this was important. God was doing something.

Brad continued excitedly where she left off, "We saw someone who was depressed have a weight lifted off them and start smiling and laughing by the time we left. It's been amazing. I know for me personally, after seeing God do so many incredible things, I know He can do much more than I ever thought possible. In the Bible, Jesus told the disciples that if they just had a tiny bit of faith they could see entire mountains moved and thrown into the ocean. He wasn't speaking in metaphors. He really meant it!"

Brad was really on a roll. Sarah noticed that he became animated as he spoke; it was like energy was flowing through him. She could feel faith building in the room.

"Maybe all this time God wanted us to just believe His Word, to believe that if we ask Him in faith, not doubting, that we can *all* see miracles happen. It's not just limited to a few people. This is for everyone. The question we have to ask ourselves is do we really believe Him and what He said? Over the last few weeks, I have noticed my faith level jump. Just the other day I prayed for my neighbor who got hurt when he was cutting some tree branches with a chain saw. A bolt had fallen off and the chain came loose and hit his arm, and cut a big gash in it." Brad indicated with his hand a big slice across his arm where the man had been cut. "I was outside and heard him yell and ran over. I started praying for him, and within a few minutes, the gash stopped bleeding. Then it fused back together! He couldn't believe it."

The students sat in awe, digesting what they had just heard. It was clear some of these students had never heard anything like that before. Hearing this was opening a world of possibilities of the supernatural and what God was truly capable of.

Just then there was a commotion outside the room. They heard someone running down the hall and a male voice yelling, "Call 911! Someone, call 911 *right now!*"

Another teacher had their arm around a student hunched over and passed the doorway, moving quickly toward the main office.

Mr. Roberts, along with Nathan and Brad, all jumped to their feet and rushed to the door, stopping abruptly at the doorway. Sarah and others ran to look over their shoulders and their eyes widened at the scene that met them.

A trail of splattered blood ran down the length of the hall. Someone had gotten hurt—badly.

"What the..." Luke said what they were all thinking.

Nathan and Brad moved down the hall in the direction the injured student had gone, toward the main office, in spite of Mr. Roberts telling them that it would probably be best not to get in the way. Sarah and some of the other students followed, including Taylor, Mandy, and Luke. There was no way they would be missing what might happen, especially with his heightened curiosity of what God could do in situations like these.

When they reached the main office, the scene unfolded before them. A student, whom they recognized as Sean Billings, was hunched over in a chair with a blood-soaked towel wrapped around his hand. The school secretary frantically talked on the phone with the 911 operator, relaying the information that the shop teacher, Mr. Porter, was yelling to her. He held something bloody in his hand and stooped in front of Sean, who looked pale.

They all stopped outside the door, which was still open.

"Tell them again, his finger got cut off while he was using the table saw!" Mr. Porter shouted. "He's lost a lot of blood. Tell them to hurry!" He tried to match the finger up with where it had been cut off, trying without success to wrap them together as Sean cried out in pain.

Sarah gasped, and she heard several of them do the same. Sean was also a senior, so they shared several classes with him. He was known to party and drink from time to time, but overall was a good guy. He had run for class secretary and was almost elected this year.

Nobody moved. Then Brad said, "We should pray. Form a circle."

Those who had followed stepped back to make a circle in the hallway outside the office door, and they all grabbed hands. Sarah was standing between Taylor and Mandy and grabbed their hands. Brad began to pray, and Sarah could hear others in the group praying too. "Father God, we join together to pray for Sean. Please help him, touch his hand, and let him not lose this finger. Let the ambulance get here soon..."

As Brad continued to pray, Taylor tapped Sarah with their joined hands to get her attention. She looked perplexed. "Sarah, I…I feel like I'm supposed to go over and put his finger back on and pray. It sounds crazy, right?" Taylor looked as though she hoped Sarah would tell her she was crazy and not to do it.

"Really? How strong are you feeling about it?"

"I feel like I have to do it, like I *need* to…it's so weird!" Taylor whispered loudly.

Sarah replied, "Sometimes I feel like I'm supposed to do strange things, too, when I pray, and usually it's what God wants me to do in order to answer prayer or heal someone." Sarah nodded, "As strange as it seems, you should probably do it."

"I don't know…it's so crazy…what if nothing happens?"

"Then people will think it's weird, but what if something great happens? If you don't, you'll never know. Sometimes you have to just step out and do it." Sarah paused. "Besides, all they can do is tell you to get back if nothing happens."

"Okay, here it goes." Taylor took a deep breath, straightened her shoulders, and stepped into the office with determination.

Without another thought, Taylor moved past the teacher and another office worker and forcefully grabbed Sean's hand, right where the finger had been cut off. With her other hand she grabbed Mr. Porter's hand which still held the bloody appendage, and guided it back where it belonged.

"What are you doing?" Mr. Porter was taken by surprise.

"Aaaaahhh," Sean cried out.

"In the name of Jesus, heal this finger!" Taylor prayed, strong and bold.

"You can't—" Mr. Porter tried to pull his hand back, but with a strength she didn't know she had, she held it in place. Then he stopped mid-sentence as what looked like flesh-colored tentacles appeared around the cut and began to fuse the finger together. Each tentacle rose up from nowhere and covered the wound rapidly. One by one, each strand literally pulled the fingertip back into its proper position, even rotating it into perfect alignment.

Sean, whose hand was being held by both Mr. Porter and Taylor, backed himself up in the chair as far as he could go, groaning and writhing, all the while in shock and wide-eyed at what was taking place in his body. "It's hot!" he cried.

The secretary, who had stopped talking, dropped the phone with her mouth hanging open, then scrambled to pick it up, trying to explain—without success—what was happening. They could now hear the ambulance's siren in the distance headed toward the school.

Sean's finger continued to transform. Someone had grabbed a bunch of wet paper towels and handed them to Mr. Porter. He carefully wiped away the blood from Sean's hand, very gently, where it had been cut. They could all see now that there was a bulge where the cut had been and the tentacles of flesh had covered and fused the cut. But even as they watched, the bulge decreased until the finger was smooth. Just a slight red mark ringing around the finger remained, which was slowly fading.

Within a few moments three paramedics burst through the front entrance and followed the blood trail to the office. They rushed over to Sean and Mr. Porter. The head paramedic said, "Okay, let's get this young man in the ambulance. Where's the finger? We need to get it on ice right away." He grabbed a cooler filled with ice from the female paramedic who came in with him.

Sean, who was dumbfounded at what had just happened to him, held up his finger. "It's back on!" he said lamely. Even when he was trying to be serious, Sean had a knack for making people laugh.

The head paramedic scanned Sean's hands, noting that all fingers were securely attached and furrowed his brow. "Is this some kind of a joke? We were told someone's finger got cut off with a table saw."

"It did, I mean, it was...but it came back on..." Mr. Porter sounded incredulous even as he said it out loud. He shook his head. "I know it sounds crazy, but it did! Just before you got here, this girl here grabbed

his hand, put the finger back in place, and said something or other…
and it just...came back together."

"Where did all this blood come from then? Nobody's bleeding?"
the female paramedic asked.

"He *was* bleeding—a lot. That's all his blood on the floor and down
the hall." Mr. Porter swept his arm in the direction of the hallway, "but
he's not bleeding anymore."

Sean sat there, inspecting his finger, which looked completely
normal now.

The head paramedic leaned over and inspected Sean's finger,
turning his hand every which way, even pulling on the finger and
pressing on it. "Anything hurt?" he asked while another paramedic
checked Sean's vitals.

Sean shook his head. "Nope, it feels fine." A smile tugged at the
corners of his mouth. "I can't believe that just happened." He was
still amazed.

The paramedic scratched his head, "Well, this is a new one. I
guess we'll just say it was a false alarm." He turned to Taylor. "What
did you do anyway?"

Taylor smiled and shrugged. "I just took the two pieces and put
them together and prayed for it to be healed in the name of Jesus…I
felt like I had to do it…and then it started growing back together. We
all saw it."

"Jesus, huh? I wish we had gotten here sooner. That must have
been something else!"

"There's nothing too crazy when it comes to God, sir," Brad
smiled widely. "Actually stuff like this is starting to seem normal."

***

Taylor, Brad, and Nathan stayed at the main office to give
statements of what they saw happen before the paramedics left, taking
Sean with them to make sure everything was fine. Someone must have
tipped off the local media because a news crew actually showed up

and interviewed them, focusing mostly on Taylor about Sean's finger being healed, and they interviewed Sarah about the prayer group and the miracles they had been seeing. They were told that the footage would air on tonight's news.

After the reporters left, they joined a few other students who had stayed in the hallway and they all walked slowly back down the hall to retrieve their backpacks from Mr. Robert's classroom before going home.

"That was even wilder than my rash disappearing!" Samantha pushed her glasses up on her nose and flipped her long, dirty-blonde hair behind her shoulder.

"God is so amazing. I was starting to feel like certain situations were weighing me down so much that I was losing touch with what He is really able to do. I needed to see that today." Sarah shook her head yes. "So amazing."

"You said that already." Taylor grinned.

Then Samantha elbowed Sarah and leaned in closer to her. "By the way, I saw the way Nathan was looking at you before that whole thing happened. He likes you."

Sarah blushed, not realizing that anyone else saw their brief interaction as the meeting started.

"So is he your boyfriend yet?" Samantha waited for a response.

Sarah shrugged. "Not really. I mean, we both know we like each other. I guess there's been so much going on that we haven't had much time to really figure it out yet." They hadn't gone too far down the hallway yet. She looked over her shoulder at the main office, the floor to ceiling glass wall giving her an unrestrained view of Nathan and the others. He glanced in their direction and caught her watching him, their eyes locking again. Sarah couldn't help the smile tugging at her mouth as she looked at him.

Samantha seemed to be enjoying this far too much and chuckled. "Oh yeah, you both got it bad."

Chapter Twenty-six

Sarah had such mixed emotions the next few days. She was overjoyed at what happened with Sean and his finger, yet she was still burdened for Maria and Andrea. She felt an urgency to do something—but what? She woke up trying to figure out a way to get through to Maria.

Nathan wanted to talk about it after she got home from Maria's apartment Monday night, but she was too overwhelmed to talk for more than just a few minutes. Before they hung up, he prayed for her, and she could feel hope and strength through his words. Her mom sat with her a long time Monday night too, talking, praying, and giving advice and wisdom from mother to daughter, but she still felt unsettled.

There was a sense that they were racing against time, both with Maria's mom and the baby's uncertain future. Tuesday's events were amazing and gave her new hope that God was in control; she just needed His direction, and soon.

She only saw Nathan at school for a few minutes on Wednesday, so they hadn't had time to talk much, and before and after the service she was spending time with her new friend, Casey. On Thursday Nathan caught up with her at her locker before her first class. He smiled as he approached.

"I'm still so pumped up about Sean's miracle. Wasn't that great?"

"It was. I still can't believe we saw it happen…I mean I can…It was just really cool." She smiled, but then her expression faded. "But I wish I knew how to help Maria and her mom."

"Yeah, I've been thinking about that a lot too." He reached up and moved a lock of hair back from her face.

"I just wish there was something we could do..." She trailed off, not needing to say any more.

They started walking slowly down the hall. There was a minute or two before class started, plenty of time for both of them to get to class just a few doors down.

"I think I have an idea."

"Really?" Sarah perked up. "What is it?"

Nathan peeked at his watch to see how much time they had. "We'll talk about it more later, but I was thinking that they just now changed those rules. If we go back to the hospital today, maybe they haven't started enforcing them yet. I mean, it can't hurt to try, right? The worse they can do is tell us to leave."

Sarah wasn't sure she liked the idea. "Hmmm, I don't know. I don't want to get Pastor Jake in trouble; he already told us the rules...I'll think about it and catch you later before we go home."

"Okay, fair enough, I wasn't thinking about what it might do to the Martins. You have a point there." Just then the bell rang. Good thing their classes were right across the hall from each other.

"See you later," they both said in unison before ducking into their classrooms.

***

All day long Sarah was distracted. In math, she started the wrong assignment until her teacher pointed it out to her. In English, she couldn't keep her mind on the reading and had to read the same page over about four times before she actually knew what it said.

She contemplated Nathan's idea. Maybe he had a point. They could only tell them to leave. Along with her concern for Maria's mom, she couldn't shake the feeling that Maria was seriously contemplating aborting her baby. But when? Would she wait until after Thanksgiving or would she go before?

She spent most of the time at school that day quietly interceding for guidance and direction.

As she closed her locker at the end of the day, Nathan snuck up behind her and whispered in her ear, "Have you decided yet?"

Whirling around, she found herself staring into Nathan's hazel eyes, just a few inches away. He grinned from ear to ear, knowing he caught her off guard.

Sarah shoved him playfully on the shoulder, putting a few more inches of distance between them. Not because she wanted to, but because she needed to. "You scared me!"

His eyes twinkled. "You didn't answer my question. Have you decided if we should try to see Maria's mom after school?"

"Did you talk to Brad about it? Can he come too?"

"I mentioned it to him, and he said he would come if we ended up going. He said Taylor will already be leading Impact today anyway."

"Good. I think it's worth a shot but I think we should tell Pastor Jake first."

"But what if he tells us not to? What do we do then?" Nathan paused a moment. "Besides, if he's in a meeting or something he may not get back to us for a few hours. You said you felt like something needs to be done soon, so I think we should just go for it."

Sarah bit her lip. If they were really racing against time, the sooner they got there the better. What if Andrea wouldn't make it much longer? Reluctantly she agreed, "Okay, but how do we get there?"

Nathan leaned in closer. "We can walk, it's really not that far." He raised his eyebrows.

Highland Falls Memorial was probably ten blocks away, much closer from here than from home. Sarah still felt a reserve.

Something felt off.

Nathan seemed to be reading her mind and sensed her hesitancy. "Look, if we leave now we can be back in time to take the late buses home. It'll be fine."

"All right, let's go."

"Good, I'll text Brad."

Before long, the trio made the ten-block journey to the hospital. Sarah was glad she had her gloves in her pockets or her hands would have been frozen by the time they arrived.

They entered the hospital's main entrance and headed toward the sign-in desk. A white-haired woman looked up at them over the rim of her glasses. She had signed them in a few times before when they had come with Pastor Jake, but this was the first time they had come without him or Charlotte. She had been cordial with them in the past, so maybe she wouldn't give them trouble today. The woman smiled as she greeted them.

"Can I help you?"

Sarah glanced over at Nathan and Brad and spoke up first. "We're here to see Mrs. Romano...um...I mean Andrea Romano."

"Just a moment." the woman typed something into the computer and tipped her head back to read whatever was on the screen through her bifocals. As they waited, Sarah noticed a new poster next to the sign in the window that read: EFFECTIVE IMMEDIATELY: VISITORS WILL ONLY BE ADMITTED BY REQUEST OF PATIENT OR THEIR IMMEDIATE FAMILY MEMBERS.

Sarah nudged Nathan and nodded to the sign. He read it and shrugged, looking hopefully back to the woman at the computer.

"What are your names?" the woman asked. They each told her their name and she shook her head, "I don't see any of your names listed here to be admitted as visitors for Andrea Romano. I'm sorry, but I can't let you see her until she or one of her family members puts your names down." She pointed to the poster. "It's part of our new visitation guidelines." She offered a sympathetic smile. "I'm sorry."

This new system still felt so foreign to Sarah; maybe she could use the woman's kindheartedness to gain access to Maria's mom. "Look, Andrea is really sick and we just want to pray for her, that's all. Could we just see her for a minute?"

Just then a deep male voice from behind them joined the conversation, making them all jump. "Not according to our new regulations, you can't."

They turned to see a doctor and nurse standing there, not looking too happy. The name tag on the doctor's uniform stated "Dr. Kramer," and the nurse's tag showed that her name was Rachel. They recognized Rachel as the grumpy nurse on Deanne's floor. It looked like maybe they had just come back from taking a break.

Dr. Kramer continued, "I'm pretty sure I have seen you three here before with Pastor Jake Martin, correct?"

Nathan cleared his throat. "Yes, sir, that's right. He's the pastor of our church."

"Right." Dr. Kramer sounded impatient. "I was told that he was going to inform you of the new regulations for visitors. Did he not do that yet?"

"Um, yeah he did, but we thought maybe it hadn't started yet. We just wanted to pray for someone we know who's really sick right now."

The nurse, Rachel, rolled her eyes and huffed. She touched Dr. Kramer's arm. "I'll let you handle this. We'll talk later," she said before striding down the hall at a rapid pace.

"Well, as you were *informed*, you can't see someone now unless they request you to be here, and if I heard the conversation correctly, that has not happened yet." He crossed his arms, a clear indication that this was the final verdict on the topic.

Brad, sensing Sarah's disappointment but also knowing they weren't going to make any headway here, spoke up. "I'm sorry, Dr. Kramer; we'll make sure to follow the new rules. Sorry for any inconvenience," he said to the white-haired woman.

She offered an apologetic smile in response. Clearly she wasn't one of the people who had helped put the new rules into motion.

"That's good, and I'll make sure Pastor Jake knows that he should touch base with you three again about the new rules too." He forced a smile before turning to head down the hallway.

Sarah was ready to tell him that wasn't necessary, but with his hasty exit she decided to leave instead. Nathan and Brad followed.

They started back toward the school and walked a few blocks in silence before Nathan turned to Sarah. "I'm sorry, Sarah. I feel like I pressured you into coming and I shouldn't have done that. Not only did we waste time but I'm pretty sure the Martins won't be too happy with us either."

Sarah shook her head. "No, I knew something wasn't right and that we shouldn't have gone, but I didn't stop us from going. I was so caught up with trying to help Maria and Andrea and all...it's just as much my fault as yours."

Nathan gently reached over and laced his fingers with Sarah's, not caring that Brad was present. They were sure by now that Brad knew they had feelings for each other. Sarah had not put her gloves on yet, but the warmth of Nathan's hand in hers was enough to keep her warm from head to toe. She looked up at him as they walked and they grinned at each other.

"So...I guess I'm the third wheel now, huh?" Brad was eying their interlocked hands.

They both laughed, but Nathan didn't release her hand; instead he said, "You could hold my other hand but that would just be weird."

Brad cracked up, holding both hands up. "No offense, but I'll keep my hands to myself."

The rest of the way back to school they talked about what Pastor Jake was going to say after the doctor called him and what their next plan of action concerning Maria and Andrea would be, which didn't produce much results. Maybe talking with Pastor Jake and Charlotte about it would be a good thing, and they would know what to do now.

Chapter Twenty-seven

Come on in, everyone. We can pull a few chairs in from the classroom next door." Pastor Jake had arranged for Sarah, Nathan, and Brad to meet with him and Charlotte in his office after church that Sunday morning. "I'll try to keep this short because I know everybody is probably eager to get home."

Sarah noted that even though he smiled warmly, there was something else in his eyes. Was it hurt? Disappointment?

This was the first time they had seen him since before Thursday when they attempted to go back to the hospital to pray for Maria's mom. They hadn't received a call from him that night or Friday, so she hoped that maybe Dr. Kramer hadn't really called him after all.

They filed into his office and were greeted by the combination scents of the leather furniture and the apple cinnamon candles that were burning.

Sarah moved across the plush, deep red carpeting and lowered herself into the black loveseat next to Charlotte, giving her a side hug before the meeting started.

Pastor Jake leaned back against his slick mahogany desktop and cleared his throat. "I got a call from the hospital Thursday evening from a Doctor Kramer, and he said that the three of you had gone back to see a patient who did not have your names down for visitation. He seemed pretty upset that you already knew the guidelines and didn't follow them. I assured him that I had clearly conveyed to you what the new rules were and that I didn't even know that you had been there."

He clasped his hands in front of him, absently fiddling with the shiny gold wedding ring on his left hand. "I wanted to talk to the three of you about this because I don't want to see things like this happen again. As much as I am proud of you for taking a stand and being bold about what you believe, you don't need to disobey rules that you know have been set in place. It can destroy your witness to the community. Not only do you represent this church, but you also represent Christ when you are outside these doors."

Sarah glanced at both Nathan and Brad, who both had their eyes downcast toward the floor. Charlotte offered her a consoling smile.

Pastor Jake placed his hands, palms down, on either side of him on the desktop, straightening his arms and leaning forward a bit. "So why did you feel like you had to go right then? Couldn't it have waited until we could go together?" He waited for a response.

Nathan looked over at Sarah and shrugged. "I guess we could have. It's more my fault than theirs. Thursday morning Sarah was very upset because she found out that Maria Romano's mom, Andrea, is dying of cancer in the hospital, and she felt like we needed to go pray for her. I guess we were hoping that they hadn't put the new rules into place yet." He shrugged again. "I know it's been really eating Sarah up and, you know, with her healing gift and all, maybe Andrea would have been healed. I just was thinking that we don't know how much longer she would be alive."

Pastor Jake nodded slowly, putting a few of the pieces together in his mind. "Yes, I remember Andrea and Maria. They stopped coming not long after we came here. I'm pretty sure I tried to get in touch with them after they left but never got through."

"Andrea was a really sweet woman," Charlotte interjected, "I remember her too."

"I talked to my mom about the whole situation the other night, but I am not sure what to do about it." Sarah shared about Colton's vision and how she tried to talk to Maria about her mom and the baby, how Maria had been rejected by the baby's father, and that if Maria's mom died, nobody would be there for her.

By the time she finished, tears were running down her cheeks. Charlotte wrapped an arm around Sarah in support.

Pastor Jake sat for a moment. It was evident that Sarah was deeply moved by Maria's situation.

"Even though you shouldn't have gone to the hospital, I can't ignore this situation with Amanda and Maria." He turned to Charlotte and tilted his head. You know, honey, I think last night Colton shared a vision with me that he had about them. Maybe Colton should be here too." Charlotte nodded in agreement as he spoke. For now, he directed his attention back to the three teens in front of him.

"Before we go any further, I just want you three to agree that you won't try something like that again. I don't want to get any more calls from the hospital that you tried to go against their policies. Is that clear?" Pastor Jake looked at them for a response.

"Yes, sir." Brad's reply was echoed by Nathan and Sarah.

"Great. So now that we have dealt with that, there is a bigger issue at hand. And I'm not sure how to deal with it. For starters, I want Colton to be in here too. He is obviously part of what is happening with the Romanos…whether he likes it or not." He chuckled. "Brad, why don't you round him up."

"Sure thing." Brad jumped up and headed out the door to find Colton.

They returned a few minutes later. Colton looked at Sarah and Nathan with a question in his eyes. Brad probably didn't have time to fill him in on what was happening—not that Brad knew about what was going on next.

Pastor Jake clapped his hands together lightly and looked over at his son. "So, Colton, last night you shared a vision with me that you had told to Sarah about a girl who's facing some really hard times. It seems like the vision revealed some things about what she's going through so Sarah could try to help her. God gives some people visions to help reveal and give warning about future events to help them prepare for it. I think God is using you to give warning to this situation so we can get a game plan to know what to do."

Sarah was going to correct Pastor Jake that Maria wasn't exactly what you would call a friend; friends don't slam doors in your face and scream at you to leave them alone, but she stopped herself. One day she really hoped Maria would be her friend again.

"Yeah, Sarah knew what it was about as soon as I told her, even though I didn't know who it was or what was happening." Colton nodded.

"Well, I'm not sure what can be done for Maria or Andrea just yet, but I know we can pray. God will show us what to do." He stood, and they all followed, joining hands around the room. They all began to pray quietly, lifting up Maria and Andrea to the Lord.

One by one they all prayed aloud, even Colton. After about twenty minutes, they felt a change and the heavy weight of the situation lifted.

After the prayers ceased, they talked for a few minutes about what could be done. By this time their parents had come looking for the teenagers so they could go home, and they joined the discussion.

After a brief update about the Romanos' situation, some ideas were thrown out about how they all could help. Even though they did not have a concrete plan set in place, it felt like God had already heard their prayers.

Stephanie jumped in to help the other moms organize taking turns making meals to bring to Maria's apartment, making sure the young girl had plenty of nutritious food to eat. Maria had been hostile, so they figured the best way would be to have it delivered to her door when she was gone or have a third party bring it anonymously. This way she would have a hard time rejecting the food. They huddled together, planning meal options and how they would give a nice Thanksgiving Day dinner as well. Even a small gesture such as providing food could make a big difference.

As they were leaving the church, Nathan walked alongside Sarah. "Do you mind if I stop by later? Maybe we can take a walk or something."

Butterflies erupted in her stomach at the thought of having some time alone with Nathan, and she felt heat rush to her cheeks. "Sure, that would be nice."

Although it was the Sunday before Thanksgiving, the weather had been mild. It was supposed to be in the high fifties by later in the day, a perfect day to be outside and maybe the last time before the bitter cold of New York winter set in.

"Cool, see you later then." Nathan grinned widely before heading toward his parents' car. Sarah watched him jog over to Colton and Brad on the way and give them each a fist bump.

"That Nathan is a great kid." Sarah jumped at her dad's voice. "I like him a lot. I think you do too," he teased.

Sarah leaned over, playfully knocking her shoulder against his arm. "Daaaaad..."

David grabbed her in a half-hug and smiled as they turned to walk to the car together. "I have eyes, you know."

***

Nathan showed up at about four that afternoon, giving everyone time to eat lunch and rest for a while. Sarah didn't tell him that she had watched and waited the whole afternoon for his arrival. It seemed like forever and she tried to fill the time with brushing Shadow, reading her Bible, and watching something on TV, but the clock ticked slowly.

She changed into a thin black jacket layered over a long-sleeved moss green shirt with lace trim at the neckline of the same color. Dark blue jeggings and black boots that went almost up to her knees with a two-inch heel to complete the outfit, but she was starting to wonder if she had overdressed. Sarah went back and forth with herself about changing into something else for the last hour before he came. When she saw Nathan walking up the driveway, her stomach flip-flopped in anticipation of being near him again.

After he knocked, she waited a few seconds to open the door. She didn't want him to assume she was standing right next to the door, although she really was. He pushed his bangs out of his eyes and smiled. "Hey, Sarah, how's it going?"

She was anxious for their walk but wasn't sure if he wanted to warm up first. She opened the door a bit wider. "It's going great. Do you want to come in?"

She felt better about the outfit she had picked out now, being that Nathan looked like he was dressed up a bit more than his normal casual attire, like they were going on a date rather than just a walk. He had changed into his favorite jeans that looked worn but were actually pretty new, paired with a blue button-down shirt with a black wool coat she had never seen before to keep warm.

He looked *really* good.

"Maybe later." He tipped his head, motioning her outside. "It's so nice out. You want to go for a walk?"

"Sure." Sarah closed the door behind her and Nathan laced his fingers with hers as they started down the driveway, sending warmth through her body in spite of the crisp November air. Leaves crunched under their feet as they walked down the street. The bare arms of nearby trees gave stark evidence that winter was on its way.

"So that meeting wasn't as bad as I thought it was gonna be." Nathan looked over at her.

"No, it wasn't. I didn't think it would turn into a prayer meeting." Sarah smiled. "When Pastor Jake first brought us in I thought he was really mad about what we did." After a pause she added, "I like the meal plan. I can imagine it's hard for Maria to be eating well with all that's going on."

Sarah and Nathan walked a while in silence, enjoying each other's company and lost in their own thoughts. They turned into one of the town's parks which had evergreen trees planted all around. Over the Christmas season every tree was lit up with different colored lights and people could either walk or drive through to see it all. They could tell that the lights were already in place, waiting for the opening day, which was usually the day after Thanksgiving. It was especially beautiful when there was snow covering the ground and blanketing the trees.

Today, the evergreen trees gave some privacy to Nathan and Sarah as they walked hand in hand around the park.

Sarah contemplated Maria's dilemma before breaking the silence. "I still wish we knew a way to go and pray for her. And I feel like I still need to get through to Maria about the baby. I keep thinking..."

Sarah stopped walking and sighed, "what if she really is going to go through with it...the abortion. What can I do to convince her not to?"

Nathan turned to face her. "You're an amazing person, Sarah Wright. I know God will show you what to do at just the right time." He raised their clasped hands up to his lips and kissed the back of her hand sweetly, sending shivers up and down her spine.

"Oh, hey, you're cold. Here, you can use my jacket." Nathan released her hand and unzipped his jacket the rest of the way down.

"It's okay. I don't need it."

In spite of her protest, he shrugged out of the coat and placed it around her shoulders with his hands remaining on either side of her neck after she had slipped her arms into the sleeves.

Sarah looked up and found herself lost in the depths of Nathan's warm hazel eyes. Slowly he moved his thumbs from the jacket to her jaw, lightly stroking her skin and sending her heart into triple time. She could feel the heat from his breath on her face as they slowly inched toward each other, their eyes still locked together. Her lips parted.

***

Nathan had never kissed anyone before, which made him a little nervous because Sarah had dated Nick, who was obviously an experienced kisser. He had dreamed of this moment for a long time now, wondering what it would be like. They had come close to kissing a couple times before, but the last time they had almost kissed, Sarah held back because she said she had needed to make God her first love before getting involved deeper with him.

This thought caused him to hesitate a bit now. *Was it time yet? Was she ready for a relationship or would it be too soon?* He didn't want to come in between her and the Lord, that's for sure. At the same time he couldn't pull his gaze away from her face, her eyes, her lips.

Their mouths were just centimeters apart now so he waited. If she was ready, then it would happen.

Sarah's eyes slid shut and she closed the short distance between them, her lips warm and soft against his. At first her lips brushed lightly over his, sending a rush of heat through his body that he'd never felt before.

Closing his eyes, he framed her face with his hands and instinctively tilted his head, their mouths fitting perfectly together like they were made for each other. Slowly and deliberately he kissed her, feeling an overwhelming love and care welling up for this girl who had so captured his heart since they were young. He threaded his hands through her silky hair and he felt her fingers travel up his chest and around his neck, bringing them even closer together.

A soft groan escaped her throat, adding more momentum to the moment. She tilted her head the opposite direction and he followed suit, deepening the kiss.

Reluctantly he moved his hands back to her face and slowly pulled back, resting his forehead against hers, their breaths coming in rapid succession.

***

Sarah kept her eyes closed, not wanting this moment to end.

Her first kiss with Nick had been so different. It had felt lustful and she had to stop him each time they kissed so things didn't progress too far. Nathan had actually been the one to pull away first and his hands never moved below her neck, something she couldn't say about Nick.

She willed her heart to stop pounding, but it was no use. Their foreheads still touched and Nathan's thumbs gently stroked her jawline.

She could feel the rumble in his chest as he whispered, "That was so much better than I ever imagined it." He lifted his head and placed a

235

lingering kiss on her forehead before they opened their eyes, his pupils shrinking back down with the daylight.

Slowly a wide, lopsided smile spread across Nathan's face and he chuckled, looking down at the ground then back up at her. "That was awesome."

Sarah couldn't help the huge grin on her face that mirrored his. "And how many times have you imagined it?" she asked playfully.

Nathan's face turned a few shades of red and pink, and he ducked his head sheepishly before answering, "Probably a few hundred... at least."

Sarah raised her brows in astonishment. "Oh...wow."

"Hey, I'm just being honest." As they turned back toward home he held her hand again, interlocking their fingers together.

"Just so you know," Sarah said as they walked, "that was the best first kiss I've ever had."

He looked over at her, grinning. "Me too. That was the best, and only, first kiss I've ever had."

Sarah stopped, looking up at him quizzically. "You'd never kissed anyone before?"

"Well, maybe I kissed my mom, but not like that, like on the cheek." He laughed.

"You know what I mean." Sarah shoved his shoulder lightly. Then she smiled. "So your first kiss was with me."

"I wonder if a second kiss is as good as a first kiss." Nathan stepped closer.

Sarah chuckled. "Calm down there, Romeo. Better not right now. I still can't think straight after the first one!"

"Me too." Nathan stepped back a bit and smiled as they continued back to Sarah's house.

Chapter Twenty-eight

Sarah was on a cloud all that next day at school. At any time she could close her eyes and still feel Nathan's lips on hers. Even though it wasn't her first kiss, it had almost seemed like it. Whenever she saw him in the hallway her legs felt weak and she couldn't help grinning from ear to ear.

Once she almost walked into a pole in the lunchroom as she headed to her table. She had spotted Nathan through the glass wall separating the cafeteria from the hallway and wasn't looking where she was going. Apparently he had the same ailment too, from the way he looked back at her. He bumped into someone right after she almost hit the pole, and they laughed at each other's clumsiness.

Just before her last class, however, she was brought back to reality as she heard four girls who were walking down the hallway in front of her talking about Maria.

"So, her mom's doing worse I heard," one girl was saying. "Maria said the doctors told her to prepare for the worst; she said her mom can't even talk anymore."

"Yeah she's still in the hospital. Maria goes there like every second she can be there. I don't think the doctors know what to do," the girl next to her said.

"That's sad. I don't know what I would do if my mom died." The first girl shook her head back and forth.

"Wanna hear something else? I heard Nick talking to his friends and he said he knocked her up," another snickered. "Figures that slut ended up getting pregnant."

"Yeah, I heard about it so asked her if it was true, and she said it was. Good thing she's planning to do something about it soon. The last thing she needs is a bratty kid running around," remarked the fourth girl.

Sarah stopped walking, her blood boiling.

The girls ahead kept walking, oblivious that Sarah had been listening, their conversation lost in the noisy hallway.

She had half a mind to go and tell those girls off, the protective instinct surfacing in spite of all the horrible things Maria had done to her over the years. Those girls were supposed to be Maria's friends and that's how they were treating her behind her back? And Nick was telling the rest of the school about his "accomplishment" at Maria's expense?

The anger gave way to compassion and she couldn't wait to get home. She had to spend some time in prayer and get some direction from God for how to help Maria, and soon.

***

Sarah got off the bus and hurried up the driveway. Her mom came around the corner of the kitchen as Sarah came through the front door and bounded up the stairs.

"You're in a hurry," Stephanie noted.

"Hi, Mom." Sarah was breathless. "I want to get out to the stable as soon as I can. I need to pray for Maria for a while."

"Okay, sweetie," her mom called after her. She knew that Sarah's sanctuary was in the stable and that she would find peace spending time there. "Your dad is still at work and Jordan is at practice. I have to run to the grocery store to get everything I need for Thanksgiving and I'm making a meal for Maria for tomorrow, but I'll be back in time to make dinner."

Sarah stopped at the top of the stairs. "Okay, Mom. I'll make sure to lock the house up when I go to the stable and bring my key so I can get back in. What's for dinner?"

"I thought I would bring home a couple of rotisserie chickens."

"Sounds good." Sarah's stomach rumbled already just thinking about the savory chicken so she figured she better bring a granola bar to the stable to hold her over.

As the car rolled backward down the driveway, Sarah waved to her mom and headed to the kitchen.

Grabbing a water bottle and a chocolate chip granola bar, she headed out to the stable, fingering the key in her pocket before locking the back door behind her. She had brought her study Bible to read as well.

She opened the stable door and was greeted by the familiar scents and sounds of Shadow nickering to her from his stall. She put her Bible and snack down on a hay bale and let Shadow out into the paddock to get some much needed exercise while she mucked out his stall, all the while humming to herself or praying quietly.

After laying down a fresh layer of bedding in the stall, she found Shadow at the paddock gate, beckoning to her by shaking his big head up and down and snorting.

Sarah set down the rake she had been using and stepped over to the large animal, wrapping her arms around his neck and resting her face against his silky neck. He playfully nipped at the back of her sweater. "Oh, I know what you want." She leaned over to a basket of red and green apples sitting on a crate nearby and grabbed a green one, holding it up for Shadow, who took the whole thing in his mouth and chomped on it happily.

Sarah smiled and stroked the length of his long face before she sat down on a hay bale and leaned back to spend some time in prayer. Her heart was heavy for Maria and Andrea; and in spite of the recent miracle at the school, she wondered how God was going to break through in these situations.

Figuring that she would take Shadow out on a quick ride after she prayed, Sarah bridled and saddled Shadow, firmly tightening the girth under Shadow's belly again after a few minutes. As she did all this she asked God to give her wisdom, direction, faith...something.

Suddenly it was like light illuminated her left knee and memories of that first miracle flooded back to her along with the childlike faith she had possessed at that time. God spoke to her heart.

Just believe and you will receive what you ask for. Ask in faith, nothing wavering.

Just believe; so simple, yet sometimes so hard to do. With a renewed faith welling up inside her, she did just that; she asked God to bring a breakthrough: For Maria to keep the baby, for Amanda's divine healing, and for their family's friendship to be restored.

After a few minutes her cell phone rang, startling her. She looked at the number. It was a local one but not a number she had saved in her contact list.

"Hello?"

"Sarah, hey, this is Colton. Sorry to bother you, I got your number from my dad. Listen, I think something is seriously wrong with that girl, the one from my visions...Maria, is it?"

Sarah perked up. "Yeah, that's Maria. What are you seeing now?" Worry creased her forehead.

"I fell asleep after school 'cause I stayed up too late last night, and I had this dream. Maria was lying on a bed and crying. She was saying, 'It's too late! It's too late!'" Colton paused. "I have this feeling that something is getting ready to happen, and that you need to find her *right now.*"

Sarah's mind raced. It was a thirty minute walk to Maria's house and she was in no shape to run there. Her parents were both gone along with the cars. It hadn't been long since her mom left and she could be gone another hour or more. How would she get there fast enough?

"Are you there? Sarah?" Colton's voice was urgent.

"I'm here, just trying to figure out how to get there quickly."

"Well, however you do it, just get there fast. I don't want anything bad to happen to her." Colton paused a second. "I mean, it seems like bad things are already happening to her, but it doesn't have to be worse."

It sounded like Colton was concerned about Maria. He had never met her, just seen her in these visions and dreams. "I'll figure something out. Thanks, Colton." She hung up.

Sarah glanced at Shadow. She had already saddled him. Riding him on the street would be risky—he was not accustomed to traffic and could get spooked. Perhaps she could stick to riding through yards, but there might be fences, and people wouldn't like hoof prints in their grass. On horseback she could get to Maria's house in just a few minutes. She would need to keep a slower pace so his hooves wouldn't slip on pavement or driveways, but it would still be much quicker than trying to run all the way there.

There was no other option. She grabbed Shadow's reins and led him out of the stable to mount, lifting her left foot into the stirrup and swinging her right leg over his broad back.

"Come on, boy, were taking a different trail today." Adrenaline rushed through her body. The urgency in Colton's voice concerned her.

Sarah guided Shadow around the front of the house and his ears pivoted, listening to the different sounds coming from the road, something he wasn't very accustomed to.

Giving a little kick to the large horse's flanks, she coaxed him into a trot and then a canter. She kept to the soft grass beside the sidewalk as much as possible, taking note of the clip-clopping sound mixed with the thuds of his hooves going through yard to yard and crossing driveways along the way. It was hard to ignore the stares and pointing fingers from those passing by and people arriving home from work. Nobody expected to see someone riding a horse down the street!

They turned around a corner and noticed a row of mid-thigh height bushes that went all the way to the sidewalk coming up fast. There wasn't time to slow down and angle Shadow onto the sidewalk. She had trained Shadow to jump small obstacles, but it had been a while since they had practiced. She counted the strides, just like they had done before: one...two...three...squeeze and jump.

Shadow swiveled his ears back, listening to her voice and responded by clearing the bushes. He did it!

Sarah patted his neck and slowed him down to a trot again to move further right to the sidewalk to avoid a tall fence coming up two yards down. Just another turn at the fourth street and they would be at Maria's apartment building.

As they rounded the corner and the building came into view, Sarah spotted Maria walking from her building and heading toward a waiting car, shoulders slumped. She recognized the driver as a girl named Leah from school.

She called out, "Maria, wait!"

Maria stopped, having just reached her car and her mouth gaped open at the sight of Sarah approaching on horseback. "Whaa..?"

Sarah slowed the animal down and slid down from the saddle a few feet away from Maria. Keeping the reins in one hand, she came closer to Maria. "Maria, please don't do what you are about to do."

Maria bit her lip and looked at the car as though considering jumping into it and leaving. Then she turned to Sarah with a sneer. "How do you know what I am about to do? You think you know so much. What's wrong with me going...to visit my mom at the hospital?"

"That's not where you were going and you know it."

Maria took a step back, her arms crossed over herself. "And where do you think I was going, huh?"

"To get rid of the baby." Sarah look at her, unblinking. "Maria, please don't do it. It's a human life, not just a mass of tissue like they try to tell you."

Just then the driver rolled the window down, "Are you coming or not, Maria? I don't have all day!"

"Just give me a second, Leah!" Maria's brows furrowed and she took a step back toward the car. "I already made the decision, Sarah.

I can't live like this. My mom is barely alive, and I can't have a baby while I'm in school. I have no family other than my mom…"

Maria's voice trailed off. Her hands were trembling now and she could see tears brimming in Maria's eyes as she continued, "You don't know what it's like to see your mom so drugged up that she doesn't even know you're there…to know she'll never hug you again…"

Maria's whole body shook as she stepped forward, pointing at Sarah with tears streaming down her face. "You don't know what it's like to know that you'll never hear your mom tell you that she loves you ever again."

Maria's voice escalated as the pain she had kept locked inside broke open like a flood. "Can't you see? I don't want to spend the last part of my mom's life throwing up in the bathroom or worrying about how I'm going to take care of a baby and go to college. It's easy for you to say I should have the baby. You're not the one going through all of this...hell on earth!" Maria was practically screaming now, getting the attention of every other passerby in the parking lot and causing Shadow to paw the pavement nervously.

Leah, however, didn't seem to care about what was going on with Maria and was checking her makeup in the rearview mirror.

"Just go away! This is the only way to at least fix one part of my screwed up life, can't you see that?" Maria angrily dug into her purse in search of some tissues as the tears continued to come. She took another step closer to the car.

Sarah lifted up a quick prayer, *What should I do, Lord?*

Love her, came the quick reply.

Without another moment, Sarah obeyed. She stepped up to Maria and folded the broken girl in her arms. She rubbed her back and whispered in motherly tones, "It's gonna be okay. We're here for you...I'm here for you."

At first Maria stiffened, but after a few moments she dissolved into sobs in Sarah's arms, her shoulders heaving as she cried in her anguish.

With a huff, Leah rolled her window back up and drove off, shaking her head.

Sarah breathed a prayer of thanks and closed her eyes, her own tears of joy making their way down her face. What a sight it must have been, two girls hugging and crying in a parking lot with a horse standing nearby! Sarah was still holding the reins, but allowed some distance so Shadow wasn't standing directly next to them. This didn't seem to matter to Shadow.

After a few minutes he came close, nuzzling both Sarah and Maria with his soft, velvety nose while noisily mouthing the metal bit in his mouth. He was always trying to comfort Sarah when she was sad; now he was comforting Maria too.

Maria sniffed and wiped the tears from her eyes, smudging her makeup, but not caring. She looked up at the large horse. "Is that Shadow? I remember when you first got him. We used to spend hours in the stable." Her voice had lost all its animosity.

"Yeah, it's Shadow." Sarah stroked his neck. He gave a little snort in response, and reached his big neck over to Maria. He remembered her too!

Maria giggled as Shadow lipped at her ear, the little hairs on his muzzle tickling her neck and leaving some horse slobber behind.

"Ewwww! You need a big tissue, Shadow!" Maria laughed while wiping her neck with her sleeve, then reached to pet him again. "He used to do that to me all the time when we were little."

Her voice had a different sound to it now—more like the Maria that Sarah had grown up with. She watched in amazement as God used Shadow to help heal Maria's heart.

Sarah grasped Maria's hand. "Maria, I want to help you with the baby. You don't have to feel alone. In fact, my mom said she can be available to take care of the baby while you are in classes once he or she is born."

Relief and gratitude washed over Maria's face. She looked down and shook her head, the tears coming again. "I don't deserve a friend like you, Sarah. After all I did to you, after everything I said to you, you still care…I know I was horrible to you…" Maria's voice broke into a sob. "Will you please forgive me?"

Joy welled up in Sarah's heart. "Of course I will." They hugged again, and for the first time in a long time, Sarah saw hope in Maria's eyes.

Maria reached into her purse and pulled out a small tissue bag, giving the first few to Sarah and another for herself. "Here. I know I must look like a mess."

"Thanks. And you look fine, just a bit of mascara under your eyes." After Maria wiped her eyes and nose, Sarah took one of her clean tissues and dabbed under Maria's right eye to get a spot she missed.

Maria chuckled. "Now that's a sign of a true friend. Some of my 'friends' at school let me walk around like a dork with stuff on my face all day."

She sobered and looked down, then back up at Sarah. "I really didn't want to...you know...get rid of the baby. Everyone around me has been telling me what I needed to do so I could have a 'great life.' I was so afraid to tell my mom. I didn't want her to be ashamed of me in the last few days of her life." Maria swallowed. "I still am not sure if I should tell her right now. She may...she may be gone before I even start showing. I'm not even sure if she would know what I'm saying… most of the time I wonder if she knows I'm even in the room when I visit her."

"If you put my name down to visit her, I can be there with you if you want to tell her." This was the breakthrough! Maybe now Maria would put all their names down so they could come and pray for Andrea.

Maria nodded, sniffing. "I will. I don't think I can do it until tomorrow though, I have to do that at the administrative office." She looked at the time on her phone quickly, "and they closed at five."

"That's okay. Can you put my mom's name down too, and possibly Nathan and Brad?"

Maria laughed. "Sure, but I think only one person can come in at a time now."

Sarah grabbed Maria's hands. "That's okay. I believe God is going to do something great in your life, and your mom's."

Chapter Twenty-nine

Maria's heels clicked on the tile as she walked down the hospital corridor to her mom's room. She was almost getting used to the sterile smell that greeted her each time she was here. They must have chosen the soft green and cranberry colors for the walls and tiles to try to take the edge off the harsh odors of the medical facility.

Maria had left school halfway through the day, wanting to make sure she had plenty of time to get the new names on the visitation list. The administrative office was always bustling with activity and it was easy to end up waiting a long time there.

Before she headed to the office she wanted to see her mom and tell her about what happened yesterday, even if she couldn't respond. Maria knew there was a long road to go to where she needed to be with school, with friends, and with God, but accepting Sarah back into her life was a start.

She went in the room and noticed that Dr. Marcotte was there checking on her mom, who looked even paler since she saw her yesterday. He looked over to her and smiled as she stepped closer. Her mom looked dazed from the medications she was on, her eyes glassy. She slowly turned her head toward Maria and looked at her, then her eyes drifted to the ceiling. Her breathing was more labored than it was the day before. Maria's heart sunk again, like it did so many times the last few weeks as she watched her mother shrivel into someone she barely recognized.

Maria leaned down and kissed her mom on the cheek with a heavy heart. "Hi, Mom. Hello, Doctor Marcotte."

"Nice to see you again, Maria." He was older and reminded her of how a grandfather would look with his white hair, large nose, and warm smile that crinkled the corners of his eyes. Her own grandparents had passed away when she was young.

Andrea turned her face toward her daughter, her eyes briefly flashing recognition as she tried to smile. Maria was glad she knew she was there.

"I know I'm early." She squeezed her mom's hand. "I needed to get here to put some names on the visitation list at the administrative office. Some friends want to come see you." Maria stroked her mom's arm. "I wanted to see you before I went down to the office, though."

Dr. Marcotte cleared his throat. "Actually, before you do that I need to talk with you. Why don't we sit down?"

He pulled one of the chairs in the room over as Maria sat in the chair by her mom's bed. He spoke softly, with concern. "As you can tell, the cancer has not been responding at all to the treatments; in fact, your mother's condition has gotten worse. By the time we discovered it, the disease had already progressed so far into her body that the chance of recovery was slim, as we said from the beginning."

He paused. "There's really no easy way of saying this, but unfortunately, from a medical standpoint there's no reason to continue giving her treatments that aren't helping. We will make sure she can be as comfortable as possible in the short time that she has left with you, Maria."

Maria wanted to cover her ears to block out what the doctor was saying, but that childish response wouldn't take away the reality of what he was trying to tell her. She blinked hard, fighting the tears that sprang to her eyes and trying to be brave for her mom. She wondered if her mom understood what the doctor was saying, but one look at her mom and the tears already streaming down her mother's pale cheeks confirmed that she had.

A sob escaped Maria's lips as she clapped a hand over her mouth, shaking her head in disbelief.

Dr. Marcotte reached over and placed a hand on Maria's arm in condolence. "I'm so sorry, Maria."

His soft concern just made the tears flow faster.

After a few moments he patted her arm and continued. "Maria, because you are eighteen and the closest family member listed to Andrea, you are her power of attorney in this situation. She's not in any condition now to make decisions for herself. We know a cold hospital room is not the most pleasant of environments, so we want to give you and your mother a few options. Either we can have her set up at a facility that will care for her around the clock, like a nursing home, or there is the option for her to go home and have a more comfortable time during the last part of her life. We can have a hospital bed delivered and have an ambulance bring her home, as well as set up hospice nurses to be there when you need help taking care of her."

Maria whispered, her voice quavering, "How long?"

Doctor Marcotte responded gently, "It could be a few days to a few weeks. Time will tell."

Maria looked at her mom, who squeezed her glossed-over eyes shut while she digested the news. "Oh, Momma..." Her voice caught and she felt her mom lightly squeeze her hand.

Andrea opened her eyes and Maria could see a look of pleading. She wanted to go home.

Maria nodded through her tears and turned back to the doctor. "We'll go home," she whispered. She knew that when Sarah and her family learned of it, they would probably help her out too.

Doctor Marcotte rose and placed a hand on Andrea's shoulder. "I'm so sorry, Andrea. You've been a wonderful patient here." Then he turned to Maria and put his hand on her arm. "We can rush the paperwork along and have a hospital liaison come within an hour or so to talk to you both about all the details. We can have you home by five o'clock tonight."

He crossed to the door and stopped with his hand on the knob. "If you have relatives or friends who can help out or who may want to see her while she is still alive, you may want to give them a call." Then he pulled the door shut after he left to give them time to take in everything they had just heard.

"Are you sure this is what you want to do, Mom?" Maria asked through her tears.

Andrea nodded slightly and a smile tugged at the corners of her mouth, a look of relief crossing her face before she closed her eyes to sleep.

***

Maria tapped the screen of her phone and found Sarah's number. She was so glad that they had exchanged numbers after they had reconciled their friendship. She paced the shiny tiled floor of the waiting room, waiting for Sarah to pick up.

"Hi there, Maria!" Sarah's cheery voice came over the line and Maria inwardly thanked God again for giving such a great friend back to her.

"Hey, Sarah." Maria had been crying all afternoon since the doctor had given them the news. There had been papers to sign, family and her mom's close friends to call, her mother's belongings to pack, and meetings with people telling them what would be happening next. Everything had been so emotional that she was already spent, but she wanted to let Sarah know they were going home.

"Are you okay?" It was amazing that after this many years Sarah could still tell something was wrong just by the sound of her voice.

"No, I'm not," she admitted openly, stifling a sob. Maria took a moment to compose herself, and Sarah waited patiently for her to continue. When she did speak again it was strained past the lump in her throat. "They said they aren't going to treat the cancer anymore… they're just going to make her comfortable now. They're sending her home…today."

"Oh, Maria! I'm so sorry. I wish I were there for you right now… does your mom understand what's happening? I know you said she's not really with it from the medicine they are giving her and all."

Maria dropped into a maroon padded waiting-room chair with her elbows on her knees and pressed the phone to her ear. "Yeah, she knows. I can tell she's scared though. She hardly wants to let go of my hand unless she's sleeping. I mean, who wouldn't be scared—knowing they could die any day?" Maria choked up again.

Sarah waited a moment. "I asked my mom what the church could do to help you guys out and she said there is a whole group of ladies who help people out in situations like yours. They come and clean, drop off food, and they can sit with your mom while you're at school or if there are things you need to do. She said they can read the Bible and pray with her, or just be close by if she needs something. I'm sure they would do that at your house too."

"Is that who's been leaving food at my apartment every night the last few days?"

"Yeah, we thought if you knew who it was coming from, you wouldn't take it, so we let it be anonymous. But now that you know… hope the food was good."

"I can't eat a lot right now, but what I tried was really good. There's still a ton of leftovers in the fridge."

"Well, they can still bring food and help out too. I am going to come over as much as you will let me. And I know my mom will help a lot. She loves to do things for other people."

"That would be great, Sarah. Thank you." She sniffed and grabbed the tissue box that was sitting on the coffee table in front of her and blew her nose. "Now that Mom won't be in the hospital anymore, I was thinking maybe tomorrow you guys could come by to visit, like you and the others who pray for people. I know it's the day before Thanksgiving, but if there's really a chance…."

"Sure, what time do you want us to be there?" Maria could hear the excitement in Sarah's voice.

"Um, how about one o'clock?"

"Perfect. We'll be there." Sarah paused. "Maria, I've been praying for your mom ever since I heard she was sick, and I just have this feeling that God is going to do something great tomorrow."

Hope wanted to spring up into Maria's heart, and she truly wanted it to come, but so many years of disappointment and broken promises had hardened her. Subconsciously she stuffed the hope back down and replied, "I hope you're right, Sarah."

***

The doorbell rang and Sarah rushed to the door to greet Pastor Jake, Charlotte, and Colton. Both Brad and Nathan were already at her house. After getting the call from Maria this afternoon about her mom coming home from the hospital, she thought a prayer meeting would be a good idea. Arriving at Maria's house tomorrow by one o'clock would give them time to talk, pray, and visit. Maria had agreed that Pastor Jake, Colton, Nathan, and Brad could come over as well, so Sarah had called everyone up and asked them to come over after dinner.

Leading the Martins to the family room where everyone was gathered, Sarah sat down and glanced around the room while everyone greeted the newcomers. Her eyes rested on Nathan, and they shared a smile.

Pastor Jake and Charlotte sat down in an overstuffed green microfiber love seat and spoke, "The other day we prayed for a breakthrough and it looks like we got one."

Brad asked, "Isn't Andrea's condition worse? That's what I thought Sarah said on the phone."

"Her condition might be worse, but now we have access to visit her without anyone interfering to say how we can pray or what we can or can't do. I truly believe this is a breakthrough."

"Okay, I see what you're saying now."

Pastor Jake spoke again, "I want to share something before we pray. It's something that I have been studying lately that has totally revolutionized how I pray. If you have a Bible app on your phone, let's look at Hebrews 4:14-16. I'm going to read it in the New Living Translation."

He paused for a few moments, allowing them to get their apps opened to Hebrews 4 before he started reading.

"So then, since we have a great High Priest who has entered heaven, Jesus the Son of God, let us hold firmly to what we believe. This High Priest of ours understands our weaknesses, for he faced all of the same testings we do, yet he did not sin. So let us come boldly to the throne of our gracious God. There we will receive his mercy, and we will find grace to help us when we need it most."

When he finished, they all looked up at Pastor Jake. His eyes danced with excitement. "I know you have probably read that before. I think I read it a thousand times before God illuminated what it truly means. I grew up in a Christian home, like all of you have, and I'm so grateful for that. But recently I began to see that how we did things in my home was based on Old Testament ways, instead of the New Testament, or new covenant patterns that Jesus taught."

Sarah was confused. Nobody she knew was practicing animal sacrifices or keeping Jewish customs, except maybe a few people from school whom she knew were Jewish—one girl at school had had a Bat Mitzvah party when she had turned thirteen.

Pastor Jake seemed to register the confused looks on the younger faces. "Okay, let me explain. In the Old Testament, people had to follow a long list of rules and guidelines and they had to do certain things after they sinned to have it atoned for. Except they couldn't do those things themselves—they had to go to the priest, who performed certain sacrifices and rituals. But the only one who was allowed to enter the place in the tabernacle or temple where God's presence dwelled was the High Priest. He would go in once a year to the most Holy Place and put blood on the mercy seat of the ark of the covenant to atone for the sins of all the people of Israel. He was like a mediator, speaking to God on behalf of the people. Through a long process, they were right with God, until the next time they sinned." He looked at them in the eyes. "You follow me so far?"

They all nodded their heads, not sure why they were getting a lesson in Old Testament rituals when he was talking about prayer.

"Probably made them think twice before they did something they shouldn't." Brad smirked, and they all chuckled at his comment.

Pastor Jake scooted forward a bit in his chair, his enthusiasm evident on his face. "So when Jesus came and died, *He* became the final sacrifice. He put His own blood on the mercy seat. The veil in the temple was ripped, indicating we no longer need to go through a human priest to come before God; we can go directly to Jesus! Now the Bible tells us that Jesus is our High Priest at the right hand of the Father in heaven, acting as a spokesperson for us. When we pray and ask God for forgiveness or help, Jesus is there speaking to God, reminding Him that our sins are covered by His blood, and presenting our needs before the Father. Now look at Hebrews 4:16 again."

Sarah looked down at her phone and touched the screen to undim it, reading the verse again while Pastor Jake read it aloud.

"So let us come boldly to the throne of our gracious God. There we will receive his mercy, and we will find grace to help us when we need it most." They looked up as he explained, "The Greek word there for *boldly* really came from the idea of standing in a public presentation without having shame on your face. It really means having full confidence that you should be there. Sometimes when we pray, well, I don't know about you, but sometimes when I prayed in the past, there was this feeling of begging, pleading, hoping that God would maybe answer, if I was good enough or had done enough praying or pleading. It wasn't with confidence. It was still that Old Testament 'if I'm good enough, if I've done the right things, maybe...possibly God would answer my prayers' type of thinking."

Nathan spoke up, "Sometimes I feel like that when I pray, like I'm not really sure if God heard me for one reason or another, so I start begging Him to do something."

Pastor Jake replied, "I think we've all done it before. I know this was how I lived for a long time. But then God started illumining how much He loves me, and how I am not just a slave or servant, I am His son; He sees us as sons and daughters, His children. How many times have you messed up and your parents still love you, still open their home to let you live there free of charge, and still give you the things you ask for?"

He let that sink in for a bit. Nathan was the first one to answer.

"Wow, when you put it like that, it makes it real. If God loves me more than my parents do, and they love me so much in spite of all the problems I've given them..." he shook his head. "He must *really* love me!"

"So when we pray, we are supposed to go to Him with *full confidence* to get what we need, knowing that He loves us and He wants to help us. Sometimes He wants us to *expect* Him to answer. James chapter one says that a person who doubts shouldn't expect to receive anything from the Lord."

He took a breath. "The enemy has been trying and succeeding for centuries to get God's people to believe that God doesn't really want to help them. From what we read and talked about today, God *wants* to help us when we need it most. And tomorrow we are going to need Him most. Sarah shared with me what the doctors told Maria—her mom might only have a few days left to live."

Sarah hadn't shared this with Nathan and Brad; she had only said they let Andrea go home and she didn't have much time left. She could see that the guys were taken aback with this news. There wasn't much time at all.

"So let's pray for tomorrow." Pastor Jake and Charlotte stood and reached their hands out to either side. The others followed and they formed a small circle with their hands clasped together.

Pastor Jake closed his eyes and tilted his face toward heaven. "Father God, we're here today as Your children, not as slaves or servants begging. Thank You that You sent Jesus to be our High Priest, to make the way open for us to come to You. Lord, we have a really big need and we know Your Word says that You want to help us with it. Tomorrow as we go to pray for Andrea Romano, we are asking for her healing. You love her so much; help us to show her Your love and heal her body so she can spend the rest of her life loving and serving You."

They stood silently for several moments, each of them saying their own prayers and touching the Father's heart on behalf of Andrea and Maria. Sarah could feel the presence of the Lord filling the room.

Suddenly Colton gasped.

"I see His face," he said barely above a whisper. "He's right in the middle of us, and He's smiling...He's so beautiful..."

Sarah looked over at Colton and saw tears streaming down his cheeks, his eyes wide open at the image that only he was seeing right now.

For several minutes they just stayed in that position, enjoying the moment. Colton kept his eyes open, examining the image in front of him that the rest could not see. After a while he closed his eyes and said, "That was awesome."

Brad cleared his throat quietly. "Pastor Jake, this is kinda weird, but...I feel like I'm supposed to bring my guitar tomorrow, and we're supposed to worship."

Pastor Jake nodded. "That's fine, Brad." They all sensed that the prayer time was ending so they released each other's hands.

"No...I keep feeling like that's the *only* thing were supposed to do...just worship. I get the feeling that God wants to just touch her by Himself as we worship."

Pastor Jake nodded again, more slowly this time. "That's... different, but if that's what you are feeling God is saying for us to do, then I guess we need to do it His way."

Sarah had grown to appreciate Brad's sense of direction when it came to spiritual things. He had a gift of discernment that was growing stronger and stronger. Pastor Jake must have noticed it too.

Sarah looked down at her phone; it was already past nine.

Before everyone left Sarah's house, they made plans for the Martins to pick everyone up in Charlotte's minivan on the way to Maria's house. Since tomorrow was a half day of school, they'd be picked up around noon. Sarah secretly wanted to sneak in a good-bye kiss, but since Nathan was being dropped off by the Martins, the opportunity evaporated.

As she hugged him good-bye, they embraced each other for a bit longer than usual as the others were walking to the car.

It must have been longer than she realized because Colton called out from where he stood next to the car, "Come on, Lover Boy. Time to go!"

They parted abruptly and she noticed Nathan's cheeks were flushed beneath his ear-to-ear grin as he slowly walked backward. "See you tomorrow, Sarah."

"See you tomorrow." She waved as they drove away and crossed her arms in front of her, pulling her sweater closer around her in the crisp night air.

Puffs of vapor rose up above her as she stood there, still feeling the presence of God and the excitement about what He was getting ready to do—what she now understood that He wanted to do. She couldn't wait until tomorrow!

Chapter Thirty

Sarah grasped the handles of the pot that held a savory stew her mom had made to bring to Maria's house. Stephanie had wanted to come with them, but was busy with tomorrow's Thanksgiving Day preparations. As cold as it was outside, the steam rising from the heavy pot felt good as they walked up the sidewalk to the Romanos' apartment building.

Maria greeted them warmly, giving Sarah a half-hug so as not to spill the food she was holding.

"Maria, do you remember Pastor Jake Martin and his wife, Charlotte? And this is their son, Colton."

Pastor Jake grasped her hand with both of his. "It's so good to see you again, Maria.

"You look so grown-up now, Maria. What a beautiful young lady you've become!" We've been praying for you and your mom." Charlotte said as she hugged Maria.

"Thank you, I think I remember you guys," Maria replied. She turned to Colton and shyly stuck out her hand. "Nice to meet you."

Colton shook her hand and replied back with a smile, "Nice to meet you too...finally." His gaze never left her face.

Realization dawned on Sarah. This was the first time Colton was meeting Maria face-to-face. Before he had only seen visions of her distressed, screaming, and crying.

"Finally?" Maria asked. "What do you mean?"

Sarah interjected, "Do you remember when I told you that someone had a dream about you..." she lowered her voice to a whisper and leaned in, "and the baby? This is the one. This is Colton."

"Oh, now I see." Chuckling a bit, she remarked without thinking, "So I'm the girl of your dreams, huh?" Then she immediately realized what she said and straightened, her face flushed. "I'm sorry; that was just a joke. I didn't mean for it to come out that way."

Colton's cheeks took on a pinkish tone of their own as he said with a grin, "That's okay."

The Romanos' apartment had the standard tan carpet and white walls, but Andrea had decorated it with a very clean modern look. The prints on the walls were abstract and there were a few black and white candid pictures of Andrea and Maria, surrounded by sleek black frames.

Nathan and Brad followed Sarah into the apartment with grocery bags containing a full array of paper products and plasticware so there would be no dishes to clean, along with grape juice and sodas, apple pie, and warm, yeasty dinner rolls. There was even some savory broth for Andrea because she could only handle a few spoonfuls of liquid at a time. They set everything down on the glass-topped kitchen table. The aroma was tantalizing.

The living room contained a plain-looking red sectional on one side. On the other side was the hospital bed that Andrea was lying on covered up with a warm, fuzzy blanket. Her head was tilted back, mouth hanging open. Her skin looked pale and her eyes were glossed over and a bit sunken.

Andrea's head rolled to the side and she closed her mouth as Sarah approached and gently embraced her, saying, "Hi, Mrs. Romano. It seems like forever since I've seen you. Thanks for letting us come." She held onto Andrea's hand as she drew back.

Andrea's mouth curved upward slightly and she lightly squeezed Sarah's hand in response. Then her gaze went to the others behind her. Sarah looked over her shoulder, saying, "Do you remember Pastor Jake and Charlotte Martin? They came too."

The pastor and his wife stepped forward and traded places with Sarah. Charlotte carefully grasped Andrea's hand and made introductions. "It's great to see you, Andrea. This is our son, Colton, and you might remember the Stone family from when you used to come to church. This is their son, Nathan. And this is Brad Williams; his family is a bit newer to the church." She motioned toward each person as she introduced them.

Andrea blinked slowly and continued to smile. Sarah couldn't tell if she really recognized them or not. It was sad to see Andrea in such a state. She remembered her as a vivacious woman who loved life.

Pastor Jake placed a hand on Andrea's shoulder. "Sarah's mom, Stephanie, made a wonderful lunch for all of us, including a nice broth for you if you're hungry. Stephanie says she loves you and is praying for you."

Andrea's eyes misted, and Maria stepped forward. "That's so sweet of her. I'm afraid she won't be able to eat very much, but we appreciate it so much. Mom, I can get you some broth."

Maria kissed her mom on the forehead before going to the kitchen to retrieve the broth. While everyone else got their food, she returned and sat next to Andrea to spoon-feed a few teaspoons of the savory liquid into her mother's mouth until she couldn't take any more, then she fixed herself a plate.

With everyone's plates full, they sat in various parts of the living room on the sectional or chairs they had pulled in from the kitchen. In between bites, Pastor Jake and Charlotte asked Maria questions about school and other things, keeping the topics light.

After everyone had eaten and cleaned up, putting any leftover food away in the refrigerator, Pastor Jake clapped his hands lightly, grasping them together. "Last night we spent some time praying about our time here today. We had intended to come and pray, but God gave us a different direction. He told us to just spend some time in worship while we are here, so Brad here is going to go get his guitar," he said while nodding in Brad's direction, "and we're going to sing."

Sarah looked over at Maria and could see disappointment written on her face. Pastor Jake must have seen it too because he explained, "Sometimes God asks us to do things that don't really make sense, and it's a test of our obedience, just like when He tested Abraham and asked him to sacrifice his son, Isaac. God didn't want Abraham to actually kill his son; He wanted to see if he would do whatever He asked him to do. It may not make sense to just sing when we all know that you are in such desperate need of a miracle, but what worship does is invite God's presence into this place. It doesn't matter the words we say, because when He's here, He can touch someone without anyone praying anything. I've seen it happen time after time in our church over the years, and it can happen today."

Maria nodded and said, "That's fine then. I love to sing anyway."

Brad had returned with the guitar and he sat forward on the edge of the sofa and did a quick tune up before they started. When he was confident the instrument was pretty well in tune he strummed a chord, the rich sound filling the room and already inviting the presence of the Lord.

Brad's tenor voice started out quietly, cautiously, becoming stronger the more they worshiped. They began with a few songs about faith and how nothing is impossible for God, then Brad easily transitioned into a chorus about the beauty of the Lord, and God's presence changed the atmosphere as they worshiped.

***

Colton wasn't totally sure why his dad had insisted that he come with them today. His dad kept telling him that God wanted him to be part of what He was doing with Maria and her family. Of course after meeting Maria face-to-face he didn't mind being here one bit. When they first met she had joked about being the girl of his dreams and quickly apologized, but with her long, dark hair paired with a set of captivating brown eyes, she just might possibly be the girl of his dreams.

Colton never thought love at first sight was possible but he was second-guessing that after meeting Maria. He felt like he couldn't stop staring at her. He'd been stealing glances at her discreetly, but Nathan had caught him looking at her once already and was grinning at the realization.

Now as everyone was singing, he tried to focus on their purpose for being here rather than on Maria. He closed his eyes.

As a child, he had been a big part of the church and asked Jesus into his heart at the age of seven, but since then his faith had waned from living under the scrutiny of people in the church who thought he should act certain ways as the P.K. (preacher's kid), and having every detail about his life open for discussion and correction. As a result, he struggled with being critical of the church and the people in it.

Add that to the visions and dreams he frequently had, and the misunderstandings that he had had with his parents and everyone else—until recently, that is. It was the first vision he had of Maria, and Sarah's confirmation of the validity of what he was seeing, that got his dad's attention to show him that Colton wasn't just making up the stuff he saw. In fact, even though his dad had preached and talked about miracles happening, it wasn't until his dad started seeing them happen right before his eyes that he started acting like they really could, and would, happen.

Colton had no desire to follow in his father's footsteps into any type of ministry, but in the last few weeks he was being drawn back to God in a way that he didn't even understand.

Brad was now singing about heaven and the beauty of Jesus.

Colton furrowed his brows, even though his eyes were still shut. Why would Brad be singing about heaven around someone who was on their deathbed when they were supposed to be praying for their healing? At first it didn't sit right with Colton, but as the song progressed he could feel something descending into the room. It was like breathing in the greatest excitement he had ever felt, covering him like a blanket.

Suddenly he had the feeling that he was being watched, but not in a creepy way. Someone was looking right at him and he had an overwhelming urge to open his eyes. Slowly he cracked one eyelid open, and then opened both eyes wide.

There, directly in front of him, was Jesus. There was a misty golden aura surrounding Him. He was larger than life-size and it seemed like he was floating, visible from the waist up, as though the bottom part of Him was under the floor. His dark hair fluttered as though a breeze was gently blowing, even though there was no air movement in the room. Tiny golden beads seemed to emanate from every part of Him and dissipate as they got further away. There was a gentle smile on Jesus' face, but what really captured Colton was the love that was flowing from His eyes directly into Colton's heart.

"I see Him again," Colton whispered.

Pastor Jake opened his eyes and looked over at his son, realizing that Colton was seeing another open vision. "What do you see, son?"

"It's Jesus. He's right in front of me. He's looking right into my heart...putting love in it. He's beautiful." It wasn't a word Colton used often but it was the only word he could use to describe Jesus as the vision continued in front of him.

Colton watched as Jesus slowly turned toward each person in the room, beams of love coming from His eyes, twisting gently through the air and filling each person's heart one by one as the music continued.

"He's looking at each of us and putting love into our hearts. It's like there's beams going from His eyes into each person...it's so cool," Colton said, trying to explain the amazing sight.

Brad slowly fingered a riff on the guitar and strummed a mellow chord before singing spontaneously, his smooth tenor voice filling the room. "I saw the Lord. I saw Jesus' face, and He loves me, yes, He loves me." He gained momentum with the guitar chords and repeated the lines again. "I saw the Lord. I saw Jesus' face, and He loves me, yes, He loves me."

As he repeated the short song over a few more times, they all joined in, Maria adding a beautiful harmony to the simple chorus.

Colton didn't know she could sing like that; of course, he didn't know much about her at all, yet. Brad drifted into a series of anointed, drawn out vocal sounds, spontaneous and free, and perfectly synchronized with the guitar. The rest hummed softly or just basked in the beauty of the moment.

Colton kept watching the scene in the center of the room.

The last person Jesus turned to was Andrea. Jesus reached out His hand and touched one finger over her heart so that his finger and the beams of love intersected.

Being the only person with their eyes open, Colton saw her body give a slight jump at that very moment and tears began to stream down from her tightly shut eyes.

In one sweeping motion, Jesus turned back to Colton and a wide smile broke out over His face before the image totally dissipated into tiny golden beads and disappeared.

Colton blinked several times, ensuring himself that the vision was over, and looked around the room. Brad continued to worship in his own way, eyes closed, voice rolling out a smooth melody to God. Nathan was on his knees in a corner, arms raised, face turned upward. Pastor Jake sat on the couch, head down in prayer. Charlotte sat next to him, her hands clutching each other over her heart, lost in worship. Sarah had moved by Maria and the two recently reunited friends were holding on to each other on the floor next to Andrea's bed, who still had tears coming down her face.

Colton closed his eyes again, enjoying the feel of the moment. The heavy presence had lifted when the image of Jesus left, leaving a warm, comfortable atmosphere in its place. It was so different from the feeling of a demonic manifestation.

He could stay in this type of presence all day long.

Suddenly someone's cell phone rang and Brad stopped playing abruptly. "Oh, man. Sorry, guys, I guess I forgot to put mine on silent," he said softly with an apologetic look. He grabbed his phone and looked at the screen. "I better take this; it's my dad. He wouldn't call unless it's important." Brad held the guitar neck with one hand and lifted it over his head, twisting his shoulders and head to get the strap off in one motion and jogged to the next room after gently putting the guitar down.

Charlotte looked over at Maria and Sarah on the floor, then her attention turned to Andrea and her head tilted in wonder. "Well, hello there!"

They all turned their attention to Andrea.

Colton wasn't sure if it was just him or if her eyes didn't look quite as sunken as they had when they first came in. Her cheeks were a little pink, and her eyes, still full of tears, looked coherent, like she knew what was happening. He wondered what she had felt when Jesus touched her. He didn't have to wait long to find out.

Andrea opened her mouth as though she were trying to speak. "I felt something…" She rasped and closed her eyes again.

Maria gasped and stood up, grabbed her mom's hand, and said, "I haven't heard her say anything for weeks!" She turned to her mom. "What did you feel, Mom?" she asked gently. Colton could hear both emotion and expectation in her voice.

Andrea swallowed, opened her eyes, and gestured toward Colton. "I felt…the love." Quiet sobs shook her shoulders and she closed her eyes again. Whatever happened had touched her deeply. They were all amazed that she was speaking.

Sarah stood and hugged Maria. "I told you God was going to do something amazing!" They cried happy tears together for a few moments.

Brad returned. "Pastor Jake, I really need to get home." He looked around the room. "I'm sorry, guys." Then taking a better look he asked, "Did I miss something?"

Nathan clapped Brad on the back. "Mrs. Romano talked!"

Brad looked over at Andrea who now had her hands raised toward the ceiling, praising God for touching her. "Wow, He did it! That's awesome. Praise the Lord!"

"Yes, God is so amazing; He touched her just like you said you felt He would, while we worshiped," Pastor Jake remarked.

"Wow," was all Brad could say.

Pastor Jake turned to Brad. "If you have to leave soon, we can take you home. I believe God has done what He wanted to do here today," he said, looking at his watch. "Wow, it's already four o'clock! Time flies when you're having fun!"

Colton looked at his own watch to confirm it. They had started worshiping at about two thirty, and it had felt like maybe thirty minutes, not an hour and a half. He looked back over at Andrea in wonder. He had heard about the miracles that had been happening but this was the first time he had witnessed one personally, and definitely the first time he had been part of one.

"No wonder my fingers are a little sore. I didn't realize I was playing that long!" Brad exclaimed, rubbing his hands together.

Sarah mentioned that she could have her mom pick her up later. She wanted to stay for a while longer with Maria and Andrea. No doubt they had a lot to catch up on. Nathan lived within walking distance and said he would be heading home soon.

Colton followed his parents to Andrea's bed to say good-bye. They promised to check in on her soon either by phone or in person. Colton placed his hand gently on her arm. "Jesus does love you, Andrea."

Her eyes connected with his when he touched her and she whispered, "Thank you."

As they headed toward the apartment door, Maria came over to say good-bye to everyone, shaking hands with them before they left. Colton was last to leave the apartment and he held her hand for a second longer than normal, relishing in the feel of her soft skin.

Their eyes locked for a moment, then she looked down. "I'm so glad you came, Colton. It was great to meet you. That was really cool...how you saw Jesus, and how you saw Him touch my mom."

Her excitement faded and she looked embarrassed for a moment. "So, I guess you already know about..." Colton reluctantly dropped her hand; she gently placed her hand on her abdomen where a tiny life was developing, safely tucked away inside of her. She bit her lip and looked back up into his eyes. "I don't understand all this yet...the visions and stuff, but I wanted to tell you I think it's really cool…and my baby is alive because you told Sarah to find me the other day."

Before he knew what was happening, she quickly raised herself up on her tiptoes, leaned in and kissed his cheek, whispering, "Thank you," in his ear before she drew back.

Dazed, Colton murmured, "You're welcome," and stepped out the door backward, watching as she slowly closed the door with a soft click. He didn't move until he heard the lock slide into place a moment later; then he turned to walk to the waiting car.

Colton could still feel the sensation of her soft lips on his cheek and he could tell his face was bright red from the encounter, which was confirmed when he saw the look on his dad's face as he slid into the front seat.

Chapter Thirty-One

One week later

Deanne Campbell hummed to herself as she walked down the brightly lit hallway toward the break room. The soft green walls seemed to welcome her today, dotted with paintings of landscapes in muted colors.

It had been a good day so far; in fact it had been a great week. On Sunday Pastor Jake had told the congregation about how Andrea Romano had been touched by God, so she had been over to see her as quickly as she could. She hadn't been working those last few days before Andrea had gone home. Deanne had taken some vacation time before the holiday, but Rachel had been working, so she had known what poor condition Andrea had been in before she went home.

Deanne was excited because Andrea had called last night and told her she was coming in for a follow-up checkup and a few tests with none other than Dr. Kramer, and was hoping Deanne would be able to be there for her appointment, too, as a support.

Rounding a corner, she saw Andrea heading toward her, a large smile beaming on her face. Her daughter, Maria, was helping her, although she looked like she could walk by herself, even if it were slowly.

"I'm so glad you could work your schedule around to join us, Deanne," Andrea said as Deanne clasped her hands around Andrea's thin ones.

"No problem ladies. I'll get you to where y'all are going, and I know it will be a few hours while you go through the tests they need to do. So I'll check back in with you later before you meet with Dr. Kramer. I'm glad to see Maria could come with you," Deanne remarked in her southern drawl.

"I just got off of school and I can finish my homework while I'm waiting for her tests to get done." Maria looked lovingly at her mom. "I'm just glad she's feeling a whole lot better."

"It's so amazing; isn't God good?" Deanne's eyes danced, still marveling at what God had done for this family already.

They continued together to the outpatient desk and let the receptionist know that Andrea was here for her appointment before settling into the padded waiting room chairs. When Andrea was called back, Deanne excused herself and got back to her shift. She was glad to be busy for the next few hours as it helped the time pass more quickly.

Her shift went by fast and after clocking out for the day, Deanne hurried back down to where she had left Andrea. Maria looked up from a textbook and smiled as she entered the waiting room.

"They said she should be coming back out soon and then we meet with Dr. Kramer," Maria said.

As if on cue, the door opened and Andrea came out on the arm of another nurse. She looked a bit tired from the whole ordeal but the sparkle of joy was still in her eyes.

"Just wait here, Andrea, and the doctor will be with you shortly," the nurse said as she got her seated before turning to leave.

They talked for a while, and eventually a nurse called them back to a room with several chairs and a desk. Within a few minutes Dr. Kramer and Rachel entered the room. They both had a strange look on their faces which Deanne couldn't decipher.

"Hello there, Andrea, Maria…Deanne…" Dr. Kramer looked at her with confusion. "Are you scheduled to work here tonight?"

Andrea spoke up, "Oh, I'm sorry, Dr. Kramer. Deanne is a friend of mine and I asked if she could be here with me today. Is that okay?" she asked with a worried look on her face.

"That's fine," he responded, although Deanne could tell he would probably rather not have her there. At this point, she was there for Andrea and wasn't too concerned about what the doctor wanted.

"Well, I have compared the results from the first test you had several weeks back with today's test results and I have very good news for you, Andrea. I have to say that I have never seen anyone recover as quickly as you did."

Dr. Kramer lowered the charts, set them on the desk, and sat back, his hands interlaced together. "Frankly, we had sent you home because there wasn't anything more we could do for you, and I fully expected that by now you would have passed on. I can't explain it, but it appears that the cancer is gone. Now, there are more results coming back within five to seven days, but I expect those to confirm what I am telling you now."

Deanne looked over at Andrea and saw tears of joy streaming down her cheeks. "It was God, Dr. Kramer. God healed me!" she exclaimed.

Dr. Kramer pulled nervously at his collar. "I'm…um…I'm very happy for you, Andrea. It appears He did," he admitted.

Deanne glanced at Rachel, who still appeared shocked at the news. When Rachel's eyes met Deanne's, she looked away and stood, mumbling an excuse that she had to leave, and exited the room quickly.

Deanne rose, excusing herself as well, and followed Rachel. She spotted her walking briskly down the hall and called out to her. "Rachel!"

Rachel stopped and turned with a look on her face that Deanne had never seen before; her eyes shone with unshed tears, but her face displayed a longing. "I had written that woman off as dead…but there she sits…" she waved her arm in the direction they had just come, "cancer free. I've never seen anything like that before." She looked down, struggling with what she was about to say.

Then looking straight at Deanne, Rachel admitted in a broken voice, "I've been horrible to you, Deanne. I know that. I tried so hard to stop all of you from praying for these people. Now I see that it was what helped Andrea the most. All of our technology and medical expertise couldn't help her…but your God did. Why?"

Deanne placed her hand gently on Rachel's arm and looked her in the eyes. "Because He loves her so much, and He loves you just the same, Rachel."

Rachel blinked, a tiny tear escaping and running down her cheek. She swiped at it and whispered, "Thank you." Then turned to find a quiet place to process her thoughts.

Deanne lifted her eyes, looking in her mind's eye past the ceiling and florescent lights to the heavens above. "Thank you, God!" she said softly.

***

Sarah laughed, watching Nathan trying to make friends with Shadow, who kept stomping and snorting whenever Nathan came close. "He can tell you're afraid of him. If you could get over your fear, then he wouldn't act like that."

She hopped down from where she was sitting on a nearby bale of hay in the stable and walked up to Shadow, talking to the large animal. "He just wants to pet you, big boy."

"Yeah, you make that look easy," Nathan remarked. He turned to face her and rested his elbows on the rail of the next stall over. "So how's Andrea doing? I know you said a few days ago that she was better."

Sarah smiled. "Oh my gosh, you wouldn't believe how much better she looks now. She's actually up and walking around. I don't know if I told you, but after you guys left the day we worshiped in her house, the color in her skin was already coming back. Maria told her about the baby too, and that seemed to give Andrea another reason to live, knowing she's gonna be a grandma. Maria said that her mom wants to feel her belly all the time, but the baby isn't big enough for her to feel it kick yet."

"That's awesome!" Nathan said.

"Do you remember when Colton said he saw Jesus putting love into everyone?" Sarah asked.

"Yeah, I remember that."

She tucked a lock of hair behind her ear. "Andrea said that right at that moment she felt God's power coming into her body; she could feel it working. She also said she gave her heart back to God that day and so did Maria. They have been reading the Bible and singing worship songs together every day."

"Maria can really sing, I heard her the other day when we were there."

"Yeah, I had forgotten about that." Sarah sighed. "It's so good to have her back as a friend."

"So has a doctor seen Andrea yet?" Nathan asked. "What are they saying now?"

"They were going for a follow-up visit to the doctor today, but I haven't heard anything yet. Maria told me that the care specialists can't believe how much better she looks and how much progress she's made.

Sarah sat back down on the hay and Nathan brought his arms down and followed her, sitting on a bale across from her. He rested his hands on his knees and said, "The last few months I have learned so much about faith and miracles."

"I know. Me too. I didn't realize before how much miracles depend on us," Sarah said.

Nathan looked at her quizzically. "What do you mean, depend on us? We can't do them; God does."

"Not the actual miracle, of course; only God can do the supernatural, but it's like His hands are tied if we don't believe that He can do it," she explained.

Nathan tilted his head. "But He's God. He's all powerful. How does our believing or not believing hold back His power?"

"I've really been studying it lately and it's all through the Bible. Do you remember the man who brought his son who was demon possessed to the disciples and they couldn't cast it out?"

Nathan nodded. "The guy ended up taking his son to Jesus, right?"

"Right. It's in Mark 9. The man asks Jesus to help them if He can, and Jesus says to the man that anything is possible if a person believes." She continued, "Then in another place, Jesus tells the disciples that if they just have faith the size of a tiny mustard seed that mountains can be cast into the sea. I don't think He was speaking metaphorically because when Jesus taught, He always used physical things that people could see so they could relate to what He was saying."

"I see what you mean."

Sarah continued, "Then when Jesus went to His hometown, it said that He could hardly do any miracles there because of the people's unbelief. They couldn't believe that the Jesus who grew up there could do such great things. See, it all hinges on what we believe God can do."

She paused and looked down, pulling a few loose straws from the hay bale. Looking up she said, "Ever since I was young, I never really doubted God's power. For some reason I just believed that He could do what I asked Him to do. When I talked to Pastor Jake about it, he said it was an unusual gift, a supernatural faith that God had given me. But the more I think about it, the more I am realizing that *every* believer should have faith. Maybe not always at the same level, but think about it: Jesus saves us, puts His Spirit into us, even gives us authority over sicknesses and demons, and tells us that we have the *same power that He had* and that we can do *even greater* things than He did."

Sarah paused, tilting her head. "So why do we doubt? Why do so many people know all those things but still think, *God won't do that if I ask Him for it?*"

Nathan considered that and seemed lost in his thoughts for a few moments before answering. "I honestly don't know. When you put it that way, it really makes sense."

"Can you imagine what would happen if every Christian would just believe?"

Nathan's eyebrows rose as he considered the implication of that. "We would turn the world upside down!"

"Exactly," Sarah responded.

He got up and sat next to her. "Do you know what I really believe right now?" he said, lacing his fingers with hers.

Sarah looked up into his hazel eyes. "What?" She spoke barely above a whisper.

He lowered his voice as he traced her jawline with his other hand. "I believe you want to kiss me."

"Then you would be right," she said with a smile as their lips met.

Epilogue

Colton opened the door to the sanctuary, light from the hallway giving him a snapshot of the familiar scene before the door shut behind him. Light blue padded chairs were arranged in four sections leading up to an open area in front of the platform, which was a six-sided structure with a few steps that were used for the altar area instead of the railings most churches had. A few pillars and decorative hangings with well-placed backlights made the platform look radiant when it was all lit up. Today everything was dark.

He used to come in here all the time when he was younger just to be alone, scaring his parents a few times when they didn't know where he was and discovered him sitting in the dark at the altar. It was here where he found a reprieve from the demonic visitations. Those evil spirits were not allowed into the church, particularly the sanctuary, by some sort of invisible shield.

Colton ran a hand over his hair and walked down the main aisle, feeling the contours of the chair backs to the left of him as he continued toward the front. He breathed deeply of the scent that still lingered in the air of the new carpeting, a few shades darker than the chairs, that had been installed about six months ago.

Sitting down on a front row chair, Colton sighed.

He wasn't exactly sure why he came today. He had been drawn here. All day at school he felt a tug to come to the sanctuary until finally he asked his mom to drive him here when he got home. He had greeted his dad when he arrived and told him he would be in the sanctuary so he wouldn't lock the building and leave him there alone. His dad seemed surprised but had said it would be fine.

"Well, I'm here," Colton whispered. The sound was magnified in the silence of the large auditorium.

He looked around, not knowing what to expect. When he saw nothing he decided to put his head down and spend some time in prayer.

It hadn't been more than thirty minutes before a bright light pierced through his closed lids. Squinting, Colton slowly opened his eyes, allowing them to adjust to the brightness that now surrounded him.

What filled his vision almost made him drop to the floor.

An angelic being stood facing him, sword in hand. His perfectly chiseled facial features were bracketed by long, golden hair. He wore a belted robe from the waist down, with a brilliant white sash covering one side of his chest, revealing large, hard abdomen and chest muscles, his skin gleaming like burnished bronze. It was like looking at the most amazing warrior he had ever seen.

Colton's flesh wanted to be afraid, wondering if the angel had a sword drawn to hurt him, but his spirit realized that the supernatural being was here for a different purpose. He couldn't speak, couldn't move, just kept gazing at the angel.

A multi-colored radiance beamed across every part of the room from where they were standing, lighting up the entire sanctuary in a prism of color.

The angel spoke in a smooth but strong voice, "Colton, I was sent to give you a message."

Colton wondered if this was a dream or a very vivid vision; sometimes it was hard to tell. His whole body trembled and when he finally got his mouth to work, he asked, "Who are you?"

"My name is Aryeh. I am a commanding officer in the heavenly host. I am here to commission you."

"Commission me? For what?"

"You are appointed to bring light to the darkness. There are many who are trapped by the enemy's power and they do not realize it.

You have been given the ability to see their bondage so you can help bring them out of their darkness and into Yahweh's glorious light. But you are not alone. You must work together with others for success in your mission. You cannot handle the power of the enemy alone; there are some principalities that are much too powerful for you and will destroy you if you try to abolish them by yourself."

As the large angel finished saying these things he held out his sword.

Colton instinctively bowed down on one knee and the angel brought the sword down, blade flat, and barely touched one of his shoulders, then crossed it over his head to tap the other shoulder twice. The places where the sword had touched suddenly felt like they were on fire, flaming at first then a softer burning that worked its way down his chest and moved across his heart.

Colton rested his hands on the floor and closed his eyes as the sensation continued. When he opened them the angel was gone and all was dark again.

After a while Colton rose to his feet and rubbed his shoulders where the sword had touched them; they still burned. He exited the sanctuary and stepped into the men's bathroom.

Flicking on the light, he pulled his shirt down off one of his shoulders and examined the spot; there was a mark there. It was red, but was not a welt. The skin was slightly raised in the shape of the tip of the sword. He quickly looked at the other shoulder to discover the same thing there.

It hadn't been a dream; it was real. And now he had proof.

Note from the Author

I am a firm believer that a story can be fun and exciting and can teach and train the reader at the same time. When I got the inspiration for this series in 2012 and began to write *Believe*, I had just finished reading a well-written historical fiction book. I walked away from that book feeling like I had learned so much about a place and time that I wouldn't have otherwise—but even more, *I felt as though I had experienced it firsthand!* Then I thought to myself, *Why can't we do that with spiritual things?* And the idea for this series was born; stories that teach and train Christians how to recognize and walk in their spiritual gifts.

I love it when the author of a fiction story pulls from real life experiences and historical events and drops them into their narrative. Such is the case with this story; woven into this book are experiences from my own life that I would like to briefly share with you.

Right from the beginning, the miracle that happens in the prologue with fourteen-year-old Sarah was something very similar to what happened to my brother, Matt, in high school. While playing basketball one day he went up to take a shot and came down wrong, causing his knee to dislocate. I remember him telling me that in that moment he quickly prayed and suddenly knew what he had to do to put the kneecap back in place without having any medical training. The doctor asked how he knew to do that and said that he could have suffered a lot of damage to the knee if he hadn't done that right away.

In chapter fourteen, the miracle that happened to the man with spinal meningitis actually happened to my husband, Andy. It was our senior year in college, just a few days away from my graduation, when Andy got a sudden fever that spiked dangerously high, and he told me he needed to get to the hospital. He said he felt like he was dying. I was alarmed and rushed him to the hospital. Once at the ER, the hospital staff put him through all kinds of tests, including a spinal tap, and hooked him up to an IV, trying every way they knew to get his 104.8 degree fever down to no avail. We had as many people praying for him as possible. At about midnight, a blonde nurse came in the room and checked him. He remembers her saying, "Can't get that fever down? Well, we'll take care of that." The next thing he knew, she was wheeling in an industrial fan, and within a short time, his fever broke and was normal. When the other nurses and doctor came in, they asked where the fan came from, saying that type of equipment was not allowed in that area of the hospital. They also asked about the nurse, and when Andy described her, they said there was no nurse who fit that description. Once they confirmed the fever was gone, they released Andy to come home. He felt fine! It wasn't until the next day that they got the test results back and found that he had spinal meningitis and told us that he had to be quarantined for several days until they confirmed it was totally gone. Although he felt fine, he complied. If he didn't come back to the hospital, they said they would have to get law enforcement involved and quarantine the whole college campus. We believe that God sent an angel to come and minister healing in a unique way that night.

In chapter sixteen is a girl who was healed of chronic allergies. This is a condition that I had to deal with for many years. My husband and I were the senior pastors of a church in northwest Indiana when it developed. This was troubling to me because I am a singer and worship leader, and it is very hard to lead worship for an extended amount of time with throat irritation. My doctor told me I would have to take medication every day to control it; and even with the medicine I would sometimes go into coughing fits when trying to lead worship because of the allergies. I had been taking medicine every day for about three years by the time we were at a conference with some friends of ours who are ministers. When I learned that our friend's wife had been healed from many types of allergies, I asked her to pray for me. You see, when God does something in your life, it gives you the faith it takes for someone else to be healed in that same area. Anyway, after that night I told God that I was going to simply believe that He healed me and I stopped taking the medication. To the glory of God, I have not had to take those allergy medications at all since then. He healed me!

In chapter twenty, we meet Colton Martin, who has the ability to see into the spiritual realm. This is a gift that my husband has, but not to the extent that Colton does. I have heard about ministers with an extreme measure of this gift who have a hard time stepping into a hospital because of all the demonic activity they see going on. Also, there was an instance when my husband actually did see a demon sitting on a woman's shoulder, pounding on her head as she cried about how lonely she felt. It's hard for those of us who cannot see these things to believe how much of what we deal with is affected by the spirit realm, but it definitely is. I am not one to believe there is a demon behind every bush, but I do believe that angels and demons are real and have an impact on our lives. I also believe that prayer and living righteously can help protect us from evil invisible forces.

In chapter twenty-two, there is the healing of the little boy from the blood disorder. This actually happened to my husband. At the age of two he was diagnosed with a rare blood disorder that would have taken his life. Three other children had the same blood disorder that year in Indiana, and all three of the other children died. At the time, doctors didn't know how to treat it other than injecting the patients with steroids to try to combat it. He was black and blue all over, so the police questioned his parents, thinking that Andy was being abused; they had to show the authorities the doctors' reports and records to prove they weren't beating him. One Sunday they went to church as usual, and the pastor (who didn't even believe that miracles still happened) called them up and laid his hands on Andy's little body. He prayed a very simple prayer, similar to the one Sarah prayed, and within two weeks Andy was totally healed! He still has the doctor's report stating that no further treatment was needed.

Our family traveled full time for four years around all over the U.S. We saw God's power in many ways and forms. Our experience grants us many stories of healing and restoration that we can pull from and which empower our faith.

Although you may not be able to travel and minister like we did, you have a whole world of needy people around you when you step out your front door. If you have faith that God can heal people, don't be afraid to reach out of your comfort zone and touch the hurting world around you. Remember that James tells us that faith without works—or action—is dead.

Imagine what could happen if all Christians would overcome their own doubts, worries, and fears, and simply *believe!*

If you enjoyed *Believe*, look for the second book in the series coming in 2023!

Acknowledgments

As an author, I may have written the main material of the book, but there is a whole team—and in some cases, a community—of people behind the scenes that have made this book possible. I could not have written this book without the help of the people named below and countless others who can't all be named because of space. Thank you to all of you from the bottom of my heart!

To my husband, Andy: Thank you for all the time you have given up for me to write, the gift cards that fueled my writing time, and for being a strong sounding board for my ideas and plotlines. Your wild imagination, sound realism, and godly wisdom have helped shape this story to go beyond what I was capable of doing on my own. I love you with all my heart!

To my kids, Michael and Joselyn: As I wrote this book, you were always in the back of my mind, knowing that one day you would be reading this story and that it might help shape your life and spiritual gifts. That is what drove me to write the way I did, to tell a story that can teach and train people in their spiritual gifts. One of my most ongoing prayers for you is that you each find your gifts and don't be afraid to use them!

To my dad: From the time I was young, you and Mom trained me to look to God first when trouble comes. As a family, we have gone through many faith-shaking times and we have come through it together with God's help. It was through some of these childhood experiences that my faith started to be shaped. You instilled in me that God should be first in my life, and I am grateful for it. Thanks for being there for me at every point in my life. During the writing of this book, Mom battled cancer and is now walking in perfect healing in her heavenly home. She fought long and hard. Although the woman in this book was physically healed on earth, God had a different healing for Mom, and I would never wish to take that away from her. I miss her greatly and I know she is looking on and cheering for us both as we learn to live life here without her. Thank you for being the best dad!

To my good friend and author, Kathy Dolman: How can I thank you enough? For three years from 2012 to 2014, you read every chapter in its raw form, gave your suggestions, pointed out what needed to be changed, and then read it again (and sometimes again and again)! The time you have given to this project has been precious, and I highly value your input. I must admit there were moments when you gave feedback on my unrealistic storyline that necessitated a whole chapter rewrite and that got me flustered a bit, but I thank God for a friend who doesn't just tell me what I want to hear. This book wouldn't have been nearly as effective without your invaluable feedback. Every bit was precious to me. Thank you, thank you, thank you!

To my editors: Thank you for the amazing attention to detail that you have. Your honest critique of my content as well as your encouragement really helped to shape this work to be better than I thought it could be. Thank you for your perspective and suggestions, too!

To my sounding boards: Suzi Gorney, Nati Cabrera, Brooke-Lynn Warne, and Angela Fae, thank you so much for your input and feedback. Your expertise and advice helped this project to be as accurate and real to life as possible. You are appreciated.

To my pastors and all of the ministers who have helped shape my faith and belief: Your solid teaching from the Word has built my life in ways that Bible college and seminary could not. Much of the teaching found in this book about spiritual gifts and faith are a direct result of what God has been building into my life through the ministry of the men and woman of God in my life. Thank you for not compromising the Word while letting the Spirit flow!

To all my other family and friends: From my in-laws, to my church family, and to all the many people whom I have met all over the country, there are so many of you who have prayed for and supported me that I can't really give proper credit to all of you. Thank you all from the bottom of my heart for everything you do.

Cathy Sanders

Discussion Questions

These questions can be answered individually or used for igniting group discussion. For more discussion questions to use in a group study, look for the accompanying discussion guide.

Prologue and Chapter 1

When she was injured, Sarah chose to believe that God could heal her, and He did. It is easy to doubt in God's power when we have not witnessed or experienced it much. What is your level of faith? On a scale of 1-10 (1 being the lowest faith, 10 being the highest), how much do you believe that God can do miracles in your life?

Chapter 2

Sarah's goal in school is to fit in so others will not make fun of her beliefs or the special gift God has given her. Have you ever hidden your faith or beliefs to try to fit in with a crowd? Why?

Chapter 3

Sarah loves to spend time with her horse, Shadow, and she uses those times to think and pray. Do you have a place or time that you use to talk to God? How does this help you?

Chapter 4

Before the service, Sarah took some time to read her Bible, which she does every day. How often do you read the Bible? Do you have a reading plan or do you randomly read Scripture?

Chapter 5

It becomes clear in this chapter that Nick does not have the same values that Sarah holds. How do you think this can affect a relationship?

Chapter 6

Sarah is able to talk with her mom to help sort out things she is going through. Is there anyone in your life you can talk to about troubling issues you are facing?

Chapter 7

Anna challenges Sarah not to hide her gift, but to let it shine. Is there something God is doing in your life that you tend to hide? How can you let your gift shine more?

Chapter 8

Do you think you have more than one spiritual gift? If so, how do you think those gifts work together?

Chapter 9

Sarah tries to be nice to Maria and is only met with hostility. If there is someone like this in your life, how can you reach out to that person with kindness?

Chapter 1

Sarah had waited to break up with Nick, waiting for better timing. If she had broken up with him when she first knew he wasn't right for her it would have saved her from a lot of heartache. Is there something that you have put off doing that could become a problem later? How can you deal with it sooner?

Chapter 11

Like Nathan said, there is always someone in your life who is hurting, sick, or who might just need some encouragement. Think of someone like that and plan a way to show them that you care and God loves them.

Chapter 12

Nick once again challenges Sarah's morals by having her at his house when his parents are not home, a rule that Sarah's parents has set in place for her protection. Do you have rules and boundaries? Do you let people sway them?

Chapter 13

In this chapter it says that no human can love you as completely as God does and until Jesus becomes your first true love that you will look for love in other places and not be satisfied. What places have you or others looked for true love apart from God?

Chapter 14

Pastor Jake talks about how many Christians don't realize that they have the same power within them that raised Christ from the dead, and don't realize that God can do great things through them. Do you believe God can heal someone when you pray for them?

Chapter 15

Sarah tells Nathan that before she can have a relationship with him she needs to make God first in her love life. Is God first in your love life? If not, how can you fix that?

Chapter 16

As the people who joined the prayer group saw the miracles happening, their faith increased and they were able to pray for people and see miracles happen too. How do you think this works?

Chapter 17

Maria has a lot of hate and bitterness in her life because she has blamed God and others for her circumstances. Was there ever a time when you were angry that God allowed something to happen to you?

Chapter 18

Depression and suicide are almost becoming an epidemic. Do you know someone who is depressed? How can you be an encouragement to this person?

Chapter 19

Have you ever had a mentor? How did this person influence your life?

Chapter 20

How much do you think the spirit world affects the natural world?

Chapter 21

Maria let her "competition" with Sarah cause her to become loose in her morals and found herself pregnant as a result. How can you protect your integrity?

Chapter 22

Sarah felt like God told her to pray only a simple prayer over a serious, life-threatening condition. Has God ever asked you to do something that didn't make sense?

Chapter 23

It is becoming more and more common in this day and age for teenage girls to get pregnant. Do you know anyone in this situation? How can you help or encourage her?

Chapter 24

In the previous chapter, Colton Martin had a vision that Sarah believed was showing her what was happening with Maria. Have you ever had a dream that helped guide a situation that you or someone you know was going through?

Chapter 25

The prayer group expands to meet every day and is attracting attention because of the miracles that have been happening. If people are so curious about the supernatural, why do we have the tendency to hide the amazing things that God can do?

Chapter 26

The actions of Sarah, Nathan, and Brad end up getting Pastor Jake in a tight situation. Has there been a time where you did something without thinking of the impact it would have on other people? How did it affect your relationship with that person?

Chapter 27

Pastor Jake begins to realize that Colton's visions and dreams are not just a result of his wild imagination, but that God is in the middle of them. Has your gift ever been misinterpreted to be something else?

Chapter 28

When Sarah asks God what to do when Maria is rejecting her again, God tells Sarah to love Maria, which is the opposite reaction one would normally have to that situation. Has God ever asked you to do something that was directly opposite your natural reaction? Talk about it.

Chapter 29

Pastor Jake gives a teaching from Hebrews 4:16. Read this scripture passage again. How will this affect the way you pray?

Chapter 30

Pastor Jake and Charlotte, Colton, Sarah, Brad, and Nathan go to visit Andrea and Maria. God told them to just worship, not pray or lay hands on the sick woman. As they worship, Jesus comes in the room. Have you ever been in a meeting or service where something supernatural occurred? What happened?

Chapter 31

What do you think would happen in your community if all the Christians really believed that God can do anything?

About the Author

Cathy Sanders is a prolific writer who has authored or coauthored six books. Her writings have been on Ministry Today, Charisma Leader, and Spirit Fuel. As a former book publishing project manager, Cathy has helped produce over 300 book titles. One project directly under her care has now sold over three million copies. As founder of CS Media, Cathy is a book publishing and writing consultant who also oversees the product development of many book titles each year. Cathy has a deep passion for writing songs and worshiping the Lord. She carries masters and doctorate degrees in Christian education, graduating with honors. Cathy is a mother of two amazing college kids. She resides in Florida with her husband, Andy. In her downtime, she loves to run, swim, and go fishing.

Discover more at www.csbookdesign.com.

CS BOOK DESIGN

CS Book Design exists to help authors take the next step forward with their writing, book manufacturing, and marketing goals. With a proven track record in the book publishing industry and international writing, Andy and Cathy Sanders have what it takes to get your book project professionally completed and to the next level. We specialize in helping authors from start to finish—from the first sentence to the worldwide book launch.

We can help!

- **Book Writing:** All genres, including article writing
- **Professional Book Product Development:** The entire book manufacturing process
- **Book Marketing:** Short and long-term plans, from book launch to rebranding an already existing book, we can help in all areas of advertising and marketing.

Take the *NEXT* step forward!

Andy and Cathy Sanders are both international writers and former book publishers. One project under their care has sold over three million copies. They both function as book writing and publishing consultants. *CS Book Design is NOT a book publisher.*

For more information, contact Andy Sanders: andysanderswriter123@gmail.com.

CS Book Design
250 Palm Coast Parkway NEUnit 607-320
Palm Coast, FL 32137

Book Writing, Publishing, and Marketing Online Training Courses are now available!

Have you hit a few roadblocks or setbacks while completing your book and getting it published? Maybe something happened (or didn't) to cause the trajectory of your book to fall short of the target. We can give you a boost in the right the direction to get your book written, professionally completed, and marketed so that transformation can take place in your readers and substance returned to where it originated—you, the author.

Andy and Cathy Sanders have been connected to the international book publishing industry for over two decades. Their expertise comes from knowing the industry and how a book is written, developed, and marketed worldwide. As international writers, they will show you how to capture the reader's attention. As former publishers, one project under their care has now sold over three million copies. As book writing and publishing consultants, the Sanders are pulling back the curtain on the book publishing industry to show you vital processes in writing, publishing, and marketing. They provide inside information that publishers won't dare share—industry tips to help you navigate through publishing, and a doable marketing plan that will give confidence in the next steps you are about to take to properly complete and launch your book.

With our Online video and training courses you will learn:

- **Book Writing:** All book genres, including article writing.

- **Book Publishing:** Complex steps of book publishing are made easy to understand so you can make educated decisions for moving toward your writing goals.

- **Book Marketing:** How to confidently develop short and long-term marketing plans. Marketing is simple when you know what to do and when to do it. We will show you how to get your book to the masses.

We can help you take the NEXT step forward with writing, publishing, and marketing. For more information, contact Andy Sanders: andysanderswriter123@gmail.com.